ARTER

Sylas Seabrook

For information on other publications by the author, visit

https://sylas.art

ARTWORK

Artwork by Dustin Craig

ISBN 979-8-9863034-5-1 (hardcover)

ISBN 979-8-9863034-4-4 (paperback)

ISBN 979-8-9863034-9-9 (ebook)

Produced in Las Vegas, NV, USA

For Linda Byrns, who showed me strength beyond a birth parent.

Acknowledgements

I began this book six years ago. I haven't stopped talking about "my story" since then. Thanks goes to all of my friends and family who have listened to me as the story unfolded in my mind and took shape on these pages. Some people suffered more than others, some especially more.

To Dustin Craig, my chief sufferer, thank you. You were not only my endless cheerleader, but my strongest critic who provided a wealth of feedback which made this story stronger.

To AuraQuinn Miller, my daughter, thank you for entertaining my fancy with this story and listening to me read to you bits and pieces of it throughout. Your support was a strong foundation which helped motivate me.

To Marilyn Kay Lewis, my aunt and strong supporter, thank you for being there for me and sharing my excitement!

To Michael Lewis, my uncle who believes in me, thank you for the encouragement to push forward toward even greater achievements.

A special thank you to these other supporters who got in on the ground floor to help bring my dream to life:

Brittany Sheppard
Glen Bogue
Orion Lee
Don Miller
Kimberly Sleeth

Thanks to the support of all these great people, I'm already well into book two, Ertra. I look forward to delivering it and moving on to Terra, the third book in the series. Until then, I hope you enjoy Arter!

Part I

The Cycle of Ages

A time will come for every age.
For the first and the last, I will be with you.

An Impossible Formula

It shouldn't look like a mess, he thought. *Science is an art. It's simple and clean.* This *doesn't look like art.*

Unel held up the device with one hand as he ran the other through his short brown hair. It was about more than dreams to him. It was about communication. Dreams made it easier to connect two minds together, letting them communicate through a common vision. Once he figured that out, he would extend it to the waking mind, making it possible to communicate through thought alone.

The first step was the most challenging and frustrating part. The first hurdle, the largest. After leaping over that, the rest usually came down to refinement—making it perfect. He was still at the first, most frustrating step, a hurdle which had thwarted his every attempt.

He twirled the device in the soft amber light of the Dreamoria, the room where Arterians would share dreams through his device, watching golden tendrils of purple and green energy wisp into the air. His light, freckled skin reflected off the twisted metal frame holding two little spheres in place. And he marveled. Marveled at the beauty of it as much as its sheer ugliness.

The device was a beauty of mathematical calculation. Each twist of metal carefully engineered to direct the energy of the spheres, each sphere positioned at exact inflection points in the twisting energy.

On the other hand, it looked like two spheres surrounded by a tangle of wires that had been thrown in a bag and shaken around until only a swift cut by a sword could undo the resulting knot.

He sighed, shaking his head, and set the device on a small

scale in the middle of a sleeping table. This device was the broadcaster. Another copy of the device, the receiver, lay on a sleeping table on the other side of the room.

You can look like a mess if you work, he thought, but he felt differently. He felt that when it actually worked, it would be more than mathematically balanced, it would be... *Harmonized?* Yes, that was the word.

"I came up with a name," he said.

"What's that?" Col replied from the control room. His light blue eyes reflecting the amber of the Dreamoria were the only thing visible through the room's semi-reflective glass.

"*Draumr*. It's ancient Sumattan for dreamer."

He looked at the device on the other side of the room and took a pensive breath. It was time to test. He pulled the display bar of his headset around and checked the readout from the instrument panel. They were already in sync. That was good. It meant his changes hadn't broken anything.

It was good practice to only change one thing at a time. This time he'd gone with a scientific gut feeling, not necessarily good practice. The two spheres weren't just any spheres, they were *aten*, small orbs of energy found only on his home planet, Arter, and in different places depending on what they did. The device used two *aten*. One was a *hydaten*, a golden-green gelatin-like sphere that was bound to water and electricity. The other was the fragile, translucent *oxaten* sphere, used for its connection to air and electricity. Water for the human body, electricity for brain wave patterns, and air for the space between.

He followed his gut feeling, changing two things this time. He changed the *oxaten* for a *phoaten* and the metal for one with more tensile strength. *Phoaten* were a special *aten* that fell from the Living Rainbow, the permanent arch in Arter's aurora, as purple droplets. They brought a connection to both light and electromagnetism. The changes were based on a hunch that bringing the *aten* closer to each other, introducing magnetic attraction, and covering the space between by light instead of air would be what was needed.

So far, it hadn't hurt.

Unel tapped the scale near him causing the device to shake. The receiving device vibrated, mirroring the tap. Excellent, that still worked.

"I'm ready for the feed," he said with a little nervousness to his voice.

Behind the dark screen, Col pressed a button, sending a video feed of Mount Sumat into the broadcasting *draumr*. He pressed another button and turned on the receiving *draumr*'s camera. A moment later, the camera's feed appeared in Unel's headset.

This is where it always failed. Always. They would connect, but they couldn't actually share the vision, the dream. Connecting two visions together was his first hurdle.

A small clearing of grass and flowers at the base of Mount Sumat appeared in his headset, a short waterfall behind it, rocks on either side, and a pool below. It was a special platform few Arterians ever got close to. He'd been there with Trellia on a personal quest to find an *attaten*, the very rare *aten* of fertility. But they'd been run off by a spatiatta, a member of the Swarm, and given a stern warning. He had managed to get this footage, though. It made the risk worth it.

It didn't fail! Finally. It was working.

"Are you getting this, Col?" he said, voice trembling with excitement.

"By Sumatta itself, we are," Col called back. "It's beautiful. Where is that? I've never seen that part of the mountain."

Unel didn't answer, he just marveled. The hurdle had been jumped. The rest wouldn't be easy—it was still a marathon of creative invention—but it would be easy relative to what he'd just done, and it meant he was almost sure of success.

"Oh, I know that place. That's the Reader's platform. How'd you get that close?" Col asked.

Unel smiled with sublime satisfaction as he took his headset off. He turned his head back and forth to look at the two *draumrs* sitting across the room from each other. They were sharing a vision; they were sharing his vision. His tangled mess was finally working.

The only difference between his goal and what was happening is that the vision was being shared between the two *draumrs*. He needed it to be shared between two Arterians. The next step was sharing it with one Arterian.

"It's time, Col. I need a cup of avak," Unel said, setting the headset down on a table. He walked over to the broadcasting *draumr* and picked it up, leaned back against the table, and turned it around as if he could see the magic within it. He occasionally glanced at the other *draumr* across the room until another assistant, a short male Arterian who was walking quickly, but carefully, entered with a cup of avak. Rajellian was the man's name if he remembered correctly. Rajellian silently handed over the cup and left, almost as if he were a servant, not an assistant.

Unel took the cup, downed the hot liquid, then laid down.

He would have to make a way of attaching the *draumr* to a person, but for now he set it on his forehead and let the bitter brown root tea sink in. The tea from the Isle Of Lights was renowned for not only its sedative effects, but for inducing vivid, epic-length dreams. It tasted like seasoned mud and was utterly disgusting, but it was more effective than anything else. This would definitely be an epic dream, not only because of the tea, but because of what the dream would prove.

His dream surprised him. It took him back to the Reader's platform on Mount Sumat. The vision seemed more vibrant than the one streamed into the *draumr*. Dreams added a vagueness that seemed to enhance things, somehow making them more vivid than even a replay, despite the added vagueness.

He walked back toward the waterfall, the mist growing heavier with each step, and stopped abruptly as a spatiatta stepped through. It's skin was pearlescent, but darker and shades of blue and purple that glistened against the light. It raised it wings and flapped them threateningly while its tentacles swirled at its base.

"You are not a Reader. This is not your place," it said. It spoke in Arterian, not Sumattan, and didn't use its tentacles when speaking. Its voice seemed to flutter like its wings. It was just like the one that had warned them away when they'd visited in the waking world.

Spatiatta weren't known for speaking. Not much was known about them other than that they protected Sumatta, Giver of Life, Protector of Arter, Guardian of the Ages, and functioned like a hive. They generally stayed away from Arterians.

Unel reached out and tapped toward the sun, envisioning his tap passing through Arter's electromagnetic aurora and hitting the sun. It was his lucid dreaming trick to become aware of his dream and take control.

The only way to tell if he had taken control was to envision something happening. Whatever he envisioned would suddenly come to be, and that would tell him he was in control of the dream.

He envisioned the spatiatta vanishing. It did not. Instead, it flapped it wings threateningly and marched forward. Unel took a step back, slipped on a grassy rock, and tumbled backward, falling hard on his butt.

Unel woke, alarmed, and sat up, his skin clammy and breathing heavily.

"Did you get anything, Col?" he asked, rubbing his backside as if he'd actually fallen. Oddly, it did feel tender. He dismissed the feeling as a phantom of the dream seeming so real.

"Nothing," Col said.

"Nothing? What do you mean nothing? I don't get it. What was different?" he said. *And not that spatiatta*, he thought. "What am I missing?"

Unel scratched his rough, unshaven face as he tried to figure out what he was missing. He had already overcome the hurdle, but this seemed to be sending him back over the hurdle as if he had to re-accomplish the jump.

"Let me see the data streams," he said. He grabbed his headset and pulled the viewing bar around. Col pulled up the data streams for this last dream. The receiver was blank and the input was blank.

"You could have told me that nothing literally meant nothing, Col," Unel complained, taking off his headset and tossing it onto the sleeping table.

Col chuckled. "Maybe this will be more useful. The receiver view is from when they work together, the broadcaster view is from when you were just dreaming."

Unel put the headset back on, then tapped his fingers on the table as he watched the data. This time he was seeing the data from the *draumrs* on each receiver, not the visuals. They looked very much the same. Some variations where the dream was different, but nothing of note. Comparing the streams wasn't useful.

He was too close for there to be nothing when the two *draumrs* had worked so beautifully together. He couldn't go back over the hurdle. There had to be something else. *What am I not seeing?* he thought, his frustration coming out as an almost growling voice in his head.

"Trellia's been calling, Unel," Col said, his voice more that of a counselor than an assistant.

At first, Unel didn't catch what Col had said. He was thinking about the *draumrs*, not Trellia. Trellia, his beautiful bonded, his life mate, his living incarnation of a dream. The one woman who could put up with him forgetting about her while he thought of nothing but his project. She would be missing him. Patiently, but she'd still be missing him. He missed her, too. In those moments when he had to wait and the *draumr* didn't consume his mind, Trellia was all he thought of and longed for. He loved his bonded with all his energy. If it were possible, he'd have his *draumrs* and Trellia together, but Trellia didn't interfere with his work; she was his distraction from it.

"How long have we been here?" Unel asked.

"*You* are going on day nine," he replied, still counseling, but now in a parental tone. Col was more than an assistant. Unel felt the man truly cared for him. He could probably tell Unel was exhausted.

"I'll go soon. I'm just so close," he said to himself more than Col as the replay ended.

It was there at the end, barely noticeable. A little glitch when he sat up and took off the *draumr*. He had been watching the working *draumr* stream more than the failed one of him sleeping, but there it was in the one of him sleeping.

"Replay the last second, but extend it to a minute in length," he said. His exhaustion dissipated as excitement flooded him.

Col requeued the replay with the new parameters and played it. There it was. There were two glitches, not one. What did the glitches mean? What caused them?

"Overlay that on top of a replay of my brain waves." He was close. He was about to pinpoint it. He could feel it.

Col set up the replay, then fed it into Unel's headset. The first glitch happened when he sat up, the second when he stopped touching the *draumr* after he'd set it down. Of course! Mass and distance were involved!

"Ask her how much she weighs," Unel ordered, starting to speak so fast Col didn't catch the words at first.

When he finally registered the order, Col coughed. "You want me to ask your bonded how much she weighs?"

"Yes," Unel said, oblivious to Col's surprise. "It's part of it.

Mass and distance. I need to adjust the two to sync. Don't you see? That's why it's not working with just me on one side and a *draumr* on the other—the mass differential is too high. Check out the forty-fifth and fifty-eighth seconds in the expanded version," he said.

Col started to look over the data streams, but Unel ran to each sleeping table, grabbed the *draumrs* and took them to the back, setting them on a table. He needed to change the *draumrs'* metal weave to allow for greater accuracy and increase the tensile strength which meant making new *draumrs* of a new metal. With that, he'd have some flexibility as he adjusted their position in real time during dreaming to maintain the connection. It wouldn't have made sense to Col or the other assistants, but it was perfectly clear for him. This was a scientific gut feeling, one he knew meant he had already traversed the first hurdle even if his feet didn't look like they'd touched the ground.

As a few more thoughts came to mind, he gave Col more orders. "And, ask her to come here. And bring my tools. And tell her I love her. And hurry. This is it, Col!"

* * *

"He doesn't care about my weight, Col. He wants my mass. Tell him 74.8," Trellia said as she laughed at the question. Her Unel was too focused on his work. She'd have to steal him away for some relaxation soon. He could usually handle a couple weeks at a time, but productivity suffered after the first week. He was male, so easily distracted.

He was equally as distracting for her, she admitted to herself.

"I'll be there in about an hour," she said, closing the connection and pocketing her touchpad.

The ride only took twenty minutes, but she couldn't simply grab his toolbox and hop over. Not for her Unel. She showered, washing her straight dark hair with a special shampoo that made it sweep like a gentle wall of rain around her shoulders when dry, then went to her makeup stand.

He always liked softer colors, so she lightened her already light face to just a tad away from white and accentuated her eyes and lips with a soft pink, barely more color than her natural lips. The pink was a perfect match with her brown eyes which reflected it and seemed to grow lighter as a result.

Tossing the towel aside and letting her hair tumble to her shoulders, she went to the closet and picked out a pair of Caleston bottoms, the soft brown ones that seemed to make her glide when she walked, and a white blouse with frilly bell-like sleeves.

Checking her work in the mirror as she brushed her hair free of any snags, she smiled with approval. *This will drive him crazy*, she thought as she swayed her hips back and forth. She twirled around and headed to his workshop now that she was ready to make him think of something other than his work, ready to make him think of her.

His toolbox, containing everything from screwdrivers to frequency meters, was right where it should be. He generally kept it at home for his creativity spurts, but apparently something at the Dreamoria required a tool not already at the lab. She hefted the toolbox over to their transport and shoved it into the passenger seat, then hopped in, pulling her Calestons up so they didn't get stuck in the door.

The night sky over Sumna was calm, though not still. Arter's skies were never still. Electricity bolted between waves of amber aurora that undulated across the sky, painting buildings in a constant flowing stream of evening beauty. It would be a fast and quiet trip under the gently rolling lights.

She set course and the transport lifted up off their apartment, slowly turning toward midtown, then accelerated rapidly, zipping over the cylindrical towers of varying numbers of floors which filled the biggest city on Arter. A few were more than twenty-five floors and the transport had to adjust course to avoid them, zipping left and right, but never going over them. All civilian transports flew under thirty floors to keep a safe distance from the electricity of Arter's sky.

Was he really close this time? She always wanted to believe as much as he did that he was on the verge, that he'd overcome the last hurdle and his device would work, but she'd seen so many of his discoveries end in setbacks, and she hated seeing him when he'd suffer.

One day he would get there. She was confident of that. Maybe that day was on the horizon. Maybe it was now. Should she distract him, or would a distraction delay his discovery? She discarded the thought. Of course, she should distract him (as much as she could, anyway). Stepping away from it all let him come back to it with more vigor and creativity than if he were to keep going and lose his focus.

The transport settled down at Sumna University on the ground next to the Dreamoria Research Center. She lugged the toolbox toward the front door, but stopped when Col came running out. He was fast, running a little too eagerly.

He looked similar to Unel, sans freckles. They were both of typical height with short, dark brown hair and light blue eyes. They had square faces and medium builds. Col was a bit stronger than Unel. Where Unel had the extra girth coming from the sedentariness of studies, Col had muscle. Col was just more athletic, and clearly a better runner. Unel, with his thinner lips, had a cuter smile. Col couldn't beat that, not that there was a competition, of course.

"You shouldn't be carrying that," he yelled. "Let me take it."

"I'm not fragile, Col," she said as she let him take the toolbox. "You act like I'm pregnant or made of glass."

"Are you?" he asked, looking toward her stomach.

Trellia stood back, shocked. "If I were, Unel would be the first to know," she scolded.

Col smirked. "I would think he'd *have* to be the first to

know," he said.

"Where is he?"

"You have to ask?"

Trellia laughed. "I'm sure he does leave the Dreamoria every now and then."

Col looked humored by her suggestion. "Unless nature calls, he doesn't leave. He probably stinks."

Of course, he would stink. Another reason she needed to distract him. She opened the door and waved Col into the reception room. Marshia, the more than hefty receptionist with a fluffy brown curl for every roll on her waist and a plump, friendly smile, sat snug behind her desk.

"Trellia, it's good to see you again. I'm sure Unel will feel the same," Marshia said.

"To make sure I know my weight?"

Marshia laughed. "You know your bonded. He has two focuses in life: This place and you. I sometimes wonder if he remembers more than one at a time."

"I have my ways of reminding him," Trellia said, coyly twisting her hips.

Amused, Marshia buzzed them in. Trellia held the door for Col as he carried in the toolbox.

"Let me take that, Col. It's just around the corner and I'm sure he'll want you in the control room with the rest of the team," Trellia said.

He capitulated, handing her the toolbox, and they walked down the hall to the sleeping lab. Col opened the door for Trellia, waited for her to step in, then continued to the next door which led to the control room.

Trellia set the toolbox down and put her hands on her hips.

"I don't see you for weeks and you have *Col* call me to ask my weight and order me here? With tools?" She gave Unel a pointed, condescending, but playful glare. "Are you going to send him to kiss me on your behalf too?" she said, warming her tone and ending with an enticing laugh.

Unel jumped up from under a sleeping table, ducking just in time, and leaped over to her, hugging and kissing Trellia wildly. His rough beard scraped across her face and his words came out so fast they almost overlapped each other. "I've got it," he said. "Well, I don't know for sure, but I'm certain anyway. I, I...where do I start?"

"Col told me about the *hydaten* and something about the metal," she said, stealing a moment as he caught a breath and flipped her hair back so it would fall forward and cascade against her shoulders, catching his eyes. "That was it?"

"He did? When? Oh, it doesn't matter. Yes, those had to change, but more than that, it's mass and distance. Look," he said, handing her a headset. He didn't seem to notice her. Now was not the time to distract him.

He stopped for a moment as she flipped her hair back and put on the headset. He watched her hair tumble down around her shoulders as if just noticing it was her, Trellia, and not a random Arterian he was talking to in his lab. He seemed to forget where he was for that moment and only see her. Now she was doing a good job of being distracting.

He did stink. She'd need to bring that up with him, but not now. He was too excited. His moment of distraction wouldn't last long.

Headset on, Unel pulled the viewing bar around and told Col to start the replay near the end. He explained the two variations as rapidly as his mouth would spit out his thoughts without completely tripping over them.

He took his headset off, then helped Trellia take off hers.

"I've adjusted the *draumrs*. Now I just need to make the tables movable and, oh, over there," he said, pointing. "That *draumr* is adjusted for your mass. The other is mine." He turned to look at the control room. "Col, we need some tea."

"Slow down, Unel. You want to do this now? And you want *me* to dream with you? Why not one of the scientists? Your assistants? Col?"

He stopped rambling and looked at her, confused. "Why not? I know this is it. It has to be. You saw the data. And," he said, looking at her slightly hurt. "If I'm right, with who else?"

Trellia knew he meant it. He had two focuses in life, and she was one. No one else would even cross his mind.

With a soft smile, Trellia nodded acceptingly. "I thought you had to make the tables movable," she said.

Frustrated, Unel turned to the tables and rubbed his chin. He wanted to find a way of doing it now, even if the tables weren't movable.

"I'm hungry. Why don't me and Col go to the cafeteria while you work on the tables? I'll get you some food and you can meet us in a bit."

"Yeah, I guess that works," he said, still staring at the tables and looking for an alternative solution.

She grabbed him by the shoulders and turned him around, giving him a kiss and stealing his attention for a moment. "Thirty minutes, Unel. Promise?"

He agreed. She knew he had every intention of coming and zero chance of actually showing up on time.

* * *

Unel turned the table, rotating it until the last foot was over the microtrack, then eased it down. He hunched under the table and set a screw in one of the four holes. He drilled it in place, then grabbed another screw and drilled it into its hole. He grabbed the third screw and noticed the first was unscrewed. That was weird. Hadn't he just screwed that in?

And where had the microtrack come from? Col must have found one. He didn't remember Col bringing one, but he was tired. Maybe he'd just forgotten.

He drilled the first screw back in, then looked at the third screw. It was already in, but the second was now unscrewed. Something wasn't right. He'd drilled that in after the first, right? He drilled the second back in while he watched the first. As the second screw went in, the third unscrewed. *No way*, he thought.

He rubbed his eyes, yawned, and ran his fingers through his hair trying to figure out what just happened.

"Maybe if you take a break, they'll screw themselves in?"

Trellia? Hadn't she gone to the cafeteria? He looked up. No, those were her pants.

"I doubt that's how it works," he said. "Am I late? I thought I had more time. I'm sorry. The microtracks were here and I thought—"

"We don't have microtracks," Trellia said with a coy laugh. "Maybe that's why you can't screw them in."

He looked down. The microtrack wasn't there. He tucked his head in, holding the table to make sure he didn't bump his head as he stood up to ask her what was going on. When he stood up, Trellia wasn't there.

He rubbed his eyes and ran his hand through his hair, trying to figure out what was happening. It came to him.

I'm dreaming. I fell asleep, he thought.

Unel sighed, then tapped through the top of the Dreamoria, past the aurora skylights, toward the sun. His finger touched the sun. *Wake*, he thought, commanding his dream. His eyes opened.

He was back in the lab laying on his back under a sleeping table. He sighed and crawled out from under the table.

Fine, you win. I'll take a break.

He looked back at the room one more time before leaving. He was so close, but he did need rest. It had been nine days? She hadn't seen him in a couple weeks? The Dreamoria would still be there when he got back, and reality itself was forcing him to take a break, not to mention he was hungry.

He reluctantly headed toward the cafeteria. Either way, taking a break from the lab was worth it. Trellia was there. He admitted that he missed her. If he could have her with him and do his work, life would be as perfect as she was. She didn't share the same passion for his work, though.

He walked faster as he thought about her. Her way of walking seemed to just flow. Her smile, as soft and gentle as a spring flower. Her look when she looked at him as if he was her whole world.

He opened the door to the cafeteria and saw her sitting across a table from Col, laughing as they chatted.

"There he is," Col said, raising his cup of blolarlorah toward Unel. "Hungry?"

"Yes. I'm starving. Sorry. Did I take too long?"

Col looked at the plate next to Trellia. "Come eat. It wasn't too long."

"It was an hour," Trellia said, turning around to greet him. "Not too long for you," she said, greeting him with a friendly look that was as enticing as friendly. "But I still missed you."

He slid in next to Trellia, wrapping an arm around her waist, pulling her shoulder length hair back, and kissing her neck just below the ear. "I had a dream about you," he whispered.

Trellia raised a brow, drawing her lips into a smile that made her diamond-shaped face twinkle with amusement as she made it seem like it was just the two of them in the room. She always made him feel like he was her world, that nothing else mattered to her. He always felt she was his entire world, that nothing else mattered except her when he was around her.

"Oh?" she said. "So, you slept. I'm glad you got some rest. I don't plan on letting you rest too much when we get home. I miss my bonded."

Unel blushed. Her whole world. If anyone could make him forget the lab, forget his work, forget everything, it was her. If it weren't for her, he'd never leave the lab.

"I'm going to take a couple of days off," he said, looking at Col.

"Good. You need—"

"I need two microtracks attached to the sleeping tables. Can you get it done by then? You'll need to be able to adjust them from the control room, so we'll need them wired up."

"There he is with more work, even as he wants to take time off from it," Trellia said. She sighed, shaking her head playfully as she chided Unel. Looking at Unel's plate, she asked, "Are you going to eat?"

As if agreeing with her, Unel's stomach grumbled. He frowned, but picked up a slice of toast she had jellied for him and took a bite. It always felt good to eat, mostly since he kept forgetting to eat. He thought that for as rare as it was that he remembered to eat, he shouldn't have the paunch around his waist that he did. It was probably the constant supply of starchy drinks the staff gave to him. It didn't really matter. Only getting the *draumr* to work mattered.

"I'm sorry," he said as he chewed. "It's just that I'm really close this time. We've already crossed the first hurdle and I know why that didn't apply to just me. If only we could—"

Trellia held up a finger to his lips, silencing him as he chewed. "You smell and you have other obligations. An obligation to me, for instance. I might not know the formula for a perfect *draumr*, but I do know the formula for a healthy you. It involves food, sleep, and a little..." She trailed off for a moment, softening her voice into a seductive whisper. "Romance."

"I think that's the perfect formula for any guy," Col chimed in.

Unel laughed and took another bite. "I think I need more than a little of all three of those," he said, chewing.

"And more than a little shower," Trellia said, waving her hand in front of her nose dramatically. "You should install one in the Dreamoria. It would make it easier to sit this close to you."

Unel enjoyed the banter, but what he really wanted to talk about was the *draumr* and how close he was. He also really wanted Trellia. Two opposite desires—he couldn't have one without putting the other on hold—was a problem he couldn't solve. He would just have to take a break.

Everything He Ever Wanted

Alia fixed the door to the Bahnderia open, inviting the faithful to come worship. The building was the centerpiece of religious belief in Sumatta, the Giver of Life, Protector of Arter, and Guardian of Ages. It was known as Sumatta's home, the place where Sumatta came when it descended from Mount Sumat.

"Good morning," a tall older man with mottled hair said as Alia waved in the faithful.

"Good morning, Huol." Huol was the definition of faithful. He had been coming to the Bahnderia every day he was not sick since before Alia could remember. His reverence for Sumatta was second only to Alia's own.

"Any word from Sumatta?" he asked.

"No, Huol. If we had heard from Sumatta, I'm sure you would be the first to know."

"If only that were true. I think all of Arter would find out at about the same time," he said, chuckling. "Going to the tree? Can I walk with you this morning?"

Center to the Bahnderia was the Bahnder Tree. It was made of an ethereal metal not of Arter which housed and protected Sumatta within the Bhanderia. Arterians came daily to pay their respects to Sumatta as welcome guests in its home.

"Of course. Is something on your mind?" Alia asked, turning toward the hallway leading to the Bhanderia Tree.

"Well, yes, now that you ask," he said. His scruffy, aged voice had a playfulness to it. "Does Sumatta come at least once during every Reader's life?"

"From my energy to yours, from my knowledge to yours, Huol. No, it comes at least twice. Once when the Next Reader becomes Reader and then when the Reader is replaced by the

Next Reader. At the beginning and end, it is with us. It comes again when the Cycle of Ages calls."

Alia walked slowly down the curved hallway with Huol, following its closing spiral to the Bahnder Tree. The last time Alia had seen Sumatta was over a half century ago when it had become the Reader. It was then that he had been transformed from the young male Next Reader to the genderless representative and voice of Sumatta to all Arterians. Life had been as peaceful and uneventful as Alia's current stroll, every day just another step with idle conversation.

"Will it come again soon?"

"Are you asking if the Next Reader is ready?"

"Oh, no. Nothing like that. I like you. You're a good Reader. I just wonder if I will ever get to see Sumatta again. I'm older than you, you know."

"I'm sorry, Huol, but I'll know when Sumatta tells me. I don't know when we'll see Sumatta next," Alia said, rounding the last bend to the center courtyard.

The Bahnder Tree was a magnificent thing. It wasn't living, but its pearlescent, translucent bark glistened continuously with an electric spark that made it seem alive. Even the Complete Histories, the series of recordings made by Sumatta to train the Reader to read its complex four-dimensional speech and understand Arter's history, did not tell exactly what the tree was made of or what purpose it served when it housed Sumatta. It was this mystery that made the Bahnderia as inspiring and hallowed to Alia as it was to Arterians.

Alia felt the awe it always felt in the presence of the Bahnder Tree abruptly shaken by a young girl dangling upside down from her knees on one of the large branches. Her hair normally hung down to the small of her back, but now it hung far past her head in a ghost-like blond swath as she swayed back and forth. Her flower-spotted dress was tied at the waist and hung down like an inverted skirt covering her torso.

"Shenol, Next Reader, what are you doing?" Alia yelled,

chastising the young girl and forgetting Huol for a moment. "Get down from there right now!"

Shenol laughed, swung herself, grabbed a smaller branch and flipped herself forward, bringing her feet up between her arms and wrapping her legs around the branch, then pulled herself up on it. She inched over to the trunk and slid down the slit in the front, tumbling into the shallow pool of water at the foot.

Standing up, she shook her hair and wrung out her dress, fluffing it until she was content that it was girly enough, then strolled over, swaying her hips and laughing.

"I'm sorry, Reader. The air feels lighter there and I feel like I can do anything."

Huol stood behind the reader, arms folded, glaring down his nose at the young Next Reader. He would not dare speak over the Reader when it addressed the Next Reader.

"Until you become Reader, you're still a young lady, and young ladies do not hang upside down from tree branches. The Next Reader does not hang upside down from the Bahnder Tree. Really, Shenol!"

Shenol huffed, frowning and bowed her head. There was nothing more insulting to the young girl than to be called unlady-like—the girl fancied her gender as much as she fancied being Next Reader. It was a feeling Alia could not identify with. It had never felt like a boy; it had always felt like a Reader. Being a Reader was all Alia had ever wanted.

"Will you excuse us, Huol?" Alia said. A reason did not need to be provided and Huol, head tilted forward in parental judgment as he eyed the Next Reader, walked off a distance into the courtyard and took a seat to meditate on the tree.

Shenol was definitely not like Alia. Shenol wanted two things in life, not one. She wanted to be a woman and she wanted to be the Reader. One simply could not have both. She would have to make a decision.

"I'm sorry, Reader," Shenol said. Alia was sure that she was sorry for not acting like a young lady, not not acting like the Next Reader.

"In life, Next Reader, we all want things. Do you know what I wanted more than being the Reader?"

Shenol looked up bright with curiosity. "What?"

"Nothing. I always felt like I was a Reader more than anything and all I wanted to do and be was be the voice of Sumatta. You will have to make a choice. What do you want more?"

Shenol's glimmer of hope soured into dejection. She did not answer.

"I did not choose wrong, Shenol. There is no one on Arter better suited to be the Next Reader than you. You just have to believe that yourself."

"I guess," the young Next Reader said. She was as dejected as only a child could be at having one of her fantasies attacked, and Alia felt a little sorry for her. However, it was Alia's job to prepare the Next Reader to be ready when Sumatta came home. Shenol would have to make the choice then, and it was better that she made it sooner rather than later.

"It's time for your studies. First, you need to clean up. Get ready and meet me in my study."

Shenol kept up her silent pout as she walked away. Making the choice she was faced with was hard—it was a choice Alia had not had to make—and Alia was probably not the best to help her make this choice. Maybe it was time to find someone to help Shenol.

* * *

Unel loved a good, hot shower. The kind that made your skin scream. It was like having the grime of the day purged with fire. He pulled his white, straight-lined slacks up, buttoned them, then stood tight as the steam evaporated from his torso like a cooling salve bringing life back to his torched body. He sighed softly as he took in the relief, then slipped on a light green shirt cut with straight lines that almost matched the pants. The outfit made him look taller, but its relaxed fit made it seem more comfortable than the sharp creases lead on.

"It's ready," Trellia called from the kitchen, her voice like a gentle kiss.

Date night was about to begin and Trellia knew exactly what he wanted. He grinned and went to the kitchen, walking right up behind her. Instrumental music played some of the latest popular songs, giving a gentle background ambiance. He slipped his arms around her and reached into the bowl in front of her.

"Hey," she chastised, swatting at his hand. "At the table."

"You said it was ready," he sportively complained.

"It is. At the table." She nudged back with her hips, pushing his arms away from the bowl, but not before he snapped up a berry covered in cream.

Unel stepped back and tossed the berry in his mouth, the cream covering his lips, and bit into the sweet, delectable juiciness. It had been cut in half, breaded, and seared on the inside, giving it a crispiness as he bit down that mixed with the cream. It softened before he swallowed and tasted like the perfection of the woman who had made it.

"I love berryant," he said of the fruit dish. "But only if you make it. Others give it too much breading. It feels like you're eating bread, not fruit. You make it perfect."

Trellia stopped walking and turned around. "Well, if you're going to compliment me like that, then you deserve a kiss." She puckered her lips, waiting.

Unel grinned, stealing another berryant bite as he went in for the kiss, but this time brought it to her lips just before their lips met. He pressed his tongue on the fruit and pushed it into her mouth as they kissed. She mushed the fruit with her tongue and swallowed as she took a step back, ending the kiss.

She grinned and wiped the bit of cream left off his lips. "Not until after dinner," she said, playfully chastising him again.

Unel grinned, sitting down next to her as she set the bowl on the table and took a seat.

It was a light dinner. A little chicakroon meat in a light white gravy with some sliced water tubers and a small salad. The berryant was supposed to be dessert.

"Have you heard anything from Col?" she asked as they filled their plates.

"Not yet. It isn't ready, I guess. Isn't this supposed to be date night? No work?" She was always trying to distract him from his work—something he needed and which she was very good at—but now she was bringing it up?

Trellia took a bite of the chickaroon. "You never escape work, energy of my life. It just sometimes takes a short pause." She glanced quickly at his workshop, her smiling throwing a friendly accusation, the kind that made him feel guilty and forgiven at the same time.

He hadn't meant for her to catch him there earlier. She'd been napping and he couldn't sleep, so he'd stolen a couple of hours to work on a head device to hold the *draumr* in place. The way it hung now, it looked like a tangled mess of a diadem. She'd woke and snuck in, catching him back at his work. That was when she made him promise a date night tonight.

Unel shrugged it off. She knew him better than anyone. He accepted the guilt and the forgiveness at the same time with that shrug. "You love me for it," he teased.

"I love you because I see your passion. Your passion for your work and your passion for me. I'm not jealous of your work, Unel," she said, then took another bite.

Unel didn't know how to reply, so he took another bite too, eyes fixed on her. The statement seemed to be a conversation killer. Neither of them said anything for a few more bites, then Unel thought of something. Something not related to his work, something related to her, to them.

"I've been thinking about it more," he said. "An *attaten*. We have the money. I could ask around. I'm sure I could find one. Sumatta knows, Strypan might have one. With the *draumr* almost working, I think we're ready for a family."

She always pushed back, telling him that he needed to get to a point in his research where he'd be able to spend more time at home and less at the lab. It was a good point, and he accepted it, but he knew that after the months of pregnancy, the *draumr* would be ready, he would be ready. He could even turn some of the tasks over to Col and the other assistants at the lab. They wouldn't need him as much as he was needed now. He'd be able to step back while they worked on the project. There would still be work to do, but it wouldn't require Unel's personal presence.

"I'll think about it," she said. How she said it was as suggestive as it was reserved. Maybe she would consider it.

Unel considered it one of the more frustrating aspects of reality. All females were born infertile. It took the rarest of *aten* to make them fertile, the *attaten*. The little pearlescent eggs were only produced by a swarm of spatiatta once a decade. They were enormously expensive and finding them usually meant having good connections.

The hard part about it wasn't getting one, in his opinion. The hardest part was convincing his bonded that they were ready. More specifically, that he was ready. Why couldn't nature just let everyone be fertile and love take its course?

Unel ignored his frustrations and stood up, leaving his almost clean plate on the table, and extended his hand. "Dance?"

Trellia stood up, her plate still having a few bites of chickaroon and tubers, and took his hand.

Today she wore the perfect skirt for dancing. The one from their trip to the Isle of Lights, Arter's only island, far to the south. It was soft brown and made of a very thin tweed that curved around her body yet had a firmness that let it vibrate as her body shook. The top was light, barely covering her breasts and leaving her tummy exposed. Made of a similar material, but a soft shade of green, it also vibrated as the cloth hung from her curves.

As the music reached a crescendo, he tugged her forward and she spun, twirling and sending her outfit into a flurry of excitement. She laughed and unfurled herself, spinning backwards with equal exuberance.

"Hold on," he said.

He pushed his recliner up against hers and the living room table up against the glass window, making a little dancing floor for the two of them, then swept up next to her, putting his hands on her hips and stepping back onto the dance floor.

Unel leaned in and whispered into her ear. "A *draumr* can't do this."

She laughed at his self-deprecating taunt as he stepped back, twisting his body around, arms over his head and twirled her into him, then turned around, his back to hers before unwrapping their twisted bodies and coming around to face each other.

"Energy of my life," Trellia said affectionately, then took control of the dance, turning and twisting both of their bodies in time with the music.

They danced until he ran out of energy and plopped down in his chair, heart racing. "I love you," he said between heartbeats. "You are the energy of my life."

"It looks like," she said, laughing, "that I've taken all your energy."

Trellia went to the table, filled two small bowls from the bowl of berryant, and brought him one with a spoon. "It'll give you more energy."

Unel took the bowl and leaned back as Trellia went to the couch and laid down flat on her stomach, not nearly as winded, legs bent up, feet idly kicking. She picked up her touchpad and started idly swiping through the screens as if casually reading.

"Tell me more about it," Trellia asked after finishing her berryant.

There was a sleekness to how her clothes wrapped around her body as she lay down, cascading around her curves like gentle, enticing waves. Her hair shook slightly with her head as she turned it back and forth, looking over each page on her touchpad. It was like a bell calling him to her side.

Unel stood up, taking his bowl of berryant, and answered that call. He slid in next to her on the couch, set the bowl of fruit on the table, and drew his fingers up along her blouse, easing them slowly up to her shoulders. Tightening his fingers around her shoulders, he dug them in firmly. He turned them into her flesh, tearing at pent up stress. They crawled into the stress and dug it out, stretching her muscles and relaxing her body.

Trellia groaned, releasing tension through a groan of pleasure and relaxation.

He climbed on top of her, her scent already arousing him beyond the physical, and straddled her body. Reaching out with both hands, he dug into her shoulders, pulling away its stress as the soft cloth teased his skin.

He reached down with one hand and tugged the cord holding her top on. The cloth fell free, slipping off to the sides and exposing the whiteness of her skin to the soft light of the room.

He swallowed and drew his hands down her spine, massaging her sides as she moaned.

"I love your massages," she said.

"I love you," he said, then leaned forward to lay on top of her.

Trellia turned around as he leaned forward, her blouse falling away completely and caught him on her chest. Her soft breasts pressing up against his now wrinkled shirt.

Unel moaned and Trellia grinned. She held up a finger. "I

said to tell me about it."

It was the most infuriating statement she could say. He wanted her. He wanted his project. He wanted to talk about it. He wanted...her. It was all her now. This moment, this time, was hers. And here she was teasing him with his other love.

He reached over and grabbed a cut berry with a coy slyness, then pressed it to her lips. He lifted it, then pressed it to one nipple, then the next, before popping it in his mouth.

Unel shook his head, denying her question, and leaned down, licking at one nipple, lapping up the sweet berry juice, then turned his head to the side and licked at the other nipple, teasing up its creaminess on his tongue before curling it into his mouth.

He swallowed and opened his mouth as if anticipating an excitement he could not handle as he leaned down and kissed her berry-sweetened lips, folding his tongue into her mouth as he reached down and unbuttoned his pants.

He pressed down, forcing his pants down as he shifted his body and exposing himself to her, exposed desire, exposed his arousal. Only Trellia could capture him fully. Nothing could compare: She was his everything.

"It? My passion in life?" He grinned and pulled her skirt down, the soft band stretching as she lifted her hips helping him. "Let me show you. I...I love you Trellia. You are the energy of my life."

As she slipped the skirt off, he slipped into her with a soft sigh of pleasure, his mind, body, and sheer existence given over to her.

It was only them. Only their love. Only their passion. He could stay here forever. Stay with her forever. Here, in perfection.

Date night was not *draumr* night for him.

Shattered Dreams

"It's ready." That was all Col had sent, and it was all Col needed to send. It had taken almost a week. Ostensibly, it had taken so long because microtracks which could be wired up for remote control were in short supply. Trellia, he was sure, was partly to blame for the delay. She must have been communicating with Col and helping make up excuses. As much as he had wanted the message, he'd wanted it delayed, so he hadn't probed.

There was nothing in life like being with Trellia. The only thing close was a discovery coming to fruition. That said, he wanted his time with Trellia to never end, for the world to just pause and their time together to stream on to eternity. In that regard, he was as much to blame for allowing the delay as either of them.

What mattered is that she was with him now, headed toward the Dreamoria, his work and his bonded together, so maybe it didn't matter either way. He wasn't sure and couldn't think about it. All he knew was that the *draumrs* were ready and this was the time it would all come together and work.

Unel walked down the hallway, passing doors of the research center faster and faster as his excitement grew the closer he got to the Dreamoria.

He could see it now. Microtracks ready, *draumrs* on their foreheads (held in place with a small necklace of sorts he'd made during his time with Trellia), and the two of them asleep, sharing a dream together.

He sped up. Five years of work, hundreds of *draumr* models, and thousands of failed tests later, it was ready!

Any faster and he'd be running.

He reached the door labeled Dreamoria and flung it open.

It was like magic. Boring magic—the kind only scientists enjoy —but magic nonetheless. Everything was laid out in place, waiting for the magician and his assistant to arrive and the show to begin. Not even the *draumrs* looking like knotted messes could detract from this moment.

He flipped around like a magician welcoming his assistant and peered down the hall with surprise. He paused for a moment while Trellia caught up.

"Ready?" he asked.

Trellia laughed. "No, I need some avak. I don't usually run before bed," she said. "Col?"

"It's on the table in the back," he said from the control room. "Hot and no sweetener."

Trellia grabbed two cups and brought one to Unel. She toasted the control room window. "To success!"

She took a sip, grimacing as the bitter root flavor tingled her tongue, then shivered as it settled into her muscles and mind. She'd only had avak a couple of times before and Unel knew it took a lot more cups than that before someone could drink it without a visceral reaction.

Unel was used to the flavor and could almost sense the taste of another herb to it, but he burned his lip when he took a sip. Hot tea was better for putting you to sleep, but why did it need to be so hot? Being hot enough to burn your lips and taste buds didn't make it taste less like dirt.

He shrugged, realized he missed the toast, and offered up his own toast with a motion of the cup.

"Thanks. I'll need to drink a couple of cups to calm down enough to sleep," he said. He gulped down the rest, accepting the hot burn on an already burned palate, then poured another cup. Ignoring the burn, he downed it too, then wrapped the broadcasting *draumr* over his forehead as the tea soothed and relaxed his mind.

Unel looked over Trellia, smiling at her beauty, but not distracted enough to skip over the *draumr*. She had naturally placed it on perfectly and lay there relaxed, peaceful, beautiful.

It was time. They were on other sides of the room. Soon they would be dreaming. Dreaming together. Sharing a dream. For the first time, two Arterians would communicate by mind only.

He smiled as the avak root sank in, lulling him to sleep, and closed his eyes.

"Let's go back to yesterday," he whispered.

"Mhmm," Trellia agreed.

Col dimmed the lights, Unel yawned, and sleep came.

Unel looked around. The world was a blur of colors not yet in focus, but he still recognized it. Sumna City Park. They had been there yesterday for a picnic before he came back to work. It was an encouraging start to the dream.

"Trellia?" he said.

He looked back and forth as the park came into focus, the vagueness of a dream making it seem more real than real. Blackish tree trunks appeared, their branches and colorful leaves quickly following suit. Small bushes peppered with yellow and orange flowers focused into clarity, followed by little white flowers, then the uncut grass underfoot flowing in the soft breeze. He could even hear the sound of bird calls fade into the dream, filling the air with a playful tune.

He looked out farther and the sky became clearer, the Fire Rainbow full of fury as it scorched a path across the Arterian aurora, phosphorescent waves of teal just like they had been the day before. And in the distance he could see their cylindrical apartment building looming far above the trees. Normally he wouldn't be able to figure out which building was theirs, but in a dream, everything important stood out.

Their apartment was a center of technology far removed from the nature of Sumna City Park. It was comfortable and inviting, but the park was another level of relaxation beyond what any building could provide. They came here to escape all the trappings of everyday life and just relax. Even their touchpads were left at home so that there was no way to interrupt their shared peace.

Looking around the park again, he saw her. In the same white skirt and blouse she wore yesterday—but without yesterday's grass stains—legs waving as she swayed back and forth in the swing. She saw him at the same time and waved him over.

It was then that the fog of the dream lifted fully and he realized that she was here! Here in a dream! She was here in a dream with him!

He ran to her. He ran faster than he could run in the waking world, gliding over the ground as his feet moved in vast strides. He ran by force of will, not the force of his feet.

He didn't stop with as much grace. He stopped abruptly, just before colliding with the swing. He held his legs tight, ready to stop the swing so that he could lean in and kiss her as the swing came down and slammed against him. He almost tumbled forward into her, but somehow evaded gravity and kept his balance.

In his excitement to see her, he'd almost forgotten where "here" was. He took a step back, eyes focused on Trellia, closed his eyes and wished that this were a dream they were sharing and not just a dream of his. He had to stay focused and not get too distracted by her.

He opened his eyes slowly, reached out, and touched the sun, visualizing the two of them in their apartment.

The world blurred around him, but didn't switch. He couldn't control where they were.

What did that mean? He was an expert at lucid dreaming. Why couldn't he change the dream? He had tried to change the dream with her. If she were actually here, could he change the dream for her and himself or did it take consent?

She was looking at him. Amused. Giving him time to think it through. That pleasant, patient smile was part of what made her perfect. How he longed to have a child with her, a family. And they were so close.

It's a dream, he told himself. *Figure out if she's here or not.*

Visualizing the first thing that came to mind, he lifted his fingers and a pearlescent *attaten* orb appeared between them, the fertility *aten*.

Trellia smirked and watched as he let the visualization go and it dissipated. She continued to sit there quietly musing as he worked his way through the problem. He could control some things, but not everything. How would he know if she were the real Trellia or not? Maybe it was as easy as asking.

"Are you real? The real Trellia?" he asked.

Trellia didn't answer. She was new to using a *draumr*, but Unel had shown her how to lucid dream. She tapped her eyelids, looked around and frowned. Her trick hadn't worked either. She continued mimicking him, making an *attaten* appear between her fingers.

"I can't change it either," she said, then raised the *attaten*. "This? Did you know I was given one? I don't think I got a chance to tell you," she said coyly. She took a deep breath as she took in his body with her eyes. "We didn't talk much the last two days."

Unel forgot the dream for a moment. She'd gotten an *attaten*? That meant she would have taken it, except... he thought back and realized she had never said she hadn't taken one; she'd simply said she would think about it. Obviously, she had been thinking about it, but had she taken it? Had she placed it to her lips and let the energy flow into her body bringing to life her womb, making it so they could have a baby, a family?

"Wait, you did? When? I mean, when can we?" He almost stammered over the words.

Trellia laughed. "I already took its energy... And we already have," she said as the little fertility sphere glimmered before vanishing from her fingers.

"I think we're sharing a dream, Unel. I can't prove it, but I feel it. I feel you're my Unel, not my mind's Unel."

Trellia reached out, wrapped her arms around him, and pulled him in for a kiss.

Unel's brain swam. Forget the dream. Forget sharing a dream. Forget everything! She ate an *attaten*? And they'd made love. Quite a bit, in fact. She was right that they hadn't talked much the last two days, but she could have made time to mention that fact. An *attaten*—a fertility spore—and she'd... They were going to be parents! Yes, she could have found time to mention that! She was so coy, so wonderful, so surprising, so much everything he wanted.

Unel found himself embarrassingly aroused. He stepped back enough to break the kiss, but leaned in and whispered. "I want to—"

Something in the back of his mind kicked in. A little sensibility. If this was a dream, then Col would be recording.

"Col, if the receiver is working, a little privacy please," he said loud enough for anyone in the park to hear and hopefully strong enough Col would pick it up on the relay video.

Trellia threw her head back laughing. "Again? Here?" she asked as she leaned forward, letting her laughter die and lifted her leg up between his, slowly, enticingly.

"If you want that to be our first shared dream..." She trailed off, shrugging, then leaned in, putting her hands at his hips and sliding them up, lifting his shirt.

Unel felt a joy like nothing he'd felt before. This was like a dream he'd never had, but always should have had coming true. Trellia and the *draumr*. Every passion of his life coming together at once. It was almost too much to expect. It was definitely too much to actually have.

As she lifted his shirt, a fire from inside him lit up as if though he were incinerating. The pain shot up through him and a lightning bolt of pain slammed into his abs, piercing his body. Unel's scream was silenced by his own body shattering. His last vision was that of the shock on Trellia's face as shards of his body pierced hers and light consumed his world.

Unel jolted up, almost tumbling as he leaped off his sleeping table and ran for Trellia. The vision of his body exploding into her was seared into his mind and blinded him as he darted across the room, instinctively knowing where his bonded lay.

In a moment he was at her side, hands around her shoulders and shaking her as he tried to blink away the memory. He cried as he called out her name. "Trellia! Trellia!"

She didn't move, didn't respond to his shaking, didn't respond to his screaming. She was breathing, but not moving. She was caught in the dream world.

He threw her *draumr* across the room and turned toward the control room to call for help, but smoke flooded out where he could normally see Col's twinkling blue eyes.

He screamed for help, but fire alarms drowned out his calls.

He looked at Trellia's limp body, eyes blurry with tears, voice soft and hopeless. "Oh, Sumatta, what happened? Energy of my life, come back to me. Come back to me, Trellia."

Hunt

The aged commander sat in a chair made of animal skin the same shade of black as his hair. It was as soft and well-worn as the commander's skin. The commander wore a gentle smile, all too knowing for the subject matter at hand. That's exactly how he wanted to look. If you did not look threatening, but seemed as if you might be, people either gave you deference or they underestimated you. Either was an advantage. These Arterians were a trusting people and often gave deference, but the man he sat across from was not a typical Arterian, he was General Byelt.

General Byelt was General of the Armies, leader of all armed forces on Arter. Having a single general for every army on Arter was a redundancy. Even having an army for a single unified front of all city-states was redundant and introduced a weakness—trained forces were better resistance should any city-state or group of them break away.

"General Byelt, I assure you I am quite capable of taking out any threats that arise. I've been doing that longer than you've been alive."

General Byelt snorted. "I doubt that. You'd have to be at least eighty by now for that to be true."

No need to answer that, the commander thought. It would just make it harder to be underestimated.

"Be that as it may," the commander said. "My confirmed kills is greater than any on your force. All I ask is that you let me take the mission and be given a little intel. I can do the rest on my own."

"Fine. You've got it, but we don't know you and won't acknowledge you. If you get caught, don't turn our way."

"I never sell out my benefactors," he said.

The commander stood up, gave a solid salute and turned around as dismissed. He marched out like an old, experienced man, closing the door behind him.

He needed to find two men. He didn't know where they were, but he had just convinced the general that they posed a threat to all of Arter and to Sumatta itself. It had been easy enough to get what he wanted. The general underestimated him, so he gave him what he asked for and he had asked for more than he needed.

Finding two Arterians amongst billions would not be easy. The gender would be male. They were always males. They would be a little odd, too. They could never exactly fit in. That would get him down to a few hundred thousand, maybe a million. Then he would find out their skills. They always had more skills than the average.

Once he'd filtered it down to a few thousand, he would have to be careful. Getting too close would tip them off and that could be more lethal than a bullet to the head.

He worked his way over to the armory and selected a specific sniper weapon and picked up some ammunition. He would need to customize this to kill these targets. He needed to kill them in more than one way or they'd find a way of staying alive. He pocketed the ammunition and folded the weapon up into a carrying case, then headed to his transport.

The transport looked as old and rickety as the commander. He had bought it off of an old farmer who now had the latest make and model. The old model had yet to be fitted with the now- required government tracking beacons. Tanseor had added a little to the anonymity by retrofitting it with a damaged identity beacon. The signal would be interpreted as just too old to read. Not being traced was as important as not having a bullet traced.

He lifted off and set in coordinates for Si'inth. He ignored the sky. The Arterian sky was impressive, but not as impressive as he'd seen elsewhere, and he needed rest, so he leaned back and slept, letting the transport take him away.

Sleeping on transports was not actually sleeping, it was like a disturbed sleep. When the thing turned left or right or occasionally veered up or down, it jostled you. *There is a reason beds don't move*, he thought as he bumped his head on an unexpected turn. It ruined dreams too, and he was enjoying his recurring dream at the moment. A vision of a nondescript Arterian taking a special bullet right to the head and dropping dead at his core.

The Arterian was only nondescript until the commander got the reports he needed and filtered it down to the right two Arterians. Then his dream would become even more vivid as he watched them felled like a tree being cut down.

A sudden loss of altitude alerted him to their descent, waking him. It landed a minute later and he stepped out with his weapon and marched to a shed to the side of the rented house in this small mountain town. He pulled out the boxes of ammunition and set them on the counter, popping open the tops and emptying them of the hard explosive. He set six of these in a row before him, then opened the table drawer.

Hundreds of *attaten* filled the drawer. He grabbed six and set them on top of the table, then opened the drawer to the right and pulled out a small iridescent metal plate. He swiped each *attaten* repeatedly in one direction against the metal plate and inverted its magnetic polarity, giving it an inverse effect. These *aten* would be deadly to any living being, Arterian or not.

The commander smiled as he popped the *attaten* into the ammunition casings, then filed them down into an aerodynamic shape.

Two targets, six shots, all lethal. This was going to be easy once he found them.

He couldn't remember how long he had sought these two. Counting the years became difficult about the same time you started forgetting your own age. How long he had been hunting them didn't matter anymore; how long he had left to hunt them was what mattered. That time was getting shorter by the second.

His touchpad signaled a new incoming message. He grabbed it and scrolled through the messages. There were fifteen thousand. He thought there would be more. *This is going to be easy*, he thought as he sat on the broken down couch, kicked his feet up, and started sifting through the potentials.

Children

"Governor Muaske thinks you're all children," Spratee shouted to the three thousand Arterians filling Attatar Stadium. The audience booed Governor Muaske, some shouting for the governor's resignation, some calling for Spratee to continue, almost everyone responding to the suggested response cues. The cues were subtle: a well-placed "attendee", colors on various broadcast signs, emotions added shown by the speechless interpreter, and the well-known signature tics of Spratee.

He stood center stage delivering the best speech of his career. He didn't need anyone to tell him that or the well-calculated audience response, he just knew. A detailed analysis of his speech would uncover a ruthless study of past speeches by the most renowned governors of Attatar, governors of the one State in Arter where being governor meant you were effectively the leader of Arter itself.

Spratee was not a politician by birth, nor was he a natural politician. Spratee was a politician by choice, on a path of his choice, one started out on from the time of his birth. The apex of that path was the governorship of Attatar. From there he would have unlimited power to finally fulfill the mission he'd chosen all those years ago.

His words were carefully chosen to instill fear, uncertainty, and doubt in the population, then give them hope of replacing that with something better. It was important not to state exactly what that was and to lean in the direction of his political party. Too much specificity meant expectations and culpability he'd never be able to fulfill, and he planned on delivering on only one promise. A promise he'd made to himself many years ago.

He was going to avenge his mother's death.

He was well on the way toward that with this speech. It, he did not doubt—and had every confidence—would cement the vote in his favor.

"He wants you bound to him, beholden to him... He wants you to rely on him for everything. You are not children! You are not his servants!

"I'm here to tell you that you can take care of yourself, that you don't need the government to take care of you, and you don't need Governor Muaske to tell you how to live.

"That doesn't mean the government doesn't have a role to play; it means the government shouldn't tell you what role to play. Look, my fellow Arterians, do you really want the government to keep telling you how to live your life? If you ask Governor Muaske to take care of your every need, if you accept his claim that he can take care of you better than you can take care of yourself, if you accept him treating you as a chil—"

Spratee was interrupted by some disturbance on stage; it looked like someone put something on the stage. He'd noticed it out of the corner of his eye and lifted his foot slightly to nonchalantly kick the thing off his stage before realizing it was a child that had crawled off a parent's shoulder. As its parents turned to grab the boy, Spratee waved them back and kneeled down.

Picking the child up, he plastered on a perfectly poised smile of confidence and calm. This would make a great campaign shot. Spratee with the short, angular brown hairstyle of the last most popular leader in a formal suit, the edges lined in a commanding red, holding a young child as he chastised Governor Muaske for babying the population.

"Yes, a child. We coddle them," he said. "Nurture them," he added, leaning down to hand the child back to its parents. "And then they grow up. We do not continue coddling them, we let them grow up. That's right, my friends. If we coddle, things do not grow..." He was back to his speech. He'd recovered from the interruption. This was perfect.

"And that's what it comes down to, my friends. When you vote, you're casting your vote to be coddled like a baby or be respected for the adults you are. The government is here to protect your rights, not *be* your rights. Vote for me. I'm your future governor, Spratee, and I will respect you. You have my word."

Those final four words were his signature line and the perfect cue. The audience erupted in a raucous standing ovation, cheering for Spratee.

He walked off the stage, half looking behind him, half looking in front of him, waving at the audience.

"Spratee!" Noselar yelled as soon as he stepped off stage. His angry bonded marched up to him, her perfectly cut dress commanding the authority it had been intended to, swaying wildly. "I told you to watch yourself! Look what you've done," she said and held up her touchpad.

He waved hers away with a scowl and held up his own, streaming the latest report of his speech. His face grew red and his chest heaved with fury at each word. The bastards had picked up on the never-delivered kick. He threw the pad down and stormed to the bathroom, his security detail slowing him down as they vetted the bathroom for threats.

What was he going to do? He washed his face, looked in the mirror, and sighed. What had they done before? Had there— yes, there had been a case like this before. But would she go with it? Of course, she would. She would have to.

Encouraged and confident, he patted his face dry and burst out of the bathroom, striding toward the debriefing room at full speed.

"Get me that family! Now!" he yelled as he entered the room.

His chief of staff pointed at a few staff members and waved them off. They went scurrying to find the family.

"Now, how did the rest of it go?" Spratee asked his chief of staff.

"They loved it. If there wasn—"

"No, we'll talk about that later and I want more than 'loved it'," he said. He was calm and commanding now, the shakiness washed away and replaced by the Spratee everyone knew. It was rare for him to lose his cool in public, though he was known for a strong temper.

He pointed at his head of public image. "Talk to me."

"You held yourself strong. Your voice was commanding, but caring. Audience response was fantastic. And your message was well received. There are a lot of great clips we can take from this speech. This will should up your standings once the family makes a public state—"

"They're not going to make a statement. They're going with me to the public debrief. Where are they? Why aren't they here by now? Can we get the kid a mouth toy?"

Spratee spun his stocky, strong body toward Noselar. "Be ready for your cue."

He leaned in and whispered in her ear. Noselar's eyes grew wide and she took a step back, then grabbed her stomach and shook her head. She quietly mouthed, "But I can't. I haven't."

He shrugged off her rebuttal, staring at her as if it were an order, not a request.

She stepped forward and whispered just loud enough for his inner circle to hear. "Spratee, one day you'll burn yourself with your lies. As sure as Sumatta gave us life, you'll burn yourself."

He turned as a group walked in, a small boy held by his birth parent in one arm among them.

"Here they are," he said warmly, extending his hand toward the birth parent. "It is great to meet you. And you, again, little one." He tapped at the boy's nose. The boy laughed and rubbed his nose. "What's your name?"

The mother rocked back and forth on her feet, extending the child out to Spratee, seemingly ready to explode with excitement. "Mar'aten, Governor Spratee."

Spratee almost smirked. She'd addressed him as governor. This would be great.

"Mar'aten. Named after the ocean and life. How inspiring." Spratee looked at the man with them, the child's other parent, and bowed approvingly. The man was strong, well-built, hair a little messy and clothes that didn't quite fit him well, as if he was wearing an outfit worn only for special occasions. The man looked as if he'd worked on a ship for most of his life. "I'm betting the name had a lot to do with you. You look like your family knows the value of good work and strong protection from the government. It's an honor to meet you."

"I'm Tonnotena, governor. Thanks," the man said, pausing to figure out what to say next. "Not much for talking, you know? I leave that to Malatee," he said, looking toward the birth parent. "You've got my vote, governor."

He said the last line in a tone of finality, as if he hoped that that would be all he was expected to say and all he would have to say.

Spratee nodded respectfully and turned to the birth parent. "I need your help. They are saying I was going to kick Mar'aten. Truth is he caught me off guard and I lost my step. You know my platform, though, and you can help me. Would you be willing to come with me to the post-speech press debrief? You don't have to say anything. Just your presence will be enough support."

Tonnotena grabbed Malatee by the elbow. She turned around and said something that calmed him a little, though he was still clearly unsettled by the idea.

"Thank you," Spratee said. "Follow me."

Surrounded by an entourage of a dozen Arterians in every direction, Spratee guided them through a backstage exit and into a small room filled with a boisterous, loud gaggle of press.

"By Sumatta itself! Let's quiet down and welcome our next governor, Spratee," Spratee's chief of staff shouted at the array of press sitting off the stage in a room too small for all of their chatter as he walked in in front of Spratee, Mar'aten, Malatee, and Tonnotena.

Spratee walked into the room holding Mar'aten and showing as much excitement as Malatee who flanked him on one side while Tonnotena kept a step behind them both. The group walked up to the microphone at the front of the room as the crowd took its time hushing.

"As I said on stage, when we are children, we are coddled." Spratee touched Mar'aten's nose. The toddler smiled as if supremely pleased, then opened its little mouth and spewed out a small explosion that splattered Spratee's suit. Apparently, he was as nervous as the rest of them. Spratee kept his poise, laughed, and held up his hand to stop his entourage from coming to assist. He took off his tie and wiped the boy's mouth as the little one reached out trying to capture the tie and pull it into his mouth like a toy to be suckled.

"And when we're grown, we are no longer coddled. So, if any of you try that, don't expect the same response." The press erupted with laughter until he held up his hand again in a sign for silence.

"I have heard the complaints and," he added, turning to Tonnotena, then Malatee. "The complaints are unfounded."

He turned back to the press and changed his tone to one of condescension, as if the audience should have known what he was about to say. "These are only character attacks. They are designed to distract you from what matters: my platform. A platform which is so frighteningly progressive that Governor Muaske's minions are afraid to argue its merits. They know they'll lose an argument of merits."

He turned back and held Mar'aten out to Malatee. "Would you? And can we get them chairs? Comfortable chairs. Not like the ones we give the press."

The press chuckled, then a question rose above the noise. "Were you going to kick the boy?"

Spratee donned a bright, skilled smile, turning to look at the press with none of the cunning he felt and all of the shock he meant to convey.

"Why would I want to kick a child when my bonded one is going to be birth parent to our first child soon?" he said, turning to Noselar.

A shocked press turned their full attention to Noselar, they seemed to collectively hold their breaths for a heartbeat.

On cue, Noselar stepped forward from the sides of the room, walking toward Spratee while holding her stomach and casting a bright, confident smile. Only Spratee would know it wasn't the smile of a woman carrying a child, but the smile of a woman carrying a secret. He clenched his jaws, letting no tension or worry show outwardly. She wouldn't sabotage him now, would she? No, she never had, and she never would, but she did love owning his secrets, even if she never used them against him.

The press got over its moment of shock and erupted with a cacophony of questions. Mar'aten started to cry. Spratee held his hand up, but there would be no quieting them now. Everyone shouted to have their question be the first one Spratee answered.

He shook his head with disappointment, went to the microphone, signaled for it to be turned up and said, "You've made a baby cry. You're worse than my opponent. You should be ashamed. I'd send you to your rooms, but instead I'm going to go to my rooms."

His entourage quickly assembled and guided them out, shielding them from the press as Spratee keep ordering them to take care of the baby. He accentuated his orders with dramatic hand motions so everyone watching the replay would see him as caring more about the baby than himself.

* * *

"Watch her as you look to help her," Strypan said, holding

out a pair of glasses.

Unel took the glasses and held them out in front of him. He could see Trellia's security cam footage streaming into the left lense. She was lying in a bed in her med room, breathing slowly, otherwise motionless, caught in a dream world that was killing her.

"I could just watch her from my touchpad. Why do I need glasses?"

"Knowing you *can* see her and *actually* seeing her is why you're still here."

Strypan was infuriating. Always speaking as if he were a philosopher, making what he said hard to understand, but always being right. Why couldn't the man just speak in plain, clear Arterian like everyone else?

"Thanks," Unel said and set the glasses down on the side. "I'll thi—"

"Unel?" a man in crisp, official looking clothing said from the door. "Can we talk?" the doctor asked.

"I'll see both of you soon," Strypan said looking at Trellia. He left the room with a nod to the doctor. Unel knew Strypan sensed his frustration. It was just hard to care on a normal day, even harder to care today.

The doctor held out his touchpad for Unel. "On the top is her brain scan. On the bottom is another similar brain scan."

Unel looked at the two, saw the similarities and looked to the doctor waiting for him to state the conclusion. The man waited.

"And?" Unel prompted.

The doctor took a deep breath, then said, "The bottom is also her brain scan. One we took when she was four and fell off the porch. Trellia is regressing, Unel."

'Watch her as you look to help her,' Strypan had just said. Unel couldn't sit here any longer. He was losing his Trellia. He handed the touchpad back to the doctor, thanked him, then grabbed his glasses and headed to his transport.

It was obvious the doctors weren't going to find a way to help her. He'd been lying to himself with hope about that. There was only one way. He was going to have to go back to the dream world and fetch her. Help her. He didn't really know what he would do there, but he knew that going in was the only way. He was afraid of the risk, but he was more afraid of losing the only one who mattered to him. He could not lose his Trellia.

Hopping in his transport, he set the destination. The only destination where he could get help. The transport lifted off and angled toward Caleston. Specifically, Trellia's parents' house. Xarat and Gemtra would be there—they were always there—and they would be the only ones with something that could help him now.

Xarat and Gemtra lived on the northern border of Caleston, far enough from the ocean to the north and far enough from the swamps to the south to be in the meadows between. It was a plush, flat land, with soil too soft for tall buildings. Their house was a simple one-story cylinder with moss growing up the walls, dark blue paint chipping away from the tattered building.

His ship turned to the right as they approached, homing in on the landing pad.

Gemtra was already walking up to meet him.

"Unel, son, how is she? Anything new?" she asked as he got out of the transport.

Trellia was breathing. He could see that. He hadn't stopped watching her since he'd left her room. She was breathing, but that was all.

"They say she's regressing. They don't know why or how or what to do about it. All they can tell me is that she has the mind of a four-year-old. I... I would never have... if I'd have known..." he said. A tear trailed out of his left eye. Infuriating tear. He'd tried to hold it back. It was blurring his view of her.

Gemtra hugged him. "I know, son. Come on. Talk to me.

I'll make some tea."

"I didn't come here to talk, Gemtra. I'm sorry. I can't." He swallowed and took a breath. "If it's true... If she's regressed, then maybe something from her childhood will help. I was hoping—"

"Yes, of course. Come on," she said, patting him on the back and wrapping her arm around him as she guided him to the house.

He stopped at the door. Trellia's childhood home. He'd always been here with Trellia. She was with him, in a way. But this was different. Another tear escaped. He wiped it away, clearing his vision, and walked in.

Whenever they visited, either Xarat or Gemtra were on some drug trip. One of them always stayed sober. It must have been Xarat's turn to trip. The hefty, normally jovial man sat in his chair, relaxed fitting pants and t-shirt on, mumbling. His eyes were dilated and he was staring at the ceiling, waving his hands as if studying them.

As Unel passed, Xarat started crying.

Gemtra stopped, whispered something into Xarat's ear and his crying changed. Unel wasn't sure how he could tell, but it changed from a sad cry to a happy one. Xarat cupped his arms together as if cradling an invisible baby.

"It's been harder on him. She was always his little girl," Gemtra said.

Unel looked at Xarat as he pinched an invisible nose and started to laugh. His cry wasn't happy, it was a comforted pain. Unel felt a connection with Xarat he'd never felt—if Unel could have Trellia back even as a vision, but knew she wasn't really back, it'd be just as hard for him. He realized as he watched Trellia through his left eye that that was exactly what he had.

Gemtra tugged at his shirt and nodded toward a back room. He followed her to Trellia's childhood room. He took a deep breath as the door opened and an array of smells slammed against him causing his head to roll back as he took it all in. Rows of colored plants in chemical baths filled the room.

Gemtra and Xarat loved their drugs, even growing their own. They'd converted Trellia's room into a grow room when she'd moved out. He hadn't known what was in the room, but he'd suspected it on their visits. Trellia had always found something else to do when he's suggested checking out her room. Now he knew why.

The array of plants was like a confessional. Psychedelics were their favorite. You could have any trip you wanted by picking the right plant here. A few of them were risky—a bad mindset and you'd have a bad trip—but most of them were known for their positive hallucinations.

Gemtra walked through the garden and over to a glass display case on the far wall.

"When your child leaves home, they leave more than memories. These were her favorites," she said. She opened the display case and pulled out a small stuffed spatiatta with dark pearlescent skin in shades of blue and green and handed it to him.

How little girls liked these dolls was beyond Unel. They were ugly. They had heads like a shroom with gills on the bottom, tentacles dangled from the sides like a sea creature and their bodies had scales that protected them like a shield. Spatiatta were only beautiful in a swarm.

He'd seen swarms of millions of them in the skies during electromagnetic storms, their translucent bodies twinkling with the aurora as if they were feeding off the electricity as it bolted amongst the soft clouds of color.

Little girls liked them, he guessed, because of their magic. Women were born infertile and spatiatta produced *attaten* like eggs. *Attaten* were toxic until mid-youth when the body started producing hormones. The more hormones present when the egg was consumed, the more receptive the woman's body would be to its energy and the more likely she would get pregnant. Trellia was an adult when she consumed the *attaten*, so she would be very fertile.

Unel closed his eyes, crying silently. Trellia was probably pregnant. By Sumatta itself, he was sure of it. Not only was he losing his Trellia, but he was losing his unborn baby.

He noticed Gemtra patting him on the back.

"What is it, son?" she asked.

"I think she's pregnant. She... Oh, by Sumatta itself, I just want her back. Do you think... Do you think..." He clutched the toy and took a couple of breaths. "I need her back, Gemtra."

Gemtra bowed her head. "We both do, son. How did it happen? Do you know?"

His voice cracked. He hadn't been able to talk about it, but sooner or later he'd have to talk about it—maybe talking about it would help him find the solution.

"It worked. The *draumrs* connected our dreams. We were sitting on a swing and she told me she'd eaten an *attaten*, then the lightning hit the Dreamoria and I exploded. Just shattered into pieces.

"I could see shards of my body cutting into her. I could see the horror on her face. She must be stuck there. I'm sure she thinks she's hurt and believes it's real. How do I get back to her? How do I bring her back? I was hoping this," he said holding up the toy, "would help. Help make her feel comfortable. Remind her of who she is."

"Can you go back to her? Can you connect to her dreams?"

"I don't know. I don't know if she's even dreaming. What if going back causes more harm? She saw me explode. I just don't know how."

"She didn't see me there, right?"

Unel let her question percolate. Gemtra wasn't there. If they could connect to Trellia's dreams, maybe her birth parent —who had been there when she was four—could connect with her. She loved Gemtra. That would be a stronger connection than a toy.

"We could try. How much do you weigh?"

Gemtra laughed. "I don't get on a scale often. I'll have to get that for you."

Unel sighed, pocketing the toy. "I'd better get back to the Dreamoria. Will you message me your weight? I'll make a *draumr* for you—that's the device that connects you to the dream world—and we can meet up with Trellia. I need to check something first. I want to make sure you're safe. I won't lose you both."

"That sounds good, Unel."

He stood up, gave Gemtra a hug, then saw himself out, Xarat still cuddling the baby, but tickling its imaginary tummy now.

If only it were that simple, Unel thought as he closed the door behind him, giving Xarat one last look. Either way, I'm going to get her back.

* * *

Unel stood next to Col in front of a display panel a couple of rooms down from the Dreamoria. They had co-opted the office and converted it into a temporary lab after the explosion. The lab itself was a place Unel didn't ever want to enter again. He never wanted to see those sleeping pads, the window that had blown out, he never wanted to see any of it that reminded him of Trellia getting hurt. It was a place of dreams turned into a place of nightmares.

He had found a place inside Attatar's obsidian cavern. The natural formation was a perfect fit for the Dreamoria. It was lower in the ground, so farther away from the dangers of the electrically-charged sky and obsidian was less likely to conduct electricity. That lab was still being set up. Couches would replace sleeping tables and the control room was being replaced by an observation deck. Nothing would serve as a reminder of Trellia's pain. In the meantime, they were using this makeshift lab.

Unel was a disheveled mess, running his hands through his oily hair as he watched. Col was only slightly better. He had slept on a couch and got some rest. Neither had showered in days and both were just as obsessed with finding out what went wrong.

On two screens in front of them, replays of the doomed dream played.

"You asked for privacy, here," he said, pointing at a line on one graph. He was talking more to himself, going through the events of the day again. Unel had lost track counting how many times they'd gone over this. What else were they supposed to see?

"Two seconds later, I paused the data recording, here," he said, pointing at a different spot. "About eight seconds later, Trellia's *draumr* surged."

Col pressed some buttons on the control pad for the viewers and the screens displayed pictures of the damaged control room. "We know the building was struck by lightning. These prove that," he said, tapping on two different pictures of an electrical panel with a burn going down the side.

"It's a little harder to tell how the electricity affected the *draumr*, but from what we can tell, the surge went into the control panel," he said, tapping the picture of the destroyed control panel, "which exploded and filled the control room with smoke. Then it shot through the wires into the microtrack and into the sleeping table before hitting her *draumr*," Col reiterated, his voice tired.

Unel hadn't expected a surge at all, much less a catastrophic one. And definitely nothing that could endanger him or Trellia. He ran his fingers through his hair as he tried to analyze the situation. He was tired, but he needed to save Trellia. If only something could have stopped the electricity. He would need something to protect them from another surge with Gemtra.

"What could we use for a *draumr* surge protector, Col? We

need something to break the connection before anyone else gets hurt."

"A surge protector? Yes, that's a great idea." He leaned his head forward and thought about it. He looked up, worried. "Do you think... Do you think we'll bring her back? I mean... I've known her—both of you—since we were... I love her. I love you. We're best friends. Can we do it?"

Col was shaken. Most of his wounds from the explosion had healed and the few remaining were healing fast, but the pain of almost losing two friends had hit him harder than the explosion.

"Col, we're not giving up. We'll get her back. Let's just focus on how," Unel said and patted his friend on the back. Col couldn't be the one consumed by emotion; Unel was fighting his own emotions and didn't have energy to help his friend fight it too.

"Yes. A surge protector? For lightning, we need a special surge protector. The energy is too much to protect a *draumr*. The problem is portability. We have to move the microtracks and have them wired up so that I can control them."

"No, we don't," Unel said.

"You're right," Col said, coming out of his depression. They were making progress. For the first time in days. "Let me look for some wireless microtracks."

If they had wireless microtracks, wires wouldn't be going through a building. The microtrack might still conduct the energy of the lightning. To stop it, they would need an insulator.

"We'll need to make sure it has a strong insulator where it attaches," Unel added.

"Yes, of course. Now let me see...."

Col tapped through screens of different supplies and picked out a microtrack and some furniture protectors with a high insulation value. "This is perfect. Not perfect, but Unel, we've got it. We can do this. Give me until..." Col tapped at the screen, ordering the hardware and picking the fastest shipping available. "Tomorrow. They don't have it in stock locally or within reasonable flying distance. I can have it for you tomorrow."

"We'll meet in the medical unit. You can prep it there. I'll make sure the doctors know to give you free rein."

They both relaxed a little. They hadn't saved her yet, but having something to do was better than fretting and it gave him hope. It gave them both hope.

"We should clean up. Gemtra won't be happy if we come in looking like this," Col said. "She's a very laid back Arterian, but I think I can smell myself, and I know I can smell you."

"Agreed. I'll get some rest too. Nothing can go wrong tomorrow. Nothing."

"I could use some soon. See you tomorrow," Col said.

Parenting

Gemtra gently opened the door to the med unit. She peeked in and saw Trellia laying on the bed, sleeping peacefully, lost in a dream world that was killing her. Unel was leaning over her, tucking the little spatiatta doll in her arms. He made it look like she was cradling it like a baby. A tear rolled from Gemtra's eye. She wiped the tear from her face, took a breath and stepped in.

"Gemtra. I'm so glad to see you," Unel said. He was sitting in a chair next to Trellia's bed in sweatpants and a t-shirt. Unshaven and hair messier than usual, he made a disheveled man look clean.

"How is she doing?" Gemtra asked.

"Nothing's changed."

Col, dressed in clean slacks and a pressed shirt, stepped forward holding out a *draumr*. His eyes were tired, but still twinkling blue sparkles of hope. "It's set for your mass," he said. "You'll need to sit in that chair. It's on a microtrack that will keep you safe."

He hadn't even greeted her. She'd have taken that as rude except they were all here for one thing. She reached out and took the *draumr*. The cord was too short to fit over her head and too big for a wrist, so it must be a headpiece. She fitted it on her head like a diadem and noted Col's approval. He handed her a cup of tea.

"This will help relax you," he said. "We have extra security precautions in place this time. You're safe."

"I brought my own tea," she said, holding up her bag and pulling out a container. "The only one whose safety I care about is my daughter's, Col. I'm willing to take any risk for her."

He stepped back, giving her some space and Gemtra sat

down in the chair next to Unel.

"I trust you on the tea," Unel said. He'd never been a fan of her psychedelic teas and she didn't really care if he trusted her or not. This tea would sedate her while also keeping her partially awake. She wasn't going to go into this blind and at the whim of a dream. Unel might have been studying dreams for a long time, but Gemtra had been mastering them for decades before he was born. She grinned and took a sip.

"The microtrack is on your chair, not the bed. We didn't want to disturb Trellia," Col said. "It will move in very small amounts. You shouldn't even notice."

Unel sat in his chair and turned, rubbing his eyes, to look at Gemtra, eyes pleading. "She has the broadcasting *draumr*, you have the receiver. You'll be going into her dream."

Gemtra took another sip of her tea. The tea enriched her senses, making her body tingle at the same time that it accentuated the colors of the room, making them brighter and seem to glow. It would slowly separate her view from the world around her and let her see into her mind's eye instead of through her eyes. Then she would fall asleep while her mind's eye stayed awake.

Unel's voice grew more choked up and raspy. "I don't know what to tell you when you're in there. I don't know what it will look like, if it will look like anything at all."

Gemtra reached out and took his hands in hers while inwardly she felt for Unel. She needed to be strong for him as well as for Trellia. "Son, I know you're worried. We all are. I need you to trust more than my tea, I need you to trust me. You might say trips through the mind are my forté."

"You're right. I do trust you," Unel said.

It was all he could say, she knew. He didn't really feel it; he felt hopeless and nothing she could say would truly help.

She let his hands go as he turned to Col and asked, "Are you ready?"

Gemtra yawned and leaned back in her chair, taking

another swig of tea. She didn't notice anything else they said. Her vision was separating, a mental shadow of Trellia being replaced by a darkness in her mind's eye. She was ready for whatever would come next. She was a birth parent, and there is nothing stronger than a birth parent's love for their child— there was nothing stronger than her love for her daughter.

Her vision went dark, then came back as she transitioned into the dream world. She wasn't looking through her mind's eye, but inside the dream, yet she could sense her waking self. It was close to being hypnotized, but hypnotized while being awake. She could open her eyes at any time she wanted; she could wake herself from the dream if it was too bad.

That was also the last thing she wanted to do.

She was in darkness. Blackness, really. The only color was little shards of Unel floating through the air, spinning slowly as they meandered around. That and a small child laying down, just floating in space.

Trellia.

How long had it been since she'd seen her baby as a baby? Four years old and sleeping soundly, her chest moving up and down in a calm rhythm. Gemtra remembered moments like that. There were two differences between now and then. Now she was dreaming and now there was a shard of Unel poking through her sleeping baby's forehead.

Gemtra gathered a birth parent's calm inside her and walked forward humming. She was never a singer. She hummed and envisioned the sound emanating from her as comforting waves that flowed through the air toward Trellia.

Reaching out left and right as she walked, she plucked shards of Unel out of the air. She envisioned her skirt having a pocket, then pocketed the shards.

It was only a few steps—and she hadn't picked all the shards out of the air—to get to Trellia. Gemtra kneeled down on the blackness, gently wiping Trellia's forehead.

"Let's clean up this mess. It looks like you're hurt. Let your Gemmy see," she said, talking in the more childlike voice she'd used when Trellia was four.

Trellia lay there, her skin cold, her breathing soft and measured, her eyes open and dilated, blurred to the world around her.

Gemtra took in a breath and with her mind's eye opened her senses to combine the real world with the dream world and the power of the tea to connect with her daughter on an unreal, but very real level. She sensed that Trellia's mind was as numb as the darkness. Trellia didn't know she was dreaming; she was simply caught in the blackness like an inescapable trap. It was like being in pain but not being able to feel it, touch it, or do anything about it—it was just debilitating.

It was hard to see her daughter in such pain. Trellia wasn't even feeling pain, but she was losing a battle to it. One that had made her mind regress to that of a child and would kill her. It was a battle her baby couldn't even fight.

Gemtra would not cry. She was here to help her baby. She was here to fight that fight. Calling on her mind's eye again, her waking body shivered as she called upon the strength of a parent—the strength to face anything for their children. It flooded her waking body and her sleeping mind. It empowered her.

She pushed Trellia's hair back and petted her face. "Now, see, Gemmy is here to make everything ok, baby. Let me see..."

Gemtra looked at the shard of Unel in Trellia's forehead and shook her head as if it had been a particularly nasty scratch on a knee. Trellia didn't know she was dreaming, but she was still dreaming. She could sense and see everything, so it had to be sincere. It had to seem real. Gemtra had to make it look like a kiss would make everything go away, so she'd put on the face she'd used so many times when Trellia had cuts and scratches as a child.

"Oh, well, it looks like Unel has been a little messy. Let's help him. Men need us to clean up after them, don't they?" she said with slight amusement. She reached out and with a quick tug, plucked the shard of Unel out of Trellia's forehead, quickly pocketing it.

"There, there. Now, we just need some magic, don't we? What do we know that's magic? That's right, a Gemmy kiss—it makes everything better again, doesn't it?" Gemtra leaned over her daughter's unmoving body and kissed her forehead firmly, pulling back and making a pop sound. "And, just like that. Magic!" she said, tossing her hands up in the air dramatically.

Trellia didn't move, but the cut on her forehead healed as if the shard had never been there.

It was only a matter of time. The cut had healed, so her daughter was getting better.

Gemtra sat back, closed her eyes, and hummed. She remembered Trellia's childhood, humming bedtime songs to Trellia, her daughter singing the words softly until she fell asleep.

"Gemmy? Where am I?" a weak Trellia asked.

Gemtra opened her eyes, smiling brightly, but trying to hold her sheer excitement back. This had to be done carefully. She had to be strong enough to hide her real emotions and only show the ones that would help Trellia. "Baby, how's your head? Do you feel better? You've been sick."

"Uh huh, but you kissed it. I'll get better now?"

"Of course, baby. Unel was messy, but we cleaned up, right? You just need a little time, then you'll be back to yourself, right?"

Trellia stared passed Gemtra and cocked her head to the side in confusion. "I see myself. Over there." Trellia pointed out into the blackness. "Gemmy, can you take me to myself?"

Gemtra turned around and saw Trellia in the distance. The adult Trellia. Her Trellia as she was in the bed in the medical unit, but smiling, loving, sweet... and healthy. The mind heals the body in mysterious ways. The things it throws at us in our subconscious are there because it knows we need them. Gemtra wasn't sure where this was going, but she trusted Trellia's subconscious to guide them. Still, she tested her connection to her mind's eye and moved her real hands into her lap.

Confident she was still in control, Gemtra looked back to her young Trellia. "Yes, baby. We will go to her in your dreams. Can you dream of yourself going to her? Dream of yourself becoming her? I bet you can. I know you can. You're Gemmy's strongest girl ever, aren't you?"

Young Trellia beamed with pride, bobbing her head rapidly. "I can dream of anything. Unel taught me. He's a messy man, huh? I..." Trellia yawned and trailed off. She closed her eyes and started humming the last song Gemtra had been humming. She then opened her eyes and lifted herself straight up, leaving her broken, sick body behind.

She looked at Gemtra and smiled. "See, I can dream of anything." Trellia reached out and wiggled her fingers and the space between them and the healthy Trellia collapsed. Trellia was facing herself.

Facing her current self, the younger self cocked her head to the side, looking at her current self as if she were a foreign concept. She didn't know what to do next.

"Now that you're dreaming, it's time to wake up," the older Trellia said to the younger, then she stepped into her younger self and the world went dark.

Gemtra sat there on her knees in the blackness and closed her eyes. Now she could release the pain of seeing her daughter in this agony. She hoped, by Sumatta itself, it had worked. She let herself cry like a baby for a moment before wiping her tears away and calling on her mind's eye to wake her.

"Trellia," Unel was saying as Gemtra woke. "Trellia, it's me, Unel."

Trellia lay there in a daze, eyes open, but not seeing. It was as if she couldn't hear Unel's pleas.

"The toy," Gemtra whispered. The tears hadn't only been in the dream world; she had plenty of them quietly streaming down her cheek now.

Unel plucked the toy from between Trellia's arms and held it up. "Do you remember this?"

Trellia's pupils dilated. She focused in on the toy and smiled, then turned her head, following the arm of the one holding it and stared at Unel.

"You're a messy man," she said in a youthful voice, then giggled. She reached out for her toy and snapped it from his hands, holding it snugly against her chest.

Unel laughed, running his fingers through his unkempt hair. "That I am. How are you?"

Gemtra pushed herself up out of her chair and walked over to the other side of the bed. She looked at her daughter, smiling with a birth parent's warmth, and drew her fingers through Trellia's hair, stroking it as if brushing it. Unel picked up on the motion and grabbed a brush from the table on his side of the bed and handed it to Gemtra.

"See, he is not always messy. Let's do your hair. Gemmy is here for you. Do you remember our conversation?"

"Uh huh," she said and yawned.

"Good. Do you remember the other you? The grown up?"

Trellia bobbed her head, smiling.

"Good. When you wake up, you're going to be her again, ok?"

"But I'm not tired, Gemmy," Trellia pleaded. She yawned again.

"I know," Gemtra said, continuing to brush Trellia's hair.

Trellia yawned, curled up against her doll, and fell asleep.

"Will that work?" Unel whispered.

"No. But it will get us started on the right path. It's going to take a few days."

"Thank you," he said, staring at Trellia. Another stream of

tears fell from his eyes as he watched her gentle breathing and sublime, happy smile.

Gemtra was sure these were tears of hope.

* * *

Alia played a single quadrigram of Sumatta speaking. Sumatta spoke with its tentacles as it sang. The tentacles formed words whose meaning was given by the song.

"Translate," Alia commanded.

Shenol looked irritated. She leaned back in her chair, folding her arms in defiance, and huffed. "It's a word none of us know. We think it means—"

"We know what it *means*. What we don't know is the exact word. Not every word translates to another word. Sometimes a single word represents multiple words, sometimes multiple words represent a single word; they always represent a concept. When we translate, we have to translate meaning, not just words. Come now, Shenol. I have told—"

A small needle in the middle of the room interrupted Alia as it rose from a pool below to pierce a sphere hovering directly above it.

Alia closed its eyes tight just as the needle pierced the sphere. The sphere erupted in a blinding flash of light, and Alia started counting in its head. The number of seconds indicated the number of minutes.

Shenol screamed, leaping around in her seat to see what happened behind her. She threw her hands up and screamed again as the bright light blinded her.

"Screaming is not how we handle that, Shenol. What do we do now?" Alia asked and waited.

The light went out. Thirty seconds. Alia opened both eyes slowly as they adjusted back to the normal lighting of the room, the haze of the brightness fading.

Shenol was staring at Alia, mouth gaping, shocked by the

question. She realized her mouth was gaping and slowly closed her mouth. She stood up, primped her Reader's robe, then announced with dignity, "I will close the Bahnderia, Reader."

Alia gave an approving nod and watched as Shenol left the room quickly. Not so quickly that she couldn't put her hands on her hips, swaying them effeminately as she hustled. Nothing Alia could do would get that girl to give up her gender. When the time came, it was going to be a tough choice for Shenol. What Shenol didn't know is what this call meant for her specifically. It meant that choice was coming sooner rather than later.

It was still easy to remember young Alia's response to the same call—it had been just as surprising and unsettling as a little boy. It was still just as surprising and unsettling, but Reader Alia hadn't reacted the same way. Reader Alia expected Sumatta at all times. Sumatta would come for one of two reasons. It would come to elevate the Next Reader, in which case Alia would retire as the Reader and become a former reader, living in the Bahnderia as an honored guest. Or Sumatta would come to signal a message from the Cycle of Ages. Alia wasn't old enough to retire yet. Retirement was at least a couple more decades off. That meant Sumatta was coming for one reason only.

Alia was nervous. It stood up and walked over to perform the duty of the Reader. Grabbing the now dull sphere, Alia turned it a third counterclockwise, sending a small electric shock down the needle and into the pool of water. It would quickly dissipate in the water, but Sumatta would sense that specific energy pulse and know the Reader was preparing for its arrival.

Alia frowned. Shenol was outside the Reader's study. She was in some kind of animated argument. Alia opened the door and saw Huol trying to push himself past Shenol to get inside.

Alia coughed, staring at him as if he'd better have an explanation. Huol stopped pushing forward.

"Reader! This one is sending everyone out of the Bahnderia! The law says no one can do that—the Bahnderia is for everyone! You have to stop *her*!"

Alia reached out and placed a calm hand on Shenol's shoulder, giving her a comforting look before turning eyes on Huol. "Huol, in the Bahnderia, when the Next Reader speaks, it speaks as if the Reader has spoken. You will address *it* as you address me."

Alia paused for effect, and Huol took a step back, bowing his head. "Yes, your Readerships. I apologize."

It was moments like this where Alia hoped Shenol picked up that the absence of gender removed gender bias. He clearly had biases against females, but gave proper deference to the genderless Reader. Being Reader was not about genders; it was about being Sumatta's voice.

"As for the law, Huol, it is the Reader's task to read and apply the law. You will now hear the law as given by Sumatta. From my energy to yours, from my knowledge to yours. 'In the place where one is bound, all are bound; in the place of all, all may call home; all are from me, my home is theirs.'"

Alia paused for effect, and Huol lifted his head, raising a finger as if Alia had just corrected the Next Reader, but stopped when he saw Alia. Alia had a look that said the man had fallen into a trap.

"Sumatta called the Bahnderia home. When Sumatta comes home, all shall give deference. Sumatta has called for its home and you answered that call by questioning its Readership. You have questioned Sumatta itself."

Huol paled and started to shake. Undoubtedly, he had expected anything other than to be told a message from Sumatta had come.

"You were the first to hear, Huol. Now you can spread the word." He bowed his head, apologized, and scurried off.

"Thank you," Shenol said, turning to look at Alia. "I—"

"You did well, Next Reader. Is the Bahnderia clear?"

"Yes, Reader."

"Then you need to change. And so do I. We have about thirty minutes before Sumatta arrives."

Shenol almost tripped over her robe as she ran off with no regard to her femininity. Alia grinned, then headed to the Reader's private chambers.

Motivations

"Now this is going to be a tough question. I've been told not to ask you, but on the Iantara Show we ask the tough questions. Are you ready?"

Spratee laughed off the question. The laugh was as calculated as every answer he'd given so far. Every answer was calculated to charm the audience, make them feel like he was one of them, while also imparting a feeling that he was different from them in the ways that mattered. The audience had to feel that he was the guy they wanted to lead them, and they had to feel like Governor Muaske had taken them in the wrong direction—they had to come away knowing that Governor Muaske was the wrong choice and Spratee was the one they'd been hoping for for generations.

"I think you got your guests confused, Iantara. My team doesn't hold you back. Should I take offense that you got me confused with Governor Muaske?" Spratee raised his hand, waving off the objection as he lightheartedly laughed. "No, no. It's fine. Go ahead. Ask your question."

"There are a lot of Arterians who believe you want to kill our social programs and that's what you mean when you say we shouldn't rely on the government. Are you going to kill our social programs?"

The studio audience clapped. It was a good question. A question whose answer Spratee had already calculated and readied.

"The actual question is will Spratee kill Arterians. Killing our social programs is killing Arterians. I'm not a murderer. No, let me answer this question to my fellow Arterians directly."

Spratee turned and looked directly at the camera.

"I will not kill Arterians. Our social programs save lives and I will not kill them."

Turning back to the host, Spratee continued.

"Don't let it be said I didn't answer the question directly," he said.

"That was pretty direct," Iantara said. "So, what will you do?"

"I think that's the question you really wanted to ask. It just makes for better sound bites if you ask about killing Arterians."

Spratee paused for the audience's laughter, then continued.

"Governor Muaske has social programs which are designed to tell you how to live. What I want to do is take away those conditions. For example, if you need help with food, we have a program for that. Governor Muaske says that you can only get that help if you're looking for a job. Now, take the birth parent of four who doesn't have the other parent as an example. She's going to get a job and do what? Leave her children unsupervised? Leave them with a stranger? Isn't it more important to leave her with her children? To build our families? Why are we telling her how to live? It's time to stop treating us like children and realize that our voters are adults who don't need to be coddled and enslaved by these Muaskian policies. I am a good man and I believe in every Arterian. I don't believe the government has the right to tell us how to live."

He wasn't a good man, but he wasn't a bad man. Spratee was driven, intelligent, and intense. He'd never striven to be good. Everyone's definition of good was different, but what it all simmered down to for him was Sumatta. He'd learned when he was very young that Sumatta wasn't good. His mother's death had proved that. He'd figured out that Sumatta was an invader from another planet and, though it obviously gave all life on Arter, it was creating a slave planet on Arter for when the rest of its species arrived. He'd spent his life secretly waging a war against Sumatta. He wasn't a good man, and he'd show Arter that Sumatta wasn't good either; he'd show them it was an enslaving monster.

Noselar appeared in the wings offstage. She held her stomach and arched her back exactly as he'd coached. He'd had to commission secret studies for every stage of pregnancy during a political campaign to find the perfect behavior at all times. She complied, begrudgingly and very vocally when in private. Noselar was what he deserved, if he were being honest with himself. She was everything he fought against—a personification of Sumatta—and yet he loved her fiercely.

If he could change her in just one way, it would be to make that false bump real, but Noselar held his temper and fits of rage against him. She'd told him before they were bonded that she'd never give him a child; she'd said she wouldn't make a child suffer him. Love had a price, he supposed. He was certain Noselar understood that too, and that's why she stood there now, faking a pregnancy she'd never let actually happen.

"Ah, there's the energy of my life," Spratee said. He stood up and strode across the stage to quickly take her by the arm and offer support as she walked to the small couch for the hosts guests. She carefully rotated into the seat, plopping down with a huff, then he leaned in and gave her a small, but affectionate kiss, carefully timed to be more than a peck and less than making out so that the audience would perceive it well. It was meaningless to Noselar and Spratee. It was another calculated gesture. She returned the kiss just as she was supposed to for proper perception.

Noselar bowed her head, leaned back into the couch, and wrapped her arms around her stomach in the fashion prescribed by the studies. Spratee had found the results of the studies odd, and how no one noticed that the prescribed fashion was far too dramatic for someone less than three months pregnant baffled him, but it was well-received and that's all that mattered. It was just another step in his war against Sumatta—everything he ever did in public was just another step in that war.

Spratee sat down next to her and carefully placed his arm around her. He turned his attention to Iantara as the audience's clapping for Noselar's arrival subsided. "Thank you. So, where were we?"

"Oh, I think we have more important questions than politics," Iantara said. "Noselar, can you feel kicks yet? Do you know the gender? You must be very excited."

On the inside, Spratee grinned. This was why she was here, and she had been coached on these very questions. On the outside, he lit up, full of energy and turned to face Noselar, sliding his other hand around her tummy and rubbing it gently.

Noselar leaned over and acted like she was whispering something to Spratee. He acted surprised, playfully throwing his hands up in surprised assent. Noselar did her part and put on a look of coy pleasure.

"It hasn't kicked yet, and when we talked about sharing the gender, Spratee said it best. Want to tell them, energy of my life?" She looked at Spratee and grinned as she passed the sharing of their secret back to him.

Spratee answered Iantara with surprise in his voice. "Gender doesn't make a person; actions make a person. I'm more interested in who our child is than which gender they're born with."

This interaction mirrored one of around 200 years ago. A few changes were applied to modernize the answer which studies had shown would not affect its reception. Gender was a hot topic at the moment. The response was exactly as predicted: The crowd erupted with cheers and Iantara waved his hands high as he clapped.

"That said," Noselar continued, taking the reins of the secret. "We've decided that just for your show—exclusive to the Iantara Show—we're going to share our baby's gender."

Iantara stood up from his host's chair and clapped, waving

his clapping hands out to the audience who were already rising in a standing ovation.

Noselar looked at Spratee and the two of them locked eyes as they counted silently to seven, then looked to Iantara and said in unison, "It's a boy."

The gender was a political calculation, of course. Mar'aten had been male, so having a boy would further quash that story. The bad press had subsided... mostly. This would quash it completely.

* * *

Unel caressed Trellia's tummy as they swung gently in the breeze on their favorite swing in Sumna City Park. The day was cool and relaxing, the uncut grass blown gently to the side and the Arter aurora flickered with an array of vibrant reds and greens. It made Trellia's face look warm and inviting. They'd spent more time together since she'd come back from her coma, including almost daily visits to the park. She was better now, the effects of the regression gone, but he still felt the need to be there for her every moment.

Her tummy had grown firm and started to bulge, their baby growing inside. It was hard to think about having almost lost Trellia. He would have lost the baby too. He would have lost everything. But he hadn't. The Dreamoria had survived. Trellia had survived. And the baby had survived. He hadn't lost everything, now he had even more. Now, he seemed to have everything.

"What do you think about 'Noal'?"

"Noal? Where did you get that from?"

"It means 'all things' in Sumattan. I feel like I have everything I could ever want. It seems fitting," he said, turning his caress into a hug.

Trellia smiled warmly. "I like it. I'd like to hear that word from Sumatta. I bet it sounds beautiful. What's the symbol?"

Unel could see the symbol in his mind. Sumatta's nine tentacles wrapped around each other as it sang a mid-pitched note. He pulled up a replay on his touchpad and held it up for Trellia to see.

"A double infinity strip around a sphere. It's an intricate Sumattan word. I'd love to see it personally too."

Trellia rubbed her belly. "'Noal'," she whispered to the baby inside as if giving him his name.

She shifted in her seat, turning to face Unel. "I want you to do something for me, Unel."

"What's that?"

"This," she said, pulling out a folded piece of paper. "It's been almost 3 months. Noal is *our* dream, but this is *your* dream. I want you to have your dream."

Unel swallowed, stuck for words. She was right; it was his dream. He didn't need to unfold that piece of paper. She had picked it up from his sketches. It was the latest sketch of the *draumr*. He hadn't stopped desperately wanting for the *draumr* to work, but how could he move forward knowing it had almost taken everything from him? "I..."

"I know, Unel. But you didn't lose me, and it wasn't your fault. It was an accident. A simple random electrical storm."

Unel opened his mouth to object, but Trellia turned, staring off in the distance, and continued to speak.

"And that random storm forced your hand—it forced your mind in the only way a mind can be forced. It made it so that you had to solve the problem in order to save me. And you did! It works! It also left behind fear, and that fear is your biggest obstacle keeping you from realizing your dream. I want you to finish the *draumr*, Unel. I want you to realize your dreams," she said. She rubbed her belly and bent her head down to look at Noal lovingly. "All of them."

Of all the things to stop me, he thought. *I haven't let funding, derision, politics, or the supposed fact that it's impossible stop me, but I'm letting fear stop me?* he thought.

"Our weaknesses give our strengths an opportunity to shine," came a voice. It was not inside Unel's head, and it was philosophical sounding. It shook him out of his reflection. He looked around and found what he expected. Strypan was there. When random philosophy showed up, that meant Strypan had shown up.

"Stry?" he said, sitting up and scooting next to Trellia.

"You were about to say she's right, weren't you? I brought you up to see the impossible as nothing more than an enticement. I can't imagine you'd let a little thing like fear make something impossible. Use your strengths, conquer your fears."

"Ever the philosopher, aren't you, Strypan? It's good to see you. We were just talking about this," Trellia said, handing the folded paper out to Strypan. "What does your philosophy say about that?"

Strypan unfolded the paper, studied it, turned the paper clockwise, then counterclockwise a full rotation. He handed the paper back to Unel, then turned to look at the park. "It all looks like a mess, doesn't it? But nature, for as random as it is, is not a mess. It is balanced. For every direction, there is an opposite direction; for every color, a complementary color; for every shape, an opposite shape. I don't see..." he said, turning his attention back to the paper, "...any balance. That's remarkable by itself. Does a total lack of balance suggest another type of balance?"

Can't he just say what he means instead of speaking in riddles? I know it looks like a mess! It's not done. Unel frowned, folded the paper up, and stuck it in his pocket. "I need it to work. It is balanced. Every twist and turn is there for a reason. It does work, actually. It just needs a little finishing. I shouldn't need to move the masses to sync the *draumrs*. Looking balanced will come once it's finished," he said defensively.

"I'm sure it will. You've always ended up with beauty,"

Strypan said, throwing a glance Trellia's way. "I might be able to help. I can come by the lab sometime and you can show me what it is supposed to do. Or maybe you can stop by my house."

Unel sighed. "Sure, Stry. What are you doing out here today?"

"Looking for coincidence. It always seems to just happen, so I thought I'd go looking for it for once. Coincidentally, I found you." Strypan said with too much seriousness for such a nonsensical statement. He suddenly seemed to recognize someone in the distance. "Oh, and another coincidence! I'd better not let this one escape. I've been hoping for a chance to speak with her."

Without saying goodbye, Strypan jaunted off in the direction of his next coincidence. Unel and Trellia looked at each other and laughed.

"It always amazes me how different you two are," Trellia said.

"It amazes me he's from this planet," Unel said, reaching around to rub her belly again.

How could he have almost lost this? Everyone knew he had two passions in life, but for the moment—for the last few days—he had only one passion, one that he'd almost lost. One he would have been lost without. No, he was not ready to go back to the *draumr*. Not yet.

He leaned into her, breathing in her soft, flowery scent and rested his chin on her shoulder as he rubbed her belly. Trellia and Noal were his world now. Everything else could wait.

Reading Sumatta

Alia waited on a slightly raised pedestal in front of the Bahnder Tree. The tree stood in a pool of water. Its pearlescent beauty rose almost forty feet in the air. It had two main branches and two smaller branches surrounded by dozens of tiny, wispy ones that seemed to crawl from the trunk. The trunk was hollow and open on one side. It glistened with an amber hue as it reflected the night sky painted in yellow and orange by the evening's aurora.

Shenol stood daintily poised on the ground to the Reader's left. She kept fidgeting with her Reader's robe as if primping, but she was nervous, impatient, and bored, shifting on her feet and swinging back and forth. For a twelve-year-old, she was doing better than expected. Alia had trained her well.

Shenol opened her mouth—undoubtedly to complain that it had been another five minutes—but snapped it shut abruptly.

The tree began to twinkle and vibrate with snaps of electricity. The pool began to vibrate, ripples bouncing back and forth between the edges and the trunk. It rose quickly.

Shenol raised her hands to her mouth, holding back a surprised scream, then started shaking a pointed finger at the pool as if Alia could not see it rising.

For all the poise Alia had learned over the years, the Reader's heart was racing, rapid breathing betraying an excitement close to Shenol's own, though more refined and controlled.

Water began to flood over the pool's walls. It created a large puddle that began to soak Shenol's shoes. She jumped up on the pedestal with Alia, grabbing onto Alia's robe for balance, but the water rose higher and covered the pedestal. Alia ignored soaked shoes and Shenol's antics. It remembered when this had happened last. It was the tree one needed to watch. Alia kept its eyes fixed on the tree.

Sumatta burst through the pool and into the hollow trunk of the Bahnder Tree. Water exploded outward and rained down from the force of the forty-foot being rocketing up into view, showering Alia and Shenol in the downpour.

Shenol screamed as the water assaulted them, ducking behind Alia and hiding her face in its robe. Alia just closed its eyes, opening them quickly as the onslaught settled into a fine mist.

Looking up, the mist became like a foggy memory as they took in the enormity that was Sumatta. The forty-foot being had filled in the tree, its head squirming into place at the top.

Sumatta unfolded its four wings onto the thickest branches of the tree, wrapping the wispy tendrils hanging from each wing around the branches. Its head popped into place above the hollow opening of the tree, expanding in the shape of a shroom with hundreds of gills hanging inside the cap. The gills moved in rhythmic waves as they breathed in the warm evening air.

It flexed its body, pressing its scaly skin against the inside of the trunk. The scales cut into the mysterious bark and melded into it. It shifted a bit as if it was getting used to the Bahnder Tree while its body wrapped around the trunk and branches.

Sumatta became one with the tree to the point Alia couldn't tell where the pearlescent bark ended and the pearlescence of Sumatta began. The tree took on a fit like that of armor shielding Sumatta's body.

Sumatta's head became conical in shape and lines of energy streamed up its body toward its head. It looked like it was pulling energy from Arter itself. The energy pooled in Sumatta's head until it glowed and hummed. The humming grew into a powerful roaring vibration which echoed against the Bahnderia's walls and made Alia's core shake.

Shenol covered her ears and winced as a high-pitched bell

tone pierced through the almost unbearable roar. A thin ray of light slid out from Sumatta's head, shooting up twenty feet above Sumatta's head. The ray flattened as if it had hit a shield around the building, then grew until it was as wide as the Bahnderia itself, curving around and down as it surrounded the Bahnderia with a shield. The high-pitched sound faded, taking the droning roar along with it, and left behind silence.

The flow of energy from Arter stopped and the ray of light broke free from Sumatta's head, zipping into the shield and sealing it closed.

Sumatta stretched, twisting back and forth slowly, pulling the roots of the Bahnder Tree up and out of the pool, then hopped into the air, pulling its speaking tentacles out of the pool, and stopped as it hovered a few feet above the pool.

Sumatta shook and a spray of water shot off of its body. Alia and Shenol only blinked as the mist came down.

Sumatta began to speak.

Sumatta's tentacles moved as it sang, the song giving meaning to the tentacles' words. It was a harmony of sound and shape spoken in four dimensions: height, width, length, and sound. Being in the presence of Sumatta made the replays seem inconsequential. Sumatta was magnificent.

"The Ancient Window of Time will hear from the Radiant Light at the next Turning. The Celebration of Cycles comes to all from All and transcends All."

Sumatta hesitated before continuing. Alia was surprised as Sumatta continued; its song gained a nervous tension. It had never seen Sumatta speak with emotion.

"The Radiant Light speaks early, its voice slow, powerful. Its message will be dangerous. I—" Sumatta shivered, its tentacles vibrating in a pattern Alia did not recognize. Was Sumatta stammering? "I fear for the children of Life," it said very clearly.

As Reader, Alia stood strong, accepting the message delivered by its god. Inside, Alia trembled. Sumatta, the forty-foot god in front of it shielded by a magical tree, was quaking at a message, fearing for its children. It was almost too much to accept. The Giver of Life, Protector of Arter, Guardian of Ages was afraid of something?

The Reader spoke as the Reader knew it must. "Arter will rejoice to receive the message from the Cycle of Ages, Bringer of Life, Protect of Arter, Guardian of the Ages, our Sumatta. In your folds, we shall find safety, comfort, knowledge, and life."

Sumatta's tone vibrated Alia's body as if a comforting blanket were being wrapped around it. "Arter and the Ancient Window of Time must be brought together for the arrival of the message. There I shall be that which you claim of me. We will know the message and we will survive it as the ages survive each other."

Alia noticed a low distant roar as it turned into a thunderous humming permeating the barrier surrounding the Bahnderia. Sumatta's Swarm was arriving, billions of spatiatta, each the size of an Arterian, flying from the eight mounts to bring home their creator. Tiers of spatiatta covered the entire sky of Attatar, darkening the sky and blocking out the aurora as they assembled around the Bahnderia.

Sumatta's head became conical in shape as it turned its head upward. It pushed up in a single thrust of its tentacles and separated from the Bahnder Tree. In a single swift motion, it crashed into the barrier. The barrier shattered and Sumatta was quickly surrounded by the Swarm. Shards of the barrier floated into the air, pulled by the electromagnetic attraction of the spatiatta. Each spatiatta absorbed one and only one piece. Those pieces would soon turn to a spatiatta egg, an *attaten*.

Alia took a deep breath and watched in awe and reverence as Sumatta turned, aiming toward Mount Sumat, and the Swarm escorted its creator back to the mountain. Sumatta's song was pure and strong enough that it rose above the buzz of the Swarm. It was a comfort to all of Attatar. Part of the Swarm broke off from the honor guard and began to echo

Sumatta's song like a chorus as it flew in every direction. It flew across all of Arter. All of Arter would hear Sumatta's song; all of Arter would know it had come with a message.

"'The strength of the message is the strength of the change, the strongest, a sign of a new Age.' We're going to die, aren't we?"

Alia turned around as the Next Reader quivered, her voice almost a shadow as she quoted from her studies. The Cycle of Ages had brought a message of technological change to Alia's predecessor. A firm message, but nothing too great. The message opened minds to the inevitable coming of advancement. The technological age would be nothing compared to a new age. Shenol should not have been able to understand enough of the message to have grasped everything the young Next Reader had grasped. She would be a great Reader... if she survived to the next age.

Alia adopted a calm, comforting, yet counseling voice. "Sumatta, Bringer of Life, Guardian of Ages, does not bring messages of death, Next Reader. Its messages are the future of life. At the turning of each age we have changed, but Arter and Arterians have survived."

Shenol, oblivious to Alia's attempt to invoke her Reader sensibilities by using her title, shook her head, still quivering. "Arterians have survived, but not every Arterian. Oh, by Sumatta itself, we are going to die."

A Reader knew things about Arter. Things it could share with no one. Shenol's time had come to learn the deeper secrets of Arter. She had come further than Alia had noticed and faster than Alia had as Next Reader. Alia pondered for a moment, wondering if the Next Reader was truly ready for the Complete History. It was a useless argument; Shenol's time had come as much because of her knowledge as because of the coming of the next age. Just like she would soon have no choice but to choose Readership over gender, Alia had no choice but to show her the Complete History now.

The Reader pulled its clothing firm, then in a commanding voice said, "Come, Next Reader. Our time comes more than once in our life. My time to become Reader came already. You have done well in your studies, and it is time for you to learn the Complete History. My final time will come soon, and then your time will come, but it will be your time to become Reader, not your final time."

Alia walked away from the pedestal and a shocked Shenol followed, scurrying to keep up as Alia walked quickly. Alia had to get Shenol away from the Bahnder Tree and away from thinking about the message as quickly as possible.

Inside the Reader's study, Alia opened a side door. It was a door Shenol had been forbidden to enter until now. It was a door to a room connected with a half dozen other rooms. It was the door to the Complete History.

"Sumatta has told us the history of Arter from the beginning. You will now study only from these rooms, and you will not study any other materials. Here you will learn the sacred and secret history of Arter. The truth is in here. Each shelf contains a thousand discs, each disk contains one story of Arter's history. Nothing you see or hear in this room may ever be repeated to anyone but a Reader. Do you understand?"

"Yes, Reader."

"Begin on that wall," Alia said, pointing to the wall on their left. "Then work your way to the right on each shelf before working your way down to the next. Just like you read a book. Every replay has a title, but not all titles are helpful in knowing what the replay is about."

"This will take me forever! How long did it take you to watch them all?"

"I'm sixty-two years old, Shenol. I have been Next Reader or Reader for fifty years. I have not finished them."

Shenol's look of surprise almost made Alia laugh. The memory of being given this task was still fresh and the overwhelming number of replays was intimidating. Watching them was enlightening on so many levels. Nowhere else could a hundred thousand years' worth of history be found and nowhere else could you find the history told in the words of your god. It was an honor reserved only for readers.

"Begin," Alia commanded.

Shenol walked over, grabbed the first disk and put it in the replay machine as Alia walked out leaving her there for her studies.

At least that would distract her from the message. And it would prepare her to become Reader. Alia sighed. It's time as Reader was coming to an end. It was a harsh thought. The only thing Alia had ever wanted was to be Reader. What would it do after?

Strypan's Spelling

Unel stood at Strypan's door waiting for Strypan to come out. He hadn't seen the man in months, but he was stuck and something in the back of his head kept coming to the forefront: "Nature, for as random as it is, is not a mess. It is balanced." Strypan was right and his *draumr* was still a mess, a knotted, almost-working mess. It just needed to work without the microtrack adjustments. He'd resisted because while it looked like a mess, it was beautiful on the inside. The physics was a perfect harmony, bringing together all the aspects of the mind and space to forge a mental connection between two Arterians. He had gone over the design more times than he could count, but when it all came down to it, he couldn't find anything wrong. A fool does not consider every factor, so he had finally given up. Now he was waiting for Strypan... he really didn't know what Strypan would show him, but with any luck, it would be useful. At the worst, it would be another useless philosophical foray and waste of Unel's time.

Strypan's house was an eccentric's playground. The door was made of thick, dried algae that was still alive and responded to those it knew; wind chimes somehow rotated in the opposite direction of the breeze, and Unel was certain that at different angles they spelled different words; *aten* peppered the walls almost like an array of eyes that could feel your presence. All of these things doing things they weren't supposed to do was unsettling. And if he asked about any of them, he would get some unintelligible philosophy that was supposed to be an explanation.

"What brings you here, son?"

Unel jerked around, almost colliding with Strypan who was standing directly behind him. Of course, Strypan would not come to the door. Had he ever come from the same direction more than once? Unel sighed. As irritating as the old man was, his irritations were a little endearing. Just a little.

"I think you know why I came here," he said.

Strypan smiled. "Why do we ask questions when we know the answer?"

The expected response was almost as old as Unel. As a child, he would be asked this question and have to provide the correct answer. Unel remained defiantly quiet, denying the expected response and instead held up a *draumr*.

Strypan stood there patiently. He was toying with Unel. He wouldn't speak until Unel answered the question. He was infuriating.

Unel capitulated and raised the *draumr* higher. "Because the answer might not be what we expect. Please?"

Strypan smiled, pleased at getting the desired response. "From my energy to yours, from my knowledge to yours, my son."

Strypan reached out and grabbed the *draumr*. He took the knotted mess and rolled it in his hands, cocking his head to the left and right, then began mumbling to himself.

"Water and light might be right."

He squeezed the metal and gave a nod of approval. "Strength to the malleable. Good, good. But it doesn't speak to me."

Strypan walked over and held the *draumr* up toward some of his wind chimes. "It's silent. Do your dreams speak to you?"

After a moment, he turned toward Unel and repeated the question. "Oh, I thought you were talking to the wind chimes. Um, yes?"

Strypan looked at Unel a bit condescendingly. "They speak to me, but I don't speak to them. What made you think I would talk to them? Are you feeling well, son?"

Unel grimaced at the chiding. This was going as well as he expected. "What is it you're getting at?"

Strypan contorted his mouth back and forth as if trying to figure out how to explain. "Follow me."

They walked up to the door and the algae fell apart, letting Strypan and Unel walk through, then it became a gel and crawled up in the space, coming back together again, closing the door behind them. Down a hallway and through another algae door, they came to a room with half the ceiling covered in a glass dome, the other half of the dome in a dark, translucent material Unel didn't recognize. Inside were parts of wind chimes laying around except for in the center where they were arrayed in three rows of three columns of three. Each chime in the center of the room represented a different letter— all twenty-seven letters of the alphabet accounted for.

"Our alphabet comes from Sumattan. You won't know that, of course. All you were told is that Sumatta gave us our alphabet. Sumatta has nine tentacles which, with its song, form all of its words. They also don't tell you that each of those tendrils represents a series of letters that spell words, not simply give them shape."

Strypan plucked a few letters out of the array and moved a few others. He played with them for a few minutes, moving them around, then stood back and looked at the display.

"There is the word for 'dreaming together'. Depending on the song, it could mean dreaming together, everyone hopes, our wishes and more."

Unel furrowed his brow. What did the alphabet have to do with the *draumr*? It didn't make sense to Unel, but Strypan seemed to think it was salient.

"Our letters are flat. We write them on paper, Stry. How do you know—"

"To Sumatta, we have a flat language. We speak without motion, we write without dimension. We have a much simpler way of communication, and we don't communicate with the same depth, same emotion. Changing that is hard, but isn't that what you're trying to do with your device?" he said.

"As for how I know, I've learned a bit in my short time walking around Arter." He took a wind chime in his hands and pressed it flat, then held it out and grinned. It was the first letter of the Arterian alphabet. He tossed it to the side. "You don't know much about Sumatta. No one really does. Well, maybe the Reader. Sumatta is so much more than Arter, but that's another story. Now, watch."

How did his parent know so much about Sumatta? He was acting as if he knew more than anyone on Arter. Unel laughed in his head at the thought. It was just another Strypanian philosophy. No one could know more about Sumatta than the Reader. The Reader had access to everything we knew about Sumatta, and most of that was not available to anyone else.

Strypan grabbed the letters making the word for "dreaming together" and started manipulating them, working them together into a small wind chime. He grabbed the *draumr* and plucked out the *hydaten* and *phoaten* with a pair of pliers, then set them in two of three open spaces of his wind chime. The metal almost perfectly formed around the *aten* holding them in place. He smiled, proud of himself, and handed the chime to Unel.

"Looks like you missed an *aten*. Let's go outside."

Unel grabbed the chime and turned it about in his hand, studying it. It had both symmetry and asymmetry to it, angles and curves, and from most angles you could see the word "dreaming together". The colorful *aten* gave it an extra aspect of life, but it didn't seem alive yet. Why Unel felt that, he couldn't explain. Maybe it was because it was made of some cheap metal? But a wind chime? His *draumr* was a scientific tool, not a wind chime. It did look simple, clean, and beautiful, but this had to just all be a waste of time—there was no science to this method, only a made-up philosophy of Sumatta's language.

"You're trying to help me by giving me a wind chime?"

"No, I'm giving you the right word," he said, turning

around and looking at Unel as if he'd just said the most ridiculous thing Arter had ever heard. "Who said that is a wind chime?"

Unel turned to point to the wind chimes hanging outside, then gave up. Whatever he said would just be contorted into something else.

"How do you know it's the right word? What if another word is better?"

"Sumattan words are concepts. The meaning of the concept is given in the song. I gave you the right concept. It also happens to be the right word. Can you think of a better word?"

Unel didn't know Sumattan, so he couldn't think of any better word. Everything he could think of was a variation of the one he held. "No," he said.

"I highly doubt that will work to replace your device, but at least you'll have the right word. It's almost balanced. Can we go outside now?"

Unel followed, baffled and frustrated. Strypan took him through a door on the side of the dome that led to the edge of the building nearest the front door.

"Why didn't we just go in through here instead of wandering around your house first?"

"Sometimes the journey matters, sometimes it doesn't. I like my house. Seemed like a good journey. Now, about your missing *aten*. I have a guess, but I think it's best if you find it. You've brought the water of life together with the light that traverses the space between everything in the universe, but there's another slot the word wants filled. Hold it up to the *atens* in my wall."

Unel debated arguing. This was not scientific, but he countered his own argument by telling himself that he hadn't come here for scientific reasons, he had come here because the *draumr* didn't look pretty. He held the wind chime up to the *atens* peppering Strypan's wall.

Siaten was glass-like. Maybe it would be a fit because it was used to see clearly. The chime did nothing when near a *siaten*. Maybe *na'aten* from the ocean would help since the body was made of salt water-like fluid. The chime didn't respond to *na'aten* either. *Ca'aten* did nothing, but that was expected. Those were as earth-like as you could get. This was useless. The only other *aten* were already in the device and *oxaten* which he'd already removed. *No, try them all,* he thought and held it up to the *oxaten*. Nothing from the chime.

"None of them work," he said.

Strypan snorted, trying to hold back far too much excitement. "You skipped the one I thought it was! Come on, son, stop messing with me. Try it."

Confused, Unel looked at the wall. What was Strypan talking about? *Attaten*, the fertility *aten* was the only one left. He turned to Unel. "*Attaten*? That's for fertility. I don't want—"

"It's for life! Who told you fertility? You youth nowadays. Always thinking about sex. Try it!" Strypan said, poised as if he was about to burst forward and hold the chime up to it himself.

Life? Where did Strypan get all these wild ideas? Another Strypanian philosophy? Whatever it was, Unel would entertain him. Sometimes the answer to a question you already knew surprised you, right?

Unel lifted the chime up to the *attaten*.

An electromagnetic shock shot out of the two *aten* in the chime and formed an electrical connection to the *attaten*, linking the three together. Unel resisted the temptation to pull back at the little bolt of electricity and just stood there in wonder, hand frozen in place.

"Don't move. I have to pee. This is too exciting. I'll be right back," Strypan said.

Unel was oblivious to Strypan's antics. He stood there staring at the future. His future. His future *draumr*. 'Dreaming together' branded in his retina as sure as the three *aten* were connected. He stared at the *draumr* in a daze, barely noticing Strypan return with pliers and extract the *attaten* from the wall and place it in the device, then hand it back to him.

"Thank you," he said in a soft, absent-minded voice. He took the device and held it in one hand as he got in his transport and headed back to the Dreamoria. The hours-long trip to Attatar seemed to happen in a flash as his mind was transfixed, one vision locked in place: A world filled with Arterians dreaming together, communicating via the *draumr*.

Behind The Scenes

Spratee shifted in his chair. He was surrounded by maps, antique signed documents, books and everything else fitting for a principal's office. A principal's office was always unsettling. It didn't help that Dise had insisted on a couple of her group being at the meeting. This meeting was an unfortunate necessity in his war.

In war, timing is as important as knowing one's enemy. Sumatta did not know Spratee, but that murderous creature had fantastic timing. Spratee had always been careful in how he handled Sumatta—it was known that he was not a believer in Sumatta, but he'd never spoken an ill word of the beast. Governor Muaske had touted his faith in Sumatta from the beginning. The announcement of a new message from the Cycle of Ages had been a knife to the throat of Spratee's campaign, turning voters toward the faithful Governor Muaske like nothing else could.

A war, however, was not fought on one front, which is what brought him to this meeting. He was ostensibly vetting schools for his unborn child. The truth was quite a bit different.

"Since Sumatta gains all its strength from electromagnetic energy, the plan is to wait until it's reading the Cycle of Ages and distracted providing the translation to the Reader, then hit it with all we've got. The first wave will be the most important. We'll cripple the monster with electromagnetic missiles—" Dise said, stopping abruptly as Spratee waved away her report.

"I don't need to know the details. I came here to learn two things and state my terms." The less he knew, in fact, the better. Something always went wrong and the more plausible deniability he could muster, the better. He had every intention of being as far away from the event as possible.

"What are your terms?" she asked through gritted teeth.

"First, what I want to learn. Do you have a plan in place to deal with the Swarm or is this a one-way mission? Second, what's my role? Why do you need me?"

Dise lost her energetic tone, becoming somber. "We don't have the resources to deal with millions of spatiatta, let alone billions. We'll be able to take out thousands of them, maybe more, but when it comes down to it, the group that attacks doesn't plan on going home. Look, that creature has told us—"

Spratee waved his hand dismissively. He knew the rant too well. They believed in the same ends, but for very different reasons.

Dise and her group felt oppressed by a being who defined Arter from the beginning and would never give up its grip on giving life by making women fertile from birth—a being that controlled who reproduced and who didn't by making the supply of *attaten* scarce and doling them out as it pleased.

Spratee saw Sumatta for what it really was: a killer. It gave his birth parent an *attaten*, yet let her die during his birth. It only hid behind the guise of being the provider of all life. No being should be able to give and take life without consequence. Spratee would be that consequence, one way or another.

Dise looked irritated by his interruption, but she changed topics. "OK, fine. Your role. As a candidate for governor, you'll be given special access and details of the event. Not you directly, of course. You're too important to deal with those details. What we need from you is for some of our staff to be put on your security team so they get those details."

"Oh, no. If your team attacks and it's connected to me, the mob will kill me before I have a chance to escape and if I do escape, I'll be finished. That's non-negotiable."

"We aren't fools, for energy's sake," Dise scolded. "The team will be your personal guard. They will, in fact, be tasked with your safe escape and they will not participate in the attack. Their primary mission is to get the information to our ground teams before the event. Only the ground teams will be implicated in the attack."

Spratee leaned back in his chair pondering. That would be good, and it could be very bad. If something went wrong and they needed a scapegoat, there'd be a team around him to facilitate that. No, he wouldn't allow that.

"They'll be where I place them, but they won't be seen around me at any time. I'll give them positions that allow them to know everything my staff knows, but at no point are they to talk to me or even look in my direction. Agreed?"

Dise shrugged. "Maybe. What are your terms?"

Spratee smiled and looked around. He wanted to clear the room, but Dise wouldn't allow that. "Give me some paper."

Dise didn't like the distrust of her people, but pushed a pad and pen toward him. He tore off a sheet and wrote a simple message: "I need a baby boy. Noselar is not pregnant."

He handed the sheet to Dise. She looked over the paper and whistled.

"I should be able to do this. Give me a week and I'll tell you if it's possible."

"When it's possible, we have a deal."

"Fine. Here," she said, handing him a different sheet of paper. "These are the leaks that will come out from this meeting. Eral is a vice principal," she said, waving a hand at the man on her left. "And Yoltia is my secretary." She said, waving her other hand at the man on her right. They were the only others in the office. "Only these two know. Only these two will know. They can be trusted."

Spratee looked at the paper. One leak was about paying for the baby's schooling, another about a private tutor to be provided. Nothing salacious. He handed the paper back to her and stood up to leave.

"The leaks are fine," he said, then saw himself out.

He had one more front to fortify in his war. Sumatta wouldn't know what hit it. That creature would pay for being a murderer.

This had introduced one problem he didn't like. He was going to have to be at the event during the attack. Maybe he could find a way to use that to his advantage.

* * *

Shenol thought she had taken it well. After all, how often does someone learn that your god is from another galaxy, crashed on your planet, and the mountains are the remnants of its ship? Learning this just before the end of your civilization made it harder to accept, but Shenol thought of herself as a student and she had accepted the Complete History in stride, as if studying any topic.

She had taken it all in stride, even discovering that there was a hole in the Complete History hadn't shaken her faith. Alia hadn't noticed the hole, or at least had never mentioned it. It stood out to Shenol like an unowned *attaten* just laying around in plain sight. Maybe Alia just wanted her to feel safe? Shenol discarded that idea. She wouldn't have access to the histories if Alia wanted her to feel safe. They had shaken up her world view. Alia simply hadn't noticed it.

If what was coming would end their civilization, start a new age, and Sumatta could create enough life to populate a planet, then why wouldn't it just repopulate Arter's continent after the new age began? It couldn't be that Sumatta didn't want its creations to die—Arterians died every day. If Sumatta had given them a story as detailed as the Complete History and yet skipped over something like that, it had left a big hole in the histories. Sumatta made no mention of what would happen at the turning of the Last Age. It was not enough that the Last Age had not come yet, that Sumatta had made no recordings about it. That kind of hole must be very important. Shenol had to find out what Sumatta was hiding. And if Shenol was wrong and there was nothing being hidden, at least the pursuit kept her busy as the end of the world crept forward.

Her studies of Sumattan had been her key to getting access to the Complete History. The history was recorded in Sumattan by Sumatta itself; it had to be replayed to be studied. In all this time, no one had taken the time to write down a translation. If that was forbidden, Alia hadn't mentioned it. Shenol didn't ask; she didn't want to be told no. About a month ago, Shenol started to transcribe the writing. It wouldn't be a perfect translation, but she wasn't making anything official anyway, she just wanted notes for reference.

One word bothered her. Alia translated it as "ship", but all words in Sumattan that were related showed their relation and the word she knew for aircraft or spacecraft weren't related. There were a few other words whose translations seemed a bit off, but Shenol focused on "ship". Maybe it was that everywhere else the word for ship was attached to the way it traveled (like airship, spaceship, watership), but the word Sumatta used didn't contain either the medium this ship traveled through or the symbol for ship. Alia's explanation that it was ancient Sumattan for a type of ship that doesn't exist on Arter and was as different as "transport" was to "airship" didn't settle Shenol's mind on the issue. Alia had just blindly accepted the given definition, but that wasn't enough for Shenol. It seemed all too much like their ability to translate came down to guessing by context clues. Shenol didn't like guessing.

The first time Shenol had encountered the word, she'd translated the phrase as "On my coming, capsules of my life I saw come to the land as towers lasting a hundred thousand years." When Alia corrected Shenol, Alia said it meant the special "ship that saved its life." The given translation seemed so far off. How could she have been that wrong? Maybe if she could prove it....

She was getting distracted. Shenol was looking for what the hole in the histories was hiding, not the definition of a single word. She was getting tired. One more history tonight, then she was off to bed. This one should be interesting. Hopefully, it was not so interesting that Shenol couldn't go to sleep afterwards. Alia said it was about how Sumatta brings life to Arter. A sacred topic, never to be spoken of. Of course, Alia said that about every history. Shenol sat back with her pad and pen as the replay came to life and the forty-foot being was reduced down to a three-foot replay on the small table in front of the couch, ready to write down the translation.

"Arter was without life on my coming. Life does not come from me. Life comes from the Foothold of my tower, a thing of Purity, but solid and dense.

"Life and Foothold are of the Igri Tufuer, the next oldest. It pulled me from my dying Space, gave the Foothold for life in this Space, and commanded life brought forth. I obey its command.

"The Foothold harnesses gravity and Arter provides electromagnetic energy to pull effervescent energies of Purity through to Arter. Arter is a barren planet without this. I use these energies with the forces of Existence to create *aten*. *Aten* are used with the formulas of species to grow life.

"All the formulas of Arter's species but one were given with the Foothold. This one, formula of Sumatta, I discovered before coming, but the Foothold does not draw from Purity the energy to grow Sumatta. I saw this Purity between Spaces, but I can no longer touch it..."

This was amazing. Sumatta, Giver of Life, Protector of Arter, Guardian of Ages, did not give life. It was more the bringer of life. Was it also Protector of Arter and Guardian of Ages or would she find out those were also misnomers? Most amazing is that Sumatta would confess this, but still leave the one hole. This revelation was of enormous proportions, so how much more so would the hole be?

Shenol knew she wasn't going to sleep. She probably wouldn't sleep tomorrow either. Tomorrow, Shenol planned to study the Age histories, a history for each coming of an Age.

Maybe there she would fill the hole and discover if Sumatta was going to let them all die or if it was going to save them and why.

Unexpected Children

The answer might not be what we expect. It was true. A *draumr* as a wind chime of ancient letters was not what Unel had expected. He was not sure he would have ever dreamed of such a design; however, it had given him what he really needed. He hadn't needed simplicity and beauty; he had needed it to work and the only hint anything was wrong had come from its appearance and the need for microtracks to fully sync them together. When he'd built the *draumr* of metal and fixed the three *aten* in place, what he had been missing became obvious. His knotted mess of a *draumr* had allowed everything to work perfectly together, but it had kept it as separate pieces working together. The wind chime version had brought the different functions together creating a truly unified piece. Instead of the sum of parts, it was a unified, whole thing. It seemed to have a balance, a harmony to it now that it would not have been able to achieve previously. Thinking about it like that seemed like circuitous logic; he had a better intuitive understanding than he had the words to explain it. This version, he knew, would work.

"Col," he said, holding the gleaming symmetric harmony in front of him, still marveling at how it had all come together. "Let's do this. You have some avak ready?"

Col yawned and climbed on his sleeping table, laying down. He had readily accepted the new role of test subject after the incident with Trellia, even before he'd found out she was pregnant. "Already ahead of you. Yours is on the counter." He flopped his hand out to the side, waiting for his *draumr*.

Unel reached out, eyes still fixed on the *draumr*, grabbed a cup of avak and sipped the rancid fluid. Taking a deep breath and letting the liquid sedation creep into his body, he downed the rest of his cup, handed Col a *draumr*, and they both set them on their foreheads as they lay on their counterpart sleeping tables.

"Where to today?" Col asked.

"The same. We were so close during the last test and the only thing we're changing this time is the—" Unel stopped as he turned his head and saw Col asleep. He closed his eyes and joined his friend.

Their vision focused as they entered the dream in familiar territory.

Col laughed. "The same place as before," he said as he lifted his leg, heavy with mud out of the mire, trudging slowly to the shore. "Why do I always start here in the mud?"

"I'm not sure," Unel said, sitting on shore and watching Col with amusement. "Maybe you were meant to be the one caught in the pit?" He laughed and leaned back as Col worked his way to shore.

It was a dream from their childhood. A game of chase that ended when Col fell from a tree into the mud pits.

None of the other staff would be watching. The *draumr* worked so well now that there was no need for a repeater to broadcast the dream into the Dreamoria. And neither device served as just a broadcaster or receiver, they did both; they were simply connected. Who controlled the dream was a result of random chance, but....

Connected. Yes, they were! It had seemed so natural that Unel had missed the import. He sat up and yelled. "By Sumatta itself, Col. We've done it! Strypan was right!"

Col seemed to gather what that meant, as if he'd forgotten he was in a dream. He stopped shaking his leg at the edge to the shore and slapped it to the ground. All the mud disappeared from his body. "That worked! We have done it! You try."

Unel stood up, reached to the sky and touched the sun beyond the waves of the blue and teal aurora. He looked across the mud pit and thought of *aten* bubbling up from the mud. The mud began to boil, then bubbles on the surface began to pop, each one exposing a different *aten*. Unel laughed at the muddy magic and noticed an *attaten* in the mix.

What he would give to have Trellia here. It seemed so long ago, but had only been eight months. She'd eaten an *attaten* and now they would be parents. A month from now he would be a parent. He closed his eyes and sighed, missing her now even though he knew he was in a dream. She would have given almost anything to be here, here when it all finally worked.

The *attaten* grew larger as Unel thought of Trellia. It glistened and twinkled against the sky as it stretched. It grew as large as Unel, the aurora clearly visible in the reflection. Then the pearly shell fell away.

Trellia stood there, eyes fixed on Unel with that ever-so-attractive smile on those soft pink lips. He found himself lost in her gaze. His Trellia was here in the dream with him. Just what she would have wanted—just what he wanted. It was perfect.

"Is that Noal?" Col asked.

Unel broke off his enamored fixation on Trellia and flipped his head toward Col. What did he just ask? Col was looking closer to the ground near Trellia. Unel followed his eyes until he saw a little boy about knee height standing next to Trellia.

He had on a small green jumper with pictures of different flowers on it that covered his whole body as if he'd just gone to bed (or was getting up from bed, Unel wasn't sure). His disheveled hair was oddly white and he had gray eyes as if all the color had been taken from him.

"How do you know what he'll look like?" Col asked.

"I don't," Unel replied. How could he? And what was wrong with his eyes and hair?

Yet there he was. He was about three years old, holding Trellia's index finger, and looked very surprised as he bounced on his feet next to his birth parent. It wasn't a look of good surprise, but like he'd just been caught doing something bad.

Unel was in awe, shock, and, he was sure, quite a few other emotions at seeing this little being in front of him. His little boy. What should he say? How did he get here? Unel's couldn't think clearly through the confusion. The boy stopped bouncing and giggled as if whatever trouble he was about to get into, he'd figured out how to get out of it and couldn't tell the secret.

"Sorry. Not here. Better go," Noal said looking at Trellia. He had a soft, sweet, innocent voice that made Unel smile.

Noal turned and waved at the shore. "Hi parent! Rain!" he shouted as he pointed at the sky. "A whole lot."

Unel looked up as a thick torrent of rain appeared. It didn't fall from the sky, it just appeared as a thunderous wall. He looked back toward Trellia and Noal, but couldn't see them through the rain.

No! You cannot take them away, he thought.

Unel screamed at the rain, commanding it to dissipate as he envisioned it gone. The dream obeyed, but when the view cleared, Noal and Trellia were gone. The *aten* peppering the mud were gone. Col was gone. Abruptly, everything was gone and he was left in blinding brightness.

Unel sat up, throwing his hands to his face and rubbing his eyes. He was covered in sweat and breathing hard. What was he doing? Was he trying to rub away the dream? What just happened? It couldn't have been the *draumr*. Could it have been real? It was surreal, for sure. It was not his dream. It was...

"I was thinking of Trellia, Col. Why were you thinking of my son?"

Col, looking confused and soaked in sweat, looked at Unel. He'd woke first and was sitting on the edge of his sleeping pedestal.

"I... I wasn't. I saw her, then him. I... I asked you how *you* knew what he looked like."

Col took a moment to gather himself and let the confusion clear away.

"What was that? If it didn't come from our dreams, where did it come from? The *draumr*? Was there a surge? Did the wavelengths get out of sync?"

Noal even looked like Col in the dream. He had a square face, eyes shaped like Col's, haircut similar to Col's, and he didn't have freckles. Just like Col. Everyone said Col and Unel looked like brothers, but Unel knew the differences. But it didn't make sense that Noal would look like Col.

If Col hadn't brought Noal into the dream, maybe it had just been Unel's subconscious? He had just been looking at Col, so maybe he'd created his unknown son from what he'd just be looking at? Was he just rationalizing now? Yes, he decided, he was. There was no way of knowing where Noal had come from or why he'd looked the way he did, but he did know one thing.

"It was not the *draumr*, Col. I think one of the dangers of dreams is that even when we're lucid dreaming, we're not always in control." He hopped off the sleeping table, shook off the last groggy confusion and tried to clear away the image of his son.

"I need to get out of here for a few days, Col. Let's take the week off. Actually," he said, pausing on a thought. "Let's take the next two weeks off. The celebration is next week. Let's just enjoy the festivities."

That would give him a break from this and a break from the memory of his son looking like Col.

"We need a break. I think I've been staring at you too long," he said.

* * *

Spratee sat at his desk in the living room study staring at

his touchpad as he delivered a speech remotely to groups spread across Arter. Noselar sat on a couch in the living room taking notes and monitoring things from her own touchpad.

"My friends," Spratee said, adopting a somber tone, "I wish I could be there with you now, but the celebration is around the corner and it just wasn't possible. We should all take the time to enjoy the festivities and appreciate the message Sumatta will deliver." He paused for a moment. He hated saying that infernal beast's name. He took a sip of his water to wash the taste out of his mouth, then continued.

"But what happens after that? Governor Muaske can only see the celebration. His myopic focus on it is a threat to the well-being of every Arterian. We need to be ready to face the problems we're facing today, not hide behind the Cycle of Ages in hopes that the message is going to solve our problems.

"Far from it, my friends! Far from it! It's called the Cycle of *Ages* and what we know from history is that it portends a new age. The question is what that age will bring. Will it bring solutions to all of our problems? Will it be a panacea to all that ails us?

"I'm here to tell you it will not! I'm here to tell you that a new age brings new problems and we need a leader who is ready to face those problems, who cares about every Arterian, and who remembers what matters most: you.

"Stand with me on election day and stand for yourself. I am Spratee and I am the candidate for governor who is ready, able, and willing to lead Arter into a new age."

He paused for effect and the display changed to audiences in different venues rising in a standing ovation, chanting his name. It wouldn't save his campaign. Governor Muaske was riding the coattails of that monster for all that it was worth and more and it showed in the pools. Spratee's chance of winning the election in the face of the celebration had taken a gunshot to the head.

Giving up was not in Spratee's blood. His speech had gone

very well (one of the best of his career by his estimation). His campaign was set to start the promotions just after the celebration quoting him and emphasizing all the problems facing Arter which Governor Muaske had ignored in favor of Sumatta's Cycle of Ages while Arterians suffered. He should be able to gain some of the electorate back, but he needed something big.

Something big was Dise's real role: She would show Arter that Governor Muaske couldn't even protect Sumatta, much less Arterians. She would show Arter that it needed a strong leader focused on truly protecting Arterians.

And she was trying to connect to him now. He didn't particularly like or dislike the woman, but every time she called him, she asked for something else. She seemed to think his part of the deal meant doing her part as well.

He waved a goodbye to the audience and closed the broadcast connection, accepting Dise's connection. Dise's voice was quietly routed into his earbuds. He waited. There was no need to move his lips and give away that he'd taken an incoming connection.

"She miscarried," Dise began. Her voice carried its typical confidence, but he detected uncertainty between the lines. "Don't worry. We'll get another, but it's not going to be the same specs I gave you before. I'll make sure it matches the ones you've released publicly."

She waited for a response. He gave none. After a moment, she caught on that he could listen, but could not speak, so she continued.

"I've heard that last minute changes would be made to the event security. I need those details."

He coughed slightly. It was more of a sigh than a cough. Just enough to signify that he didn't have what she needed. He looked around and grabbed a cup of water, taking a swig to make it look to Noselar like he needed to clear his throat after his rousing speech.

"Don't give me that," Dise said. "They can't change things without notifying your security detail and you have my team too far from you to stay informed. Get me the details or I'll get them myself. By Sum—" She cut herself off invoking the beast's name. "Or I swear I'll break our agreement and get someone close enough to you to get that information. Our agreement won't be allowed to ruin our plans."

She waited for a response. He gave none. What she took that for, he didn't know, but the tension in her voice grew more taught.

"Good. We're agreed," she said. She dropped the line before he had a chance to make any grunt, cough, or even offer silence in opposition.

Dise was a great strategist, but too talkative and too dependent on others to get the task done. She was supposed to be far away from the event when it happened, but he was going to change that. Get her close to the event, part of the event if he could. And he'd make sure she never left that event. She needed to be another victim of it or he'd be her next victim.

"You can stop grunting at me," Noselar said.

Spratee cocked his head to the side and glared at his bonded one. He thought he'd only made one sound and covered it up. She must have been moody today. She seemed as moody lately as a real pregnancy would have her be. "I was grunting at what you said, energy of my life," he said with as much sarcasm and contempt as their degraded bonding allowed. "I wasn't grunting at you."

Noselar laughed, her own contempt as obnoxious as that laugh. "Don't even start, Spratee. I'm serious. I want out when this election is over. I'll go stay with my parents. We can say that they're sick and I'm taking care of them after losing the baby. Either way, you're not the man I bonded, and I am done with whatever you're doing. You lost this election months ago and..." She finally stopped and simply shook her head. "I'm not asking, Spratee," she said and stood up, turning to walk away.

"You're going to have a baby."

She flipped her head back, then turned around to face him before laughing that forsaken laugh again. "An actual baby? With you? No, no I'm not. I will never have your child. I love you, Spratee. Sumatta knows why, but I do love you. I just can't stand you. And you're not parent material—you never have been and I doubt you ever will be."

"I didn't say *I* am going to be a parent, I said *you* are going to have a baby. You will be its parent. I want nothing to do with it. It'll give you a chance to be away from me. I'll be busy as governor and you'll be busy parenting. You can go stay at your parents' for all I care. I haven't lost this election—I'm going to win it. And that baby is still part of my campaign, so it stays."

Noselar paused for a moment, pondering his words. When she figured out what he meant, he could tell she started to consider it, then she smiled as condescendingly and obnoxiously as her laugh.

"A secret adoption? You'll be in for it more than you think, Spratee. Oh, energy of my life, you have no idea what you've just said. Proves my point, really. You'll never be parent material. Now, energy of my life, you'll just have to learn the hard way. I'll do it. If for no other reasons than to get away from you for a while and to help a parentless child. Maybe, Sumatta willing, I'll figure out why I still love you."

He knew why he loved her. She was the only one who knew him for who he truly was and despite that, she loved him. She hated who he was, but she loved him. She was strong enough to stand up to him, but was there when he really needed her. She'd do almost anything he asked and she'd never betray him. But their love wasn't like what others seemed to have. They hated each other and loved each other for it, or was it in spite of that?

For now, he'd gotten what he wanted, so he smiled, looking toward the bedroom. She rolled her eyes, but gave in, strutting toward the bedroom with airs. When they fought, it always made for a more wild night. Maybe the love they had was one based solely on the love they made?

Igri Tufuer

Alia stood before the desk in the Reader's study. The desk was equipped as a command center. Papers and notes of ancient studies had been put away, replaced by a large screen that provided a dizzying array of graphs and data charts. From the small desk, any level of manager could be reached in just two taps. Understanding the Complete History seemed a smaller task than the one before it now.

The Complete History could never be completed. Alia knew the feeling; it had not finished them. Shenol's initial interest had waned over the months and her questions had dwindled as their attention turned to the celebration. Alia was the first Reader in thousands of years to be called upon to fulfill the role of Reader. The role was more than being Sumatta's interpreter. The Reader's primary function was to read Sumatta's translation of the Cycle of Ages to Arterians when the next Age was predicted.

According to the Complete History, it had been almost nine thousand years since a Reader was called upon to fulfill this role. That had brought on the Age of Maturity. Arterians had not known science and arts at the time. They had just begun to know cities. The message had not been considered big by Sumatta's standards, and only the leaders of every tribe had been called to hear the message.

Whatever message was coming was big and Sumatta had summoned all Arterians to attend. A celebration of a few hundred would now become a celebration of billions. The logistical nightmare was larger than Mount Sumat itself. How did one bring together millions, much less billions, to witness an event the size of a dozen city blocks?

Shenol had figured it out first. The Reader had heard the

message, but the Next Reader was the one who understood. Sumatta had said that the message had come early. Maybe it had meant that it was supposed to have come when Shenol was to become Reader. She had truly grown into the role and shown she was far more ready for this than Alia.

Sumatta had said to bring the Cycle of Ages and Arter together. That didn't have to mean all of Arter to the Cycle of Ages. Bringing the Cycle of Ages to all of Arter was not a much smaller task. The Reader, voice of Sumatta for all of Arter, usually having one charge, the Next Reader, was now charged with a workforce of over a few million. Overwhelming just didn't seem like the right-sized word for it.

Shenol stood to Alia's right, staring at the screens, patiently waiting for Alia's questions and simultaneously monitoring their continued feedback as she toyed with her touchpad, sending orders and receiving responses. From her touchpad alone, Shenol could command as much as Alia from its desk.

"How do you do it?" Alia asked.

Shenol looked up from her touchpad, eyes focusing on the screens in front of Alia as she cocked her head in confusion, quietly begging the question.

"Have a sense of where it's all at? Keep the progress of the stadium, the status of the broadcasters, the state of security, the..." Alia trailed off, flipping through screen after screen of data. "...all of this?"

Shenol relaxed and looked back at her touchpad. "I take it in like I was reading a lot of books at once. Each thing is like a different book with different characters. I just know where their story is at any point and only read one book at a time."

Alia tapped the corner of the screen, unsatisfied by the answer. It collapsed down then folded up into a box on the bottom right. Alia collapsed into its chair. "I guess, but this is all one story. Anyway, we have a month left. From what I gather, you have everything in place, exactly as planned. Everything is going perfectly. So, what do I need to know?"

Shenol looked up with a degree of disbelief.

"Perfectly, Reader? I wouldn't say that. It appears everything is going as planned, but the truth is a bit different.

"I asked the various managers to have three contingency plans in place for every major task. Most have had to use at least two of them. The biggest unknown still remains, however. Scientific analysis of our relay stations suggests the stations will be able to handle the energy surge from the message and if they fail, backup relays are in place, but that only addresses the electromagnetic surge at the relay level. How we will bring the broadcast back up to all of the individual stations remains unknown.

"We've placed surge protectors to prevent any surge from traveling far, but if the surge happens at the receiver level, then the receiver is dead. Arterians would need a backup receiver and we simply cannot put a backup receiver in every house on Arter."

Alia had hoped someone would come up with some solution in the months leading up to the celebration, but none had come forward. It had been and remained the biggest problem. Every theater in Arter would broadcast the celebration, but most of Arter would be watching from the comfort of their homes. If the receiver sets in their homes failed, what else was there? This was the biggest event in Arter's history and that was the biggest obstacle—they must find a way of getting the message to every Arterian on the planet; it was their charge given by Sumatta itself. An idea came to Alia. Perhaps there was something Alia could do other than marvel at the whole situation.

"We're delivering a message to everyone. Who is better at that than marketers, Shenol?" Alia donned a huge smile. "Marketers have their message on every wall, corner, screen, ... every receiver on Arter. We need to find out if we can shut down every marketing receiver on the planet and if the local receivers are disabled by the message, activate them."

"That, …" Shenol said, pausing to consider all of the implications. "That will work! Why didn't we think of that before, Reader?" She entered some notes in her touchpad.

"One more thing," Alia added. "What is this?"

Alia picked up an envelope sitting on its desk, poured out the disk inside and set it on the replay device, then leaned forward and tapped the cube. The screen unfolded out to the left and popped up, then flipped through a few screens to bring up an authorization form.

Shenol curled her head in like a schoolgirl caught with an embarrassing secret.

"I just got that. I looked at it before bringing it to you, Reader. I think it's important."

Shenol looked up at Alia with a face atypically serious for the young Next Reader. "There's been a lot of underground chatter of an attack during the celebration. In the Complete History, there are many stories of a military leader usurping their leader. In all of them, the leader is reliant on the military for their security, so they end up falling to the military; however, in one of them the leader is prepared and when the military tries to take over, the commanders find themselves without a military. We all know the story, but what we don't know is how the leader was able to turn the tables. That person —the one in the authorization—knows. I want him to protect Sumatta; he can thwart the attack."

That was more than a lot of information, and it was more than a lot of supposition. Shenol was not a military tactician and Alia didn't know where the idea that the military was involved had come from.

"It's a backup plan, Reader. I hope it doesn't come to that, but by Sumatta itself, I swear I will do whatever I can to protect Sumatta."

"Shenol, you're asking for him to be given enough control to overthrow every government on Arter. I don't even have the authority to grant that… and I don't know that I would or even should."

Shenol blushed as if another secret were being exposed. "Look at his surnames, Reader."

What relevance could a surname have? Alia decided to humor Shenol and flipped forward to the final screens of less-pertinent data. Alia stopped abruptly. The surname stood out like an unclaimed *attaten* left out in full view. Alia glanced at Shenol with dumbfound shock, then back at the screen. "'For the first and the last.'," the Reader whispered, quoting from the Complete History. "You've been hiding here all this time?"

Alia took a long breath. It couldn't be a coincidence. Not that combination of letters. That was impossible. Alia said the surname aloud as it reached forward and pressed a finger against the screen, granting authorization: "Igri Tufuer".

The screen acknowledged the touch and scanned Alia's eyes. A dialog popped up confirming access had been granted. She tapped it closed and a single piece of paper printed off. She grabbed it, affixed the seal, and handed the paper to Shenol.

It was not a surname, but an ancient title, only spoken in the Complete History twice and never repeated by a Reader to anyone but another Reader. A title so universal that its pronunciation could be understood in both the language of the Sumatta and that of Arter, though the words did not translate in either language. Sumatta had said that it meant "next oldest". It was owned by the being which saved Sumatta and brought it to Arter in the first place.

"This is going to be a big message, Reader. Why has he come now?" Shenol stuttered before getting her voice back, now paler than ever. "Why does he feel he needs to protect Sumatta now?"

Shenol remembered the title, but had not remembered everything the Igri Tufuer had said or she'd have known the answers to her questions. Alia remembered and had different questions, the biggest of which by its estimation was why was the Igri Tufuer a simple Arterian? A being able to save the

Sumatta from the end of its world and bring it here, now in the form of just another Arterian. The Igri Tufuer could have come here as a god, but according to the screen, it was here as an old man asking to take on a secret security detail at the beginning of the Last Age... and asking for Alia's permission, nonetheless. No, the real question they both should have been asking is what was the Igri Tufuer going to do.

A nagging question in the back of Alia's head kept asking if this was real, if it was really the Igri Tufuer, but there was no way to mistake this. It had to be him.

"Get me everything you can on him. And I want to meet him."

"Yes, Reader," Shenol said as she put the paper in an envelope and sealed it. "I'll tell him." She turned and ran out of the Reader's study.

Mission

"Hey old man, Cycle of Ages is coming!" some young kid said, stopping as he ran past the streets to inform the old commander. The kid looked at the commander and saw his dark, penetrating brown eyes and shirked away, running the other direction to tell others the good news.

Undoubtedly, they thought it was good news. That's because they'd never seen a planet go through another age. Going through an age was worse than aging; a new age brought all of its pain and suffering at once. It was good news for him, though. It would provide a stellar opportunity to rid himself of an age-old foe.

So far, he had whittled his initial list down to a hundred potentials. Those would need to be investigated a little more carefully. He prepared a dossier of himself, ripe with falsehoods, and seeded with one magic set of words the Reader thought only it knew.

The Reader had a very limited world view. It thought it knew everything because of Sumatta's stories that it called history. Histories are almost never truth—he'd only seen true histories less than a handful of times ever—they're filled with what someone wants you to believe as truth. There is always some truth in every history. This one little truth would motivate the Reader to give him exactly what he wanted.

Usually, the key to getting what he wanted was to not ask for it directly. Ask for something that appeared small and let them feel that giving it was of little import. Let them underestimate the request. This request was different, a little tricky. He needed to ask for something big. The best way to get that was to make it seem as if though there was no choice but to give him what he asked for and every other alternative, including not granting it at all, would be very bad. Those two little words would do the trick.

"Next Reader," the old commander said in a scratchy voice as Shenol stepped out of the Bahnderia to check on the crowd. "I have a request, please."

There must have been something in his voice because Shenol stopped talking with others and spun around. The child had such an innocent, youthful smile. She wiped the hair back from her face and straightened her robe.

"Please deliver this request directly to the Reader. Do not make copies and do not distribute. It's for Sumatta's safety," he said, extending an envelope for her.

Shenol perked up, took the envelope, and held it up before her, eyeing it warily.

"Um, what's your name, sir?"

"Tanseor. Tanseor Igri Tufuer. Will you look at it?"

Shenol paled and reached in the envelope, slipping the papers out and caught a disk with the papers. She thumbed through them.

"The disk contains a copy of the papers," he said.

She nodded and slid everything back in the envelope. "Yes, Igri Tufuer."

Forgetting her manners, she turned and ran, leaving Tanseor standing by himself.

It was going to work. Like a charm. He leaned against the wall and waited. It seemed like he waited an hour. Did it not work? Those words should have worked, taking away any question. Had he made a mistake? That was unlikely. He was far too careful.

"Igri Tufuer," Shenol said, finally coming back out of the Bahnderia. "Your request has been accepted. Take this," she said, handing him a sealed envelope. "It contains the authorization from the Reader itself. It wants to meet you too."

"Did it say when?"

"No, actually. It didn't. I would expect the Reader would

want to see you as soon as possible."

"I will come as soon as I can. I have a lot of work to do. Forgive me, but I must get started on it now. Thank you," he said, bowing to her. She curtsied back at him and he stepped into the crowd, disappearing among the masses.

That's what the Next Reader would see. What he actually did was step into a group walking by and walk with them for four paces before turning back and crossing behind the Bahnderia. That would get him out of her sight. He walked three blocks forward and took a left. His transport was parked there. He hopped in, opened the sealed authorization and grinned. The Reader hadn't changed so much as one word. Now he'd find them. There was nowhere on Arter they could hide with this authorization.

Tanseor set course for Sumna University. It was a boring ride. Too many hours. Arterians really needed to develop faster transports. They seemed to enjoy their version of civilization and its gruelingly slow pace. That or they did not have the creativity to come up with something better.

At Sumna University, he went to the records clerk's office and opened the door slowly. He brought his cane for added effect and hobbled up to the desk.

"Excuse me, but I'm looking for a man. He attended here many years ago. He might have taught here. He is a relative of mine and I need to find him. We were researching something together and I've finally made a breakthrough, but sadly, we've lost touch in the years in between."

"I'm sorry, sir. I would really like to help you, but we cannot give out information about current or past staff or students."

"I understand," he said, pulling out the envelope. He made a show of removing the authorization and extending it to the clerk. "As you can see, it is of great importance, even to the Reader. It is a matter of Sumatta's security."

The clerk took the paper, stuttered a little before telling him to wait a moment, and took it to another Arterian sitting at a back desk. He looked over the paper and got up, walking over to Tanseor.

"This is the official seal of the Reader. I'm not sure it has the authority to grant everything on this sheet, but the Reader has more than enough authority to grant access to our records." He handed a form to Tanseor. "Please fill this out. If he can be found, I'll find him. What is the subject matter of the research?"

"Interdimensional Characteristics of Non-Arterian Orthographies," Tanseor said, the words rolling off his tongue as if he'd said them many times before. "We're studying Sumattan," he clarified as he began filling in the form.

"Interesting. I didn't know they had an alphabet."

"Most don't. It's not like ours."

"Explains why the Reader is interested, given the Cycle of Ages is coming. Honing its skills beforehand."

"Something like that," he said, then looked up and handed over the form. "You'll contact me when you find him? Time is of the essence, sir."

"Absolutely."

Tanseor left the building and hopped in his transport, heading to the Cycle of Ages. He needed to scope out the event. The Arterian the school was searching for had to be the right one. Very few would study a subject as specific as that and specifically the language of Sumatta. It was an unnatural interest. And that one would be at the event; he wouldn't miss it for the world.

An Elite Viewpoint

The celebration was a disaster. It hadn't even begun, but Spratee could see that. A stadium was meant to have a stage at its center, not a mountain. According to the reports, over a million attendees would be at the event. Spratee, being one of the political elite, had been ushered in as some of the first guests (and he'd be ushered out first as well). However, that meant a week of living in what they called Celebration Stadium. It wasn't a stadium, it was a series of cities erected on and around Mount Sumat with views of the Cycle of Ages from various angles. Cities with all of the hallmarks: sewage, stench, and sellers. Being of the elite kept him away from the sellers, but as the city grew, his rank did not keep him from the rankness.

He had an entire floor of a building situated directly across Celebration Stadium city from Governor Muaske. They were on opposite sides of the mountain with the Cycle of Ages in between. It opened to a well-decorated roof from which he had a clear view of the Cycle of Ages. Except for the heat rising and bringing with it all of the city stench, he had to admit that it was a good spot. From here, he could see Governor Muaske's transport landing on his roof. Access to a transport in Celebration Stadium was one of the perks of rank Spratee did not yet enjoy, but it meant he would not accidentally miss when Governor Muaske lost the election.

He snickered as he thought about the Governor losing the election. There was more than one way to lose an election. A loss could happen from losing votes, but a candidate could also resign or die. Governor Muaske wouldn't resign. He was going to find a different fate. With Governor Spratee out of the race, Spratee was a shoo-in—every other candidate only had a nominal vote.

The Cycle of Ages was impressive in size, but that was it. It looked like black ice filling a large, inverted pyramid gap in the mountain. It reflected the colorful aurora skylights of day and night, but other than that it looked like blackness. Soon an electromagnetic storm from the sun would light it up, somehow foretelling Arter's future. That part, he was sure, was a pile of Sumatta dung. It had to be some trick the Reader and Sumatta had schemed up to send out a message they had agreed on to keep Arterians subjugated for another few thousand years. Control and conquering was all that beast wanted, and it wanted it under the guise of being the "Giver of Life, Protector of Arter, and Guardian of Ages".

Spratee humphed. He'd never seen Sumatta dung before, but if it was going to look like anything, it would look like what he saw before him now.

It wouldn't be that much longer. He leaned back in his lounger content with himself and took in the yellow and blue of today's aurora. It was expected that the sun's energy would bring the already charged atmosphere to life. Electrical problems were expected and Arterians were told to keep everything off except for their receivers. Those in the stadium were told to keep everything off.

He wondered what would happen if the receivers went out on Arter, but that wasn't his problem. At this point, he actually didn't have any problems. Well, any except Noselar, but she was a problem he had been handling for decades. No, this was actually a very good time to be him.

Dise was arriving. A sudden appointment to Director of Education had surprised her and he was certain she still had no idea how she received the position. Spratee knew; he had pulled a few strings to make it happen. Even if she did know how, she wouldn't know why. No, one should not leave any strings behind.

He leaned forward as she stepped off the transport,

following Governor Muaske closely. She had made quite the show of being his supporter. From the looks of it, she was an obsequious whore, fawning over his every action. He appeared to trust her, oblivious to her facade, and treated her like she was in his inner circle. She had skills, that's for sure. What she was trying to get from him wasn't certain, but if Spratee had to guess, she was either finding out if the security plans he transmitted to her were legit or she was scheming up a way of getting them changed. It didn't matter. She was doing her part for him.

The baby was still an issue. Dise hadn't found a replacement. It didn't bother him. In the worst-case scenario Noselar would have a miscarriage. That would draw up some sympathy vote, but he wouldn't even need that after this week.

Laying back, he took in the entirety of his plan and smiled. It was too soon to relish his success, but success was imminent, all of his plans were coming together and better than expected.

Off in the distance, Arterians were bringing supplies into the cities. Meat, fruits, vegetables, trinkets, and a miscellany of everyday things like razors, soaps, and perfumes, many of which branded themselves as custom made for the event. There was so much stuff, that not everything could be checked by security. Spratee was most interested in the ground security, the area closest to where Sumatta would appear. The lower classes were there, and their supplies weren't being checked as thoroughly.

Even if they had been checked and any of the weaponry discovered, the Arterians ferrying it in had no idea what was in the crates and would be useless if probed. The team who would use the supplies were already on site, looking like the the lowest of the low class. They were the ones who were truly the danger, but they wouldn't stand out to anyone.

Spratee dozed off and dreamed of the celebration's sneak attack and celebrating the death of Sumatta.

Gathering

Trellia met Strypan on the roof of their building in Celebration Stadium. There was only one landing pad for every building and it was on the roof. Their area was two floors down. They had rented an entire floor. It had cost a small fortune, but all three families shared in the cost. Strypan was one of the last to arrive. He hopped out of his version of a transport—something from a couple generations back that he'd modified—and met Trellia with open arms and a beaming smile

"Strypan, you made it. It's good to see you again. You haven't seen Unel, have you?" Trellia said as she hugged him.

Strypan looked genuinely surprised. "Not since I showed him the science of wind chimes," he said with deadpan seriousness. If Strypan was serious, she knew, Strypan was not being serious—that was the conundrum with him.

"I see," Trellia said as if giving the statement its desired level of serious consideration. She motioned toward the elevator and Strypan lead the way. "He told me about that. The *draumr* looks stunning now. He says that what you did was exactly what was needed. I wouldn't expect him to admit that to you. It was fascinating to learn *attaten* are the life *aten*. I thought they were for fertility only."

"I can see how you two might think that," he replied with a glance at her stomach as the elevator door closed. He winked at her, betraying his playfulness, but maintained his serious tone. "But there is more to life than making life. When will it be born?"

Trellia turned and added a haughty tone of offense at her son being referred to without gender. "*He* will be born in eight days. Really, Strypan, I thought you knew I am having a boy!"

Strypan took offense at her offense, cocking his head back and looking at her with utter shock. "When did we start talking about *Noal*?" he asked, replacing the pronoun with the proper noun with exaggerated emphasis. "I meant the *draumr*. That's what we were talking about, right? Perhaps we were having a different conversation than the one I thought."

The elevator door opened and Trellia laughed wholeheartedly as they stepped out. "Of course, we were. Unlike the predictability of birth, invention takes its own time. I imagine anytime, though."

Strypan looked as if he'd caught her in a trap. The man always seemed to have a context under the context... at a minimum. "Then we know where he is," he said.

Trellia wasn't giving in to her bonded one's parent. She stopped laughing, lifted her head high and adopted Strypan's tone. "Of course, I know where he is. I had asked if you had seen him. I'm sure he sends his regards."

Strypan maintained his seriousness, but the edge of his mouth perked up ever so slightly. "Ah, yes, that is exactly what you asked. And I am sure he does not send his regards. Have you ever seen a serious *attaten*? No, how can an *aten* have emotion? My son seems to forget that just like an *attaten*, Life does not need to be completely serious."

Trellia scowled at Strypan. "Now, Strypan, I can't have you talking about my bonded that way. You know he loves you, but it is challenging to show love to someone you don't understand. He doesn't understand you the way I do. I know," she said, pausing to cough. "I know you happen to think Life is like an *attaten*; Life is not serious."

Strypan raised a brow, but didn't say anything in response. She decided she'd won this little exchange; she'd played off of his analogy and reversed it back at him. It was rare that she had such an opportunity—Strypan did have a few years more experience than her—so she relished the moment.

Gemtra interrupted with perfect timing and a platter of

what must be the perfect teas. "Don't take a blue cup. Those are for us," she said looking at the two of them with those all-knowing birth parent eyes. She was fully aware of her timing, she probably waited to the side while they were bantering just to enjoy the show.

Noal decided it was his time to join the conversation and gave her a swift kick just above the belly button. Trellia grabbed her stomach and took a deep, measured breath. "Hey, it's not your time yet," she said, starting to rub her stomach.

Gemtra laughed, turning as Strypan took a cup, and said, "You should sit down, dear. Your rocking chair is on the deck."

"I think I will," Trellia said. Gemtra followed her, carrying the tray of drinks and watching very parentally as Trellia waddled out to the viewing deck. She eased into her rocker and groaned with relief as she wrapped her arms around her tummy, massaging the active womb. She'd had the rocking chair brought in just for her. It seemed to calm Noal when he got more active.

Gemtra set the tray down and handed Trellia a cup of cool tea. "This will help. I made this cup for you."

Trellia took the cup and sipped the refreshing tea. It gave a slight tingle to her tongue and throat as she swallowed it, but seemed to relax her muscles. Maybe it would help Noal calm down.

"You keep talking as if the doctors pick when you'll give birth. Yes, yes, I know, they're ninety-eight point six percent right. Life has a way of not caring just how serious you are about something. Life is like an argument without a point. It just keeps going no matter what you think of it. That baby will come when it's ready, not when it's predicted."

"I think I know the real question. Is an *attaten* like an argument without a point?"

They both looked at Strypan with disbelief. Had he followed them out here just to say something so meaningless?

Gemtra threw her hands up to her mouth as she gasped.

She laughed, slightly snickering, then said, "Let's pick this up in about five minutes. It will be a more interesting pointless argument."

"Why's that?" Trellia asked.

"I said not to take a blue cup," she answered, glaring at Strypan's cup.

He shrugged and set his empty cup down on the tray. "Pointless argument now."

Trellia snorted and gave up trying to keep up the serious banter. Gemtra's tea was no joke. Strypan was in for an argument in all the glory of Life's colors. She shook her head back and forth. He was in for it. He should know that.

Xarat got out of the elevator and made his way to Gemtra as quickly as his hefty frame would allow. He swooped in behind his bonded and gave her a kiss, then looked at the tray of tea. "Where's mine?"

Everyone laughed.

Gemtra said, "I need to make you a new one. Strypan drank it. Would you like another, Strypan?"

Xarat huffed and glared at Strypan who was shaking his head for more tea. "Not until I get mine. It's almost sunset." He turned and looked over the balcony and took in a breath of appreciation for the view. "Beautiful. I love these shades of an electric sunset."

Gemtra went inside, heading to the kitchen to make some more tea.

Xarat turned around, surveyed the group and asked, "Where's Unel? Col?"

Trellia and Strypan laughed, Trellia grabbing her stomach as she laughed.

"What? That was funny? I was being serious."

They laughed even harder. Gemtra came back in with three blue cups on another tray. She looked around at everyone laughing and asked, "Now, what did I miss?"

"He wanted to know who else is coming and where Unel

is," Trellia said, breathing in and out slowly to relax her body as she tried to recover from the laugh. "We haven't answered him yet."

"Just those two. They'll be here, energy of my life," Gemtra said, shaking her head as she held out the tray for Xarat to take a cup. She turned and offered another cup to Strypan. He gladly picked it up, then she set the tray down and took the last cup for herself.

"Let's set up the balcony for the celebration. I don't like the default arrangement. It's too sterile," she said to Xarat. She turned and looked at the building itself, tracing the outline with her head. "I do like the building though. Tall windows so you can look out from the inside if it gets stormy or cold and a full half circle deck overlooking the Cycle of Ages. It's a magnificent view."

"That it is," Xarat added, taking a sip of his tea. "What do you want to do to the balcony?"

The two of them spoke more softly as Gemtra described how she wanted the deck and Xarat started moving furniture and plants around. Strypan seemed to be lost in thought as he stared at the Cycle of Ages. Maybe the tea was starting to have an effect.

Trellia wondered if Unel would even make it. He was so consumed by the *draumr* and the Dreamoria. He might miss the birth of his son if he didn't leave that place soon. She had wanted so bad to give him a child that she'd done everything she could. He would miss the birth? What if she were wrong and he didn't want a child as bad as she had thought? If he knew what she'd done... If he knew how far she'd gone... If...

No, life keeps going, no matter what you think of it or how you take it. Noal was coming and that was that. He kept kicking her to remind her of that fact.

She leaned back, hands caressing her tummy and wondered what kind of wild dream she would have as she dozed off.

* * *

Shenol opened the door to the Reader's study. "Tanseor is here, Reader. Want me to show him in?"

"Yes," Alia said with a little too much excitement and impatience. It quickly reached out and tapped the screens to cause them to fold up into the box and waited for the man to enter.

Shenol poked her head back through the door. "You can come in now," she said and swung the door wide open, bowing her head.

She stepped aside, letting a very old man slowly walk through the door, then stepped outside, closing the door behind her. His clothes were kempt, but not fancy and a little worn and dusty. His black hair had been combed, but was slightly disheveled now. His brown eyes looked bright, but aged and tired. He had been busy today for someone his age and hadn't had time to freshen up before coming to see Alia.

Alia was a little more than upset, but would not show it. Not now. Not here. Not in front of him. The fact was that Tanseor had waited until just hours before the Cycle of Ages delivered its message when Alia had asked to see him days ago. Most Arterians would come to the Reader when asked, not on their own time frame. He was the Igri Tufuer, though. He could set his own timeline. Maybe he had chosen his timing as part of his grand plan.

He smiled as he walked in and stood across from Alia. He seemed friendly, courteous, not in the slightest disrespectful.

Alia waited. The Igri Tufuer was in Alia's presence... no, Alia was in the Igri Tufuer's presence. Alia would not speak first. One does not talk before the god of one's god. The man seemed to wait in deference to Alia. What should Alia do? There were no protocols for this. It refused to speak before the Igri Tufuer. Finally, Alia gave up and motioned with a hand for him to speak. That should be acceptable, right?

"I apologize," the Igri Tufuer said.

"Apologize for what?" Alia had expected him to start some pleasantries, not an apology. Realizing they were both still standing, waiting on the other to sit first, Alia said, "Please sit."

The Igri Tufuer sat down, Alia following suit, then explained. "You summoned me and gave me the authority I asked for, then I did not come when summoned. I waited. Time was short and I had a lot of things to do to protect Sumatta. I hoped that you would be forgiving as a fellow protector of Sumatta, but an apology still seemed appropriate."

Well, he completely stole the thunder from Alia's fury. And he'd done it well. Of course he had, he's a god. Perhaps *the* God. "Thank you, ... I don't know how to address you. How should I address you?"

"Tanseor is fine," he said lightly.

Just "Tanseor"? He's the Igri Tufuer and he wants to be called by a nickname? Was it even ethical for Alia to call him that? Would it be ethical to address him differently when he'd just told Alia to do something? No, it would not. This was not going to be an easy meeting!

"Well, thank you, Tanseor. Can I ask you some questions?"

"Yes. I assume that's why you summoned me."

He said that too calmly. I summoned a god? Is that even possible? I don't have that kind of authority, Alia thought.

"I didn't want it to sound like that. I just wanted to talk with you. I apologize, Tanseor." Alia was stumbling in the presence of this man and desperately needed to get it together. Alia needed to be Reader, Protector of Sumatta, not Alia, the one tongue-tied in a god's presence. The Reader was the one who usually spoke in a god's presence. Alia took a moment to gather its wits, then asked, "You're a god. Why are you doing this this way? Can't you just do whatever you want?"

"That does seem like a logical question, but what if I did do something? Wouldn't that undermine belief in Sumatta?

Arterians would see a new god. What would that do to Arter? To Sumatta? How would I then be protecting Sumatta?"

"You could make it look like it wasn't you."

"Isn't that what I'm doing?"

And there it was. The Igri Tufuer had lowered himself to the point of explaining his grand plans and they were both simple and obvious. Alia felt like a fool. "I hadn't thought of it like that."

Tanseor ignored Alia's embarrassment, swiping it away with a hand motion as if it were nothing. "The obvious is only the obvious when it's known. Until then, it's a mystery. Any other questions?"

"I'd be afraid the answers would be as obvious as the last. No, Tanseor, no more questions. Thank you for taking the time to entertain my naiveté. I won't bother you again."

He stood and gave Alia a bow. "You have been a great help in my plans here, Reader. Thank you for all you do to protect Sumatta."

Alia, shocked at the deference to its position, bowed to Tanseor, lower than he had bowed to it.

He walked over to the door and tapped gently. A surprised Shenol let out a short scream, then quickly pulled the door open. He turned and gave one last bow of the head to Alia, then stepped out as Shenol rushed in and closed the door behind her.

The Igri Tufuer, god of a god, creator of life itself had left the building. Left after being summoned by a fool to ask a fool's questions. Alia felt numb.

"Reader?" Shenol said.

Alia could not believe what it had just done. It was so obvious that it must have been able to see that without summoning the Igri Tufuer.

"Reader?" Shenol asked loudly. It shocked Alia back to the moment.

"Yes, Shenol?"

"Three hours, eighteen minutes."

"Thank you. Everything is in place? Anything I should know?"

"We are ready."

"Then let's begin."

Shenol bowed her head, then lifted her touchpad and tapped away rapidly. "Done. I'll go get dressed."

Alia bowed her head, dismissing Shenol, and Shenol left, striding out as calm, collected, and effeminate as ever.

Alia stood, took a deep breath, then went to its chambers to prepare for the most important moment in a Reader's life. Hopefully it wouldn't flub this up as much as it had with the Igri Tufuer.

Sumatta

Trellia grabbed a cup of tea. Gemmy said it would keep Noal calm during the ceremony. It tingled the taste buds, giving a fresh airy feel. Noal seemed calm for the moment. Hopefully the tea would keep him that way. He was fond of kicking. It seemed he thought the womb was a playground.

She walked out on the viewing deck. Strypan was at the railing, staring at the black crystalline Cycle of Ages. He didn't want to miss one second of when it came to life. Knowing Strypan, he thought he could read the message. She thought for a moment. Knowing Strypan, he just might be able to read the message.

Gemmy had finished rearranging the balcony. Everyone had their own lounger, propped up so that even laying down they could see the event. A plant was set to the right of each one, just far enough back that none of the leaves blocked the view. To the left, near the knees was a small table. Each was filled with snacks and teas. Only one had blue cups and it was between Gemmy and Xarat's loungers.

She walked over to the railing and grabbed it, holding it carefully as she looked at the Cycle of Ages. Any moment and the ceremony would begin, the message would come.

Arterians at the base had assembled, but were still milling around. She was glad not to be in that mix. It was loud enough to hear its echoes reverberating in the mountains and looked far too rambunctious for her. Off to the left a long line of Arterians waited to get in.

Buildings all around the stadium were a stark contrast to the ground level viewing melee. They were mostly small groups enjoying light conversation as they waited. Not a single floor was empty. They were peaceful and friendly gatherings.

She could see herself in any of those groups.

Contrary to the long line waiting to get into the ground level area, the cities were shut down at ground level. No one could be seen down below except officers. On hers, though, that wasn't true. A man was wildly waving at their building as he ran toward it. He stopped periodically to get his breath or argue with an officer, pointing at their building.

"He's here," she said. "But why didn't he take a transport?" she whispered to herself.

"Impeccable timing," Strypan said.

Trellia looked at Strypan. Strypan was standing taller, an eager look on his face as he gave all of his attention to the Cycle of Ages. The receivers positioned throughout the mountains stopped showing the talking heads and flipped to showing the Reader's platform, a large rock sitting on a pool at the base of the Cycle of Ages. A voice boomed through the receivers' speakers.

"I am Srant, your host for the greatest celebration of our lives," the speakers blasted. "And we are moments away from the grand Cycle of Ages, a message given to Sumatta from the sun itself. Soon you will see the Reader come to the platform shown on your screens and..."

Trellia stopped listening to the speaker. He would be the only voice broadcast during the Cycle of Ages—there was only one official broadcast. More importantly, Unel wasn't there yet.

"By Sumatta itself, it's starting!" she yelled.

Gemtra and Xarat were laying back on separate recliners, theirs leaned back for a better view of the sky than the Cycle of Ages. Their eyes were dilated and faces fixed with amazement. In unison, they said monotonously, "Oh, yes, it is." Their eyes traced across the sky as they spoke. *That must be some strong tea*, Trellia thought.

Trellia turned back to find Unel. He was gone. She turned behind her and the elevator was in use. It had to be him. No one else would be using the elevator now.

The elevator door opened and Unel stepped out. He scanned the room and found the one he was looking for, not even recognizing Trellia. "Col! This is it! It works! We have to go in now. Now!" Catching his breath, he looked around, saw Gemtra's tray of teas and noted the brown ones.

"I love your birth parent," he said to Trellia as he stepped forward and grabbed the two cups of avak.

"What was that?" Gemtra asked flippantly.

"I said, 'I love you'," he repeated loudly as he marched over to Col, the banter seeming to be rote and idle, not fully catching his attention. Trellia had not caught his attention.

Trellia thought to say something to him about his initial neglect of her and Noal, but instead held that back for later. No, he was not as eager to be a parent as she'd thought. *It is what it is*, she thought, consoling herself. She felt dejected. She'd given so much of herself to him, but of his two passions, his invention was the bigger.

"The ceremony just began, Unel," she said.

"Just? Great. That means we have time. We need to do a quick test. Oh," he said, seeming to notice her for the first time. He stood upright looking at her with a beaming smile and a twinkle in his eyes, seeming to direct all of his passion at her for a moment. "I love you, energy of my life." He looked at her tummy and added, "You too, baby Noal."

Trellia smiled. Maybe the *draumr* was a relative distraction compared to Noal. Maybe it was worth it. It was so hard being only one of two passions. He wouldn't be excited for the Cycle of Ages, but he would be excited to be with her. She just needed to give him his time with his other passion first. He was so excited that maybe he'd made a breakthrough.

"Fine, but I want you with us when Sumatta appears."

He was already focusing on Col again. He'd handed Col a cup who was obediently gulping down his tea, had downed his own cup, and was laying down on one of the loungers Gemtra had moved in from the balcony. Those had been deemed not colorful enough for tonight's event.

"What about the microtracks?" Col asked.

"Don't need them. I got it. It all works now. From wherever we are. Lay down and see. Hurry."

"You have a funny way of being before you go to bed," Col said. He laid down and winked at Trellia before closing his eyes and fading off to sleep.

Trellia sighed as they went to sleep. "What am I going to do with him, Gemmy?"

"I have a tea for that," Gemtra said with a grin.

Trellia let out a deep, exasperated breath and turned to watch the ceremony.

* * *

Shenol felt powerful. Beautiful, womanly, and completely in charge. She loved this Next Reader's robe, which almost looked like a dress, but had the distinct advantage of a belt around the waist and metal weights sewn along the trim in the form of each letter of the alphabet. This gave it the very important advantage of not flying up from a gust of wind. The dress, no, the robe, had been made just for the event. It was a soft red. Outside under the afternoon sky, it would look almost blood orange and the metal alphabet would twinkle with the waves of green and red streaks flowing through the sky. She looked beautiful; she would look magical.

From her hidden alcove at the base of the Cycle of Ages, Shenol commanded the entire planet. Receivers across Arter had gone out, then just the primary ones brought back up. Srant, the official broadcast journalist for the event, was giving the preliminaries, and she was receiving scientific reports indicating the progress of the solar message through space. She also had security detail reports for Sumatta, the event, and every VIP present. By all reports, everything was going just as expected.

Only one thing was unknown. When would Sumatta appear? The first energy from the solar storm was already arriving. The aurora had lit up, twinkling like a billion stars brought to the sky from far away. From the Complete History, Sumatta had appeared, bonded with the Reader, read the message, then been swept away by the swarm. What the Complete History didn't say is how far along in the solar storm message that had happened—they hadn't developed the science to track the message at the time and there was no science to read the message as it came through now, except for the Cycle of Ages. One could not control and measure everything, and Sumatta's schedule appeared to be one such unknown.

"Next Reader?"

Shenol jumped. "Yes, Reader?"

"When we are on the platform, do not be tempted by your touchpad. You have your teams to take care of things while you are performing your duties.... Even if it is just standing there."

And just like that, Shenol felt powerless. She was only twelve and leave it to the Reader to remind her of that by scolding her before she had even done anything wrong. It was really unfair of the Reader to treat Shenol like that.

Shenol bowed her head, further stripping her of her power. The Reader was right, but Shenol couldn't help but think that this was Alia's last day as Reader. Shenol's time had come. Yet another reason not to treat her like her age. It was exciting and frightening. She enjoyed her womanhood, her dresses, her femininity. Losing that was part of the price a Reader paid, and the part that bothered her the most. She would gain respect, however. She just didn't know how she could make the choice that she was about to face.

"Next Reader?"

Shenol jumped again. "What?"

Alia looked at the sky through the opening in the alcove and Shenol followed its eyes. She dropped her touchpad as she looked at the sky. The aurora twinkled like the stars, but its coloring changed hues as if a paintbrush kept swiping across them with different colors. Behind the Cycle of Ages tens of millions of the Swarm were ascending in waves, filling the sky like an army forming an impenetrable wall.

"It is time," Alia said, turning around and waiting for Shenol to scurry up and gain her composure.

"Ready," she said, straightening her Next Reader's robe. She had forgotten to pick up the touchpad. It was too late now. It didn't matter. The Swarm of Sumatta had arrived. It was beginning.

Alia stepped forward, walking through a light mist from a small waterfall and out onto the large stone forming the Reader's platform. Arter grew quiet as the Reader presented itself for its primary duty, the Next Reader quietly standing behind it.

Above, the Swarm filled the sky over Mount Sumat and behind the mount, nine walls of spatiatta with millions in each rose, each one shorter than the one before it like a cascading fountain. Shenol had thought that all of them had come to guard Sumatta when it had visited the Bahnderia, but this group was at least ten times that size, maybe a hundred times.

The Swarm flattened out, spreading across the sky, casting a shadow over Mount Sumat in every direction and blotting out the aurora. A small group of what Shenol estimated to be about 25,000 split off, forming three rows of three columns three deep and formed what only the Reader and Next Reader would know were Sumattan words. Listening carefully, Shenol could hear the groupings humming. Unfortunately, the Next Reader had only been taught to read one word at a time. She just couldn't make out all twenty-seven words, but it appeared to be a message of safety. Could the Reader read all those words? Whatever they were saying, they were signaling Sumatta.

From behind the Cycle of Ages, Sumatta rose from the

mountain, head shaped like a diamond, and body fully plated with scales. It fully extended its wings, two large wings above two smaller wings, and colorful tendrils dangled from the wings glistening with electricity. Its tentacles swirled like a tornado, and it shot straight up into the air.

The Swarm forming a cascading fountain behind Summatta followed it up into the air, serving as an honor guard, wall after wall after wall until only Sumatta could be seen against the twinkling of their electromagnetic tendrils.

Sumatta leaned forward, turned its wings, and dove down, coasting over the surface of the Cycle of Ages and curving upward as it reached the pool below, a splash erupting and drenching the nearest spectators. It slowed as it shot up from its arch over the pool, then came down to rest just above the Reader's platform.

The Reader kneeled and bowed. Sumatta spoke the word for being ready together, then the Reader stood up and raised its arms above its head.

Shenol thought this must be the most frightening part. The Reader would bond with Sumatta so that when the message came through the Cycle of Ages as an array of twenty-seven letters like the Swarm had done over Mount Sumat, the Reader would be able to understand every word at the same moment as Sumatta.

Sumatta reached out, four tentacles going around each arm and the other around the Reader's waist. Alia's eyes dilated, then rolled back in its head. It seemed to grow larger as energy from Sumatta flowed through the tentacles, into Alia's body, and cycled back into Sumatta.

Sumatta twisted its head to look at the Cycle of Ages and began to read as the message arrived.

Cycle Of Ages

Finally, this thing was about to start. The sooner it was over, the better. That wretch Dise was laughing over on Governor Muaske's tower, doing quite the job of looking as if she were not expecting what was about to happen. They had all quieted down when the receivers started playing, but they still seemed to have a blasé attitude, as if they were above it all. Arrogant fools. They had no idea what was in store for them.

Spratee stood on his viewing deck, one arm wrapped dutifully around Noselar, with a pleased, focused look. His group was much more formal about the event, giving it the serious attention it deserved. He wanted the receivers across Arter to show him as a calm family man who was enjoying the festivities without getting caught up in them.

He watched with growing eagerness as Sumatta wrapped its tentacles around the Reader, bonding with it, then turned to the Cycle of Ages and started reading. That was the cue for the attack to begin. They hadn't known exactly how Sumatta would start reading, but Sumatta's reading would mean the beast was caught up in the translation. That would be its weakest point. Fortunately, Sumatta made it easy.

The Arterian attack team popped open crates, exposing weaponry no one would have expected. The weapons were mechanical, not electrical. Everything on Arter was based on electromagnetic or gravitational energy. Arter's security teams would have been looking for what they knew. These had been specially crafted just for this event. It was true that the Swarm might have picked up on it, but that was an unavoidable risk— The Swarm might have picked up on anything. It didn't matter now. It had worked.

The attack team efficiently unpacked a series of modified

rocket propelled missile launchers. They kept them low on the ground while another picked up the missile and armed it. Then one of the attack team yelled, "Get Down!"

Taking their cue from the scream, the launcher was picked up, placed on someone's shoulder, then the missile slipped into the launcher. This had all been practiced over and over so that the timing would be almost exact for all the missiles in the first volley to shoot.

The Cycle of Ages came to life. Inner striata which had not been visible before in the blackness twinkled rapidly as the message was received. Sumatta's tendrils twinkled with the same pattern. Neither the Swarm nor the militia were distracted by this. The Swarm saw them and someone tasked with watching the Swarm yelled, "Incoming!" just as the first volley launched.

Hundreds of rockets shot at Sumatta. The Swarm split into two groups—one group headed towards Sumatta, the other group at the attack team.

The Swarm of millions tasked with defending Sumatta descended, launching themselves in front of the missiles in a suicide mission. The other Swarm headed straight for the attack team as a sheer wall of fury.

Sumatta began reading the Cycle of Ages. Fortunately, Sumatta was enraptured by the reading as if in a trance. It didn't notice the Swarm defense or the militia's attack.

The crowd was so focused that it didn't even register the flying missiles as they shot out from the crowd toward Sumatta. The screaming began when the first missile hit.

Impact triggered a mechanical lock that turned on the power to the payload. The payload exploded into little shrapnel spheres that shot out a pulse disabling nearby electronics and demagnetizing them before exploding themselves.

Dozens of missiles plowed into Sumatta, bursting and weakening the creature as they exploded. A small part of Sumatta's scaly shield was shredded. The Swarm flew fast, putting themselves directly in the line of fire. They screamed a horrid song of agony as they fell from the sky.

Sumatta turned its head to the sky and let out a piercing musical scream as the honor guard swarm enveloped it. If Spratee was right, he thought he saw the beast collapse.

The attack team was prepared for four more volleys, but the Swarm flying directly at them didn't give them a chance. It poured out into the crowd, blanketing it in a matter of moments. Spratee thought he could see the Spatiatta opening up their bodies and a green fluid being thrown onto them. Were they dissolving them in acid? He curled his nose at the idea. Not even he would do that to his enemies. Not even Sumatta.

All shots ceased. All screaming died out. Behind the Swarm, an Arterian silence was all that was left. Only the buzz of the Swarm could be heard on the fields at the foot of the Cycle of Ages.

The Swarm didn't come for the buildings around. All the attacks had come from the fields in front of the Cycle of Ages in hopes that they would not attack innocents. It had worked. Spratee exhaled with relief and did not move. He wanted to watch what happened next.

Across the distance, Governor Muaske was doing exactly as expected, fleeing to his transport. He wouldn't make it far off that platform. That had been Spratee's other line of defense— assassinating the governor during the chaos. His ship would explode just as soon as he took off. It would be a fantastic show and officially put Governor Muaske out of the race.

An excruciating screech that sounded like Sumatta's scream being ripped in half suddenly filled the air. Spratee looked to his right toward the source. It was the Cycle of Ages. A crack was growing from the bottom of it up through the top. The crack jolted up through the Cycle of Ages and it suddenly exploded, shards of it blasting into the air and burning up as if exposure to the air was all that was needed to ignite it.

The shock wave rocked their building. Noselar stumbled and fell, hitting her head on the cement. It knocked her out. It knocked Spratee to his knees as he looked on at the surprising destruction.

Mount Sumat shook from the explosion as if it were about to collapse in on itself. Arterians tumbled to the ground, some falling off their balconies. Governor Muaske had made it to the roof and was running toward his transport when the shock wave knocked him down. He picked himself up just in time to watch his transport tumble off the side of his tower. Dise was inside. Spratee stood up, alarmed as the transport crashed below. It hadn't blown up! That was the whole plan. Now what?

Governor Muaske raised a hand for help as his tower trembled, then ducked as the top floor collapsed in. The governor went down with the roof and was buried in a pile of rubble.

Spratee laughed harder than he had ever laughed or would ever laugh again. All his work to assassinate the governor and the man died as collateral damage. It was like a mean joke being played on Spratee, yet he'd gotten what he wanted.

Sumatta was gone, the Cycle of Ages destroyed, and Dise and Governor Muaske dead. He didn't care about the governorship with Sumatta gone, so it was pure perfection that he had that too. This could not have gone more perfectly.

* * *

The Reader stepped on the platform, the Next Reader trailing behind it. Unel was still not awake. He said he would be back in time.

"Unel!" Trellia yelled, turning to look at him. He didn't stir. He seemed like he was in a coma, not sleeping. Maybe if she woke Col, that would force Unel to wake up too.

She looked at Col and yelled louder. "Col!" He was just as

out as Unel.

She turned back to the ceremony. Sumatta had appeared. It was flying up in front of the Swarm. Would Unel really miss this? If it worked, couldn't it wait? Didn't he know this was the biggest event of their lifetimes? That gave her pause. For Unel, this wasn't the biggest event of their lifetimes, creating a working *draumr* was and that's what he'd done. Well, if he'd done that, then it was time for him to spend time with her and Noal, with his family. That's the whole reason she was pregnant now—after he built the *draumr*, he was supposed to spend time with his family.

"Unel!" she yelled again, looking at her infuriating bonded as he slept. Exasperated, she looked back at the ceremony.

Sumatta was always impressive, but this was breathtaking. All those waves of the Swarm climbing up like a progressing waterfall behind it was like an organized powerhouse. No, not like one, it was one. A formidable one. And Unel was missing it.

"Unel! Wake up!" She screamed as she looked back at him. "By Sumatta itself, I swear," she said to herself.

"He's exhausted, he's gone to the world," Strypan said. "I think we have figured out that screaming isn't going to bring him back."

Trellia glared at Strypan and shook her head as she watched Sumatta descend in front of the Reader's platform. "They're dreaming. Col isn't waking either... Oh, it's..." she said and turned, stopping halfway to address Strypan. "I'm not going to scream." She completed her turn and stopped abruptly, then quickly looked around the room.

"Where'd he go?" she said.

The *draumr* was there, but he wasn't. Maybe he'd gone to the bathroom? No, the elevator wasn't moving.

"Sumatta!" Strypan screamed with a sheer terror that made Trellia's blood chill.

Everyone—even Gemtra and Xarat—turned around to look

at him. He fell backward, collapsing into his lounger unconscious. Xarat bolted up and ran for Strypan.

Trellia heard the explosions as she watched Strypan fall and turned to look toward Sumatta. Sumatta was under attack.

"Xarat," Gemtra said in quiet disbelief, pointing at the scene, but Xarat didn't look, grabbing Strypan by the shoulders and starting to shake him.

"Stry, come on. Wake up," he said as he shook him.

Noal kicked. Hard. Trellia grabbed her stomach, then sat down, eyes fixed on the massacre below as she grew nauseous. "Oh, for energy's sake." She started breathing as Noal stirred inside and her body started to tremble, contracting with a deep urge to push.

A rush of fluid came between her legs.

"He's coming, Gemmy!" she yelled, taking a deep breath and letting it out in short huffs.

Gemtra turned to her daughter and ran to her. "What is going on?" she said to herself.

Trellia groaned and took another breath. She let the breath out in three short huffs and saw an explosion of blood burst out of Xarat's neck. He grabbed his neck and fell onto Strypan, the weight of the two causing the lounger to tumble over.

"Xarat!" Trellia yelled, reaching out for him.

Gemtra turned to look at her bonded as he rolled to the floor. "Xarat!"

Trellia grunted, then gave in to the need to push as the contraction took over. She moaned. "It's happening now, Gemmy. Oh, Sumatta! It's happening now."

Tears in her eyes, Gemtra turned back to Trellia. Shock had taken over. Reality itself had just ceased. Yet somewhere in the numbness of shock, she'd called on a force without a name to give her the strength to do what she needed to. She looked down, her voice becoming calm and collected in a detached way. "His head's showing. That's it. Come on Noal. Push, Trellia. Push!"

Trellia had seen this strength in her Gemmy before. They'd never spoken of it, but she had remembered enough of Gemtra coming to save her in the dream world to know her birth parent had conquered the agony of seeing her wounded daughter. She had held back her pain and called upon this unnamed strength to do what she needed to do. It was the strength only a birth parent can have. Trellia had a name for this strength: Gemmy.

Trellia was about to be a birth parent. Would she have—

Her thoughts were interrupted as her body wrenched with another contraction and she bore down, grunting and pushing muscles that she'd never felt before. "Unel, I hate you!" she screamed as Noal's head popped out, his shoulders slipped past, and he slid into Gemtra's arms.

In a swift swing of her arms, Gemtra cleared the mucus out of his mouth and set him in his birth parent's arms. He hadn't even cried before she was on her feet running toward her bonded.

She ran up to him, collapsing to her knees and sliding into Xarat as she reached out and took him by the shoulders. She heaved his limp body up, looking in horror at the unnaturally dark, lifeless blood draining from his neck, then looked into his eyes. His eyes were dilated and glassy, but never again because of her teas. Her Xarat was dead.

"No!" she cried. "No, no, no! Not you. Not the energy of my life. Xarat, why?" she begged. She threw her head back and cried into the night. "Why? Why him?"

Trellia lay on the ground crying like a baby, her own baby crying in her arms. Where was Unel? How could he disappear at a time like this? He's missed everything. What next? Her body contracted again in answer, working the lochia out. Through her tears, she breathed again and pushed.

"Unel?" she said, her voice defeated. "Where are you? Col? Somebody? Help!"

Taking Aim

Tanseor stepped out of his transport and pulled three bags from the back, throwing them on the ground. He opened one and unfolded a camouflage tarp, throwing it over the transport. It would look like a large pile of debris from a distance. He grabbed the other two bags and walked a hundred paces to the north. He set the bags on the ground and unzipped one, pulling out another camouflage tarp. This set was just big enough to cover him. He threw it on the ground, then gathered some nearby brush and piled it around.

He lifted his weapon and checked through the scope, scanning the perimeter and distant buildings. No dangers, everyone was milling around waiting for the event to begin. He turned his sight back to the building with Strypan and watched for a moment. He'd be an easy target. He was standing there transfixed on the Cycle of Ages, barely even shifting on his feet.

There were supposed to be two of them. He'd only found one, so he was taking a risk. Taking out one would alert the rest and then he was likely to be jailed again. It had taken a long time to escape from jail and a long time to establish himself on Arter without the history of his bondage. A lot of time and care. However, if he could only get one of them, then so be it. It would send a message to them all that they were being hunted and sooner or later would have to surrender their secrets.

Tanseor laid down under his camouflage tarp and pulled the brush back around him. He had a solid location. It wasn't easy to find. He was directly shielded from the wind and within shooting distance of the building, but far enough away that when they attacked Sumatta, he would not be part of the Swarm's punishment or in the danger the rest of the stadium would face.

No one knew exactly what would happen when Sumatta was attacked, not even General Byelt. Tanseor hadn't asked directly, of course. He used the same tactics with everyone—he asked under the guise of helping Sumatta. Some had been reticent, but the Reader's authorization had disposed of their reticence as easily as he was about to dispose of Strypan.

He checked his weapon, ensuring the reverse-polarity *attaten* ammunition was chambered. The weapon would only fire one shot at a time and reloading wasn't fast, so after he fired, he would need to get out of there fast or risk the Swarm taking him as a hostile.

He rested, poised, aiming, sights on Strypan's forehead and waited for the chaos to begin. As the Swarm moved overhead, the winds kept changing. He calmly readjusted his aim as the winds changed, staying ready for his opportunity.

The explosions began and the Swarm went into action.

Through his scope, he could see Strypan's shock. Strypan suddenly screamed and passed out. *Why would he pass out? Unless... Oh, I'm out of time*, he thought. He clenched his jaws; with Strypan prone, he didn't have a shot.

A man ran over and lifted Strypan up. He was hugging him close and moving too fast. Tanseor couldn't get a clean shot. *No time*, he thought. *One shot*. He steadied his aim, adjusting for the wind and anticipating the movement of the two bodies. Tanseor fired. He could see what was going to happen before the bullet hit. It was just off. The wind had changed. The bullet took the wrong one in the neck.

Tanseor sighed, not waiting for the spray to hit the ground. He'd have to pick this up again later. He swiftly stood up, folded up his weapon into the carrying case, placed it into the bag, then folded the camouflage tarp up and placed it into the bag. He grabbed the two bags and walked back to the transport, pulling the camouflage debris off, then jumped in and set the controls for manual control. He needed time to think, recoup, and desperately needed to get away from this disaster.

Lifting the craft up, he turned south and kept just above the trees as he headed for the Isle of Lights.

Igri Tufuer

It wasn't a dream. It was colors. Colors that spread in every direction, changing, blending, pouring over in a two-dimensional array of wonder. No, the colors moved in three dimensions. No, more dimensions than that. Where was he?

"Col? Is this your dream?" Unel said.

"Col?"

Unel looked around, but couldn't see anything through the colors. In the distance he sensed a very strong wave coming toward him. It was coming at him as if from every direction, not one. It was not a wave of water, but force. It was going through every dimension. It was bigger than a tsunami. No, bigger than a planet. What was it?

"Col?"

The wave moved in as if it did not have to traverse distance. It was suddenly there, hitting him with its full force, ripping the colors apart, shattering sound into all its dimensions, ripping his consciousness from his dream, pulling him beyond himself, beyond Arter, beyond... beyond beyond.

Calm came to him. He could see clearly now. All dimensions, all spaces, all traces as they moved through time. No, not time. Time is a concept. He could see that now. He could see everything as it had been for a very long time. It was all there.

Where was he?

He sensed around. He didn't have eyes for some reason, but he could sense. He could sense everything.

He found his trace through time. He had been dreaming at the moment the Foothold was activated in the storm to start the Cycle of Ages and the energy had affected him through another dimension seen from within his dreams. The energy had not come from the sun he had been told. It came from something that appeared to be a being. It had all come together and he had been pushed into this dream and the force kept pushing until... Until he was wherever he was.

He looked at Arter, looked at the Cycle of Ages and the celebration, and saw the destruction.

He saw the truth about his parent's coma. He saw the truth of the origin of his newborn son. He saw the truth of his bonded's love.

He felt detached from it all, as if he were seeing a dream, not reality, yet he knew he was seeing reality—all of reality.

The being who sent the message approach-connected nearer to him. It was a weird sense of getting closer, but connecting directly without moving. He didn't fully understand it, but the being was definitely approaching.

It was doing many things at once. It was large enough to be able to do millions of things at once. Unel could not see its full history, but he had seen enough to know one part of the being. A manifestation on Arter.

On one edge of the being, it turned the air solid in front of Sumatta, shielding it from the attack, but the change had been done only in non-visible dimensions.

It was a beautiful solution, if Unel was being honest. It looked complicated, very hard to achieve.

He was being welcomed. It was being friendly and offering assistance. It kept calling him the wrong name, too. He didn't know the word, but it sounded as if it meant it in a welcoming, friendly way. It kept calling him Igri Tufuer.

Part II

The Last Age

You've created magnificence.
May I join your symphony?

Militant

"I've decided," Noal said as he swung his foot in a wide arc sweeping at Strypan's ankle.

"I usually find out," Strypan said as he raised his arms and leaned back. He kept leaning until he fell back, his feet almost clipping Noal's nose as he backflipped. "That my decisions accept what I knew at the beginning," he said as he landed on his feet.

"I guess that is true, mentor," he began, arching one foot forward and pulling his other leg back. He pivoted on his hands and swung his other leg up and into the air as he pushed upward, lifting into the kick to leap up onto his feet. Strypan leaned back slightly, avoiding the kick as Noal landed in a stand. "I have accepted a decision I had already made. I'm going into the military."

"You're showing off to tell me about the military? I didn't know the military was a bunch of showoffs. I wonder if they know," Strypan said, standing calmly, arms relaxed at his side.

Noal began to object, but Strypan interrupted.

"Show me what the military means to you," he said, waving Noal forward to fight him.

How could a fight show that? Understanding his mentor was sometimes impossible, the man spoke in a cryptic code of his own. Noal took a fighting stance, sweeping his foot back and raising his arms to protect his face.

Strypan lunged at Noal from his peaceful stand. Noal stepped to the side, leaving one leg back and leaning down onto his other knee for support. Strypan tripped over Noal's leg, tumbling into a somersault. He rolled out of it and into a stand, turning to face Noal.

Strypan changed strategy, marching at Noal like a wild

animal charging as he threw punches one fist at a time. Noal stood his ground until the last moment when he cartwheeled directly away from Strypan.

Strypan turned and threw himself into a cartwheel parallel to Noal. As they passed each other, Strypan reached out and grabbed Noal's wrist. He tugged and Noal collapsed to the ground face first.

"Interesting," Strypan said.

"Can we try again?" Noal asked.

Strypan pulled his belt free and whipped it at Noal in one swift motion.

Noal caught the belt, then let it go. It fell limp in Strypan's hand.

Strypan looked at Noal with respect. "You don't see it, do you? What you just said? And why it means the military is the right choice for you."

Noal shook his head.

"I did not strike, so you did not strike. I attacked head on and you gave up your position. I threw the unexpected at you and you disabled it. Every response was a balance to the attack presented. I could strike at you a thousand other ways and you'd respond the same. You try to avoid the fight, Noal. You don't have to think about it, it is part of you.

"What you fear to see there, you will see there. Arterians who want to fight and kill, they just present it in different ways. You hesitated because you don't want to lose it, that sense of balance. Now you have shown you can trust it, because it is you. You can trust yourself, Noal.

"You will always have me, Noal. Remember who you are and that only you can take that from you. Maybe you will make war a little less deadly. Your next class will be your last for now. Will you stop by in three days?"

"The military fights a fight that cannot be avoided. What then?"

"You know the answer."

Noal grinned. "Why do we ask questions we already know the answer to?"

Strypan smiled with pride. "A fight which cannot be avoided must be fought. Escalate or deescalate is the question, not if. This is the expected answer; it is the answer you know. Trust yourself, Noal. The trust is well-placed."

Noal looked down reflectively. He knew the answer. His mentor was right.

"Thank you, Stry. I think I have enough to think about today. Can I leave?"

"Just remember to come back for your next lesson," Strypan said.

"Yes, mentor."

Noal picked up his things and headed out as Strypan watched calmly. For an ancient man (he was older than his parent's parent), he sure could move. It was like he grew to look older, but under the age was still a spry youth.

Remembering who he was, was going to be tough when he had to tell his parents his decision to join the military. They wanted him to choose academia. He didn't anticipate they would be so receptive.

Opening the door to his transport, he threw his stuff on the passenger side, hopped in, and lifted into the air, setting course for the one place he truly tried to avoid, home. He loved his birth parent, but had never grown attached to his other parent. Noal had always seen the world as full of opportunities, ones that existed largely because of the last Cycle of Ages. His other parent always seemed to see the world as if it owed him a debt for something it'd taken from him a long time ago; he was jaded, angry, borderline violent. Noal was certain his other parent—the great governor of Attatar, de facto president of Arter—had never enjoyed life.

It made Noal sad. If he could give his other parent any gift, it would be to smile for just a moment. Not just any smile, not a rehearsed one. It needed to be a sincere moment of happiness. He felt the world was just a little off balance until that could happen. But what would make him happy enough to smile? Probably something that wouldn't make anyone else smile.

He arrived home, parked his transport, and trudged into the kitchen. His muscles had stiffened on the ride back. He stretched, pulling them back to their tender senses. Strypan's body must be sorer than his. They had practiced philosophy and mathematics for three hours, all while hand fighting. He smiled as he looked to his birth parent. "Hi, Nos. Do we have some nectar? I'm thirsty."

"Now, don't give me any of that," she replied and glanced at the refrigerator. "You've been traipsing through my house in your sweaty clothes for seventeen years now. You know what we have."

She was strict with him, but she did love him. And she did smile. Regularly. Sincerely. She was doing it now, in fact.

"But you look tired. Want me to pour you a glass."

Noal loved her playfulness. "Yes, thank you. Nos, how old is Strypan? Sometimes he makes me feel like the old man."

Noselar laughed. "I've never gotten a straight answer from him. He's a great mentor, but he gets lost in his thoughts too much."

"Yeah," he said, his voice fading into a pause which grew longer. He realized she was waiting for him. She was waiting for his decision. No need to hide it, but she would be the saddest.

"Military," he said, taking a glass of nectar from her as he rubbed his shoulder.

"In school, you could have lived at home. Now I lose my baby boy." Noselar huffed. "And the world gains you. I expect you'll show them I've taken care of you. I...." She dropped the sternness in her voice, tears glistening in her eyes. "I know you... You're Noal, Noal. I've always known you'd be great. Show them your greatness and always know you have a home here...." She pulled on her apron, and gained her composure, adding sternness back to her voice as she wiped her tear away with an indifferent hand. "You'd better not forget that."

Noal found quiet tears of his own well up as Noselar bared her raw emotions. He didn't want to make her sad. It had to be hard on her.

He set the cup down and went to her. He wrapped his arms around her and let his own tears stream. He knew others, especially boys, felt embarrassed when they cried. He'd tried that once, but crying and letting it all out just felt better than feeling embarrassed.

They cried as they hugged until an obnoxious yawn escaped from Noal. He'd tried to hold it back, but between the workout with Strypan and the emotions with Noselar, the yawn was too strong.

"I should get to bed," he said. "Strypan worked me over today."

"Like I said, you always have a home here. Get some rest." She patted him on the back and wiped his face with a cloth, gave him a wink, then turned away. Noal might have been too tired to keep crying, but her tears were far from over.

He went to his room and barely got undressed before passing out.

* * *

The Reader sat at her desk thinking. Thinking about the same problems she had for the last decade and a half. How could she prove Sumatta still lived? Could she recover the message? If so, how?

Shenol was a horrible Reader. She wasn't even technically a Reader. A Reader without a god was just another Arterian who lived in the Bahnderia. She could be the Reader if she had her god. That is why she refused to consider the alternative. Shenol was meant to be Reader, and that's why Sumatta had to be alive. Besides, the Igri Tufuer had come to protect Sumatta. Whatever had happened, the Igri Tufuer could not have lost. He must have succeeded. How could a god have failed? Maybe he was punishing them? If only she could find him.

Alia had been a great Reader. Alia was dead. Shenol didn't know where Sumatta had vanished to, but she had seen Sumatta fall on Alia, crushing its body before Sumatta rolled off into the lake. Alia would know what to do. It had always known what to do.

Alia had also known Bahnderia's secrets, how everything worked, but they hadn't gotten to those lessons. Shenol was left ignorant of how to do her job. She'd figured out a lot of things over the years, but nothing that allowed them to communicate through that sphere in the Reader's study like Alia did the day Sumatta came to visit.

They had searched the lake, but there were no tunnels below the surface and the lake was barely deep enough to cover Sumatta completely. The Swarm hadn't even stopped them. Sumatta and the Swarm seemed to have simply disappeared.

Shenol stood up, primped her Reader's robe and checked her appearance in the standing mirror she'd had brought in. She looked tired. Not even the makeup took that away. Too tired for someone not even thirty. Beyond that, she looked perfect. Not really like a genderless reader, she'd been able to keep her gender since Sumatta had disappeared, but a beautiful female reader. A beautiful, tired female reader.

She sighed at the mirror, then left the Reader's study, turning down the hall toward the Hive.

The Hive was a series of catacombs containing the bodies of all those who'd been taken out by the Swarm during the attack. The Swarm had not killed anyone. Instead, they had coated their enemies in a gooey green substance that solidified around them like a pod. Nothing they had tried could free the Arterians from the pods. Scientists still didn't know how or if they were alive inside the pods.

This is where Shenol had done well as Reader. She had redirected the press to portray the pods as Sumatta, Giver of Life and Protector of Arter, protecting Arterians by even protecting those who would attack it. She pledged to take care of all of Sumatta's children. This maneuver had saved the Sumattan faith and given her a mission now that her god had gone missing.

That had drummed up the faithful at the beginning, but now the faithful numbered only a few thousand of Arter's billions. In the biggest city, Sumna, there were no reported faithful. Caleston, a small city at the foot of Mount Sumat, housed the most number of faithful, coming in at just under three thousand.

Donations to keep the Bahnderia running followed the pattern of the faithful. They were strong at first, but were as dismal now as the number of faithful. She had set aside most of the donations at first, but she found herself periodically dipping into those savings now.

She walked down the rows of thousands of podded Arterians, running her hands over the solid, glossy shells as Arterians lay inside barely visible. She could just see in enough to see them resting with open eyes and vague expressions locked on their faces. She believed they were alive, that the pods were like cocoons. She didn't know when those locked inside would be able to come out. It was like a sentence issued by the Swarm for attacking Sumatta. How long would they stay imprisoned?

"Reader!" a young, tall boy with brown hair and eyes wearing a robe yelled from the other end of the Hive.

Shenol waited for him to run up, screaming for her.

"Rax, what have I told you about screaming in the Bahnderia?" she counseled. She remembered the days when Alia had scolded her the same way.

"I'm sorry," he pleaded. "I really want to be the Next

Reader. I really do. I just get so excited."

"Why are you excited?"

"Someone's knocking at the door."

"Who is it?"

"I don't know."

"You didn't answer the door."

"No."

"Why? Oh, nevermind. Rax, you can answer the door to the Bahnderia."

"He wasn't knocking at the door to the Bahnderia. The door's open, silly. I mean, Reader. Sorry." He calmed himself enough to take a deep breath. "He was knocking at your study," he said.

"Were you in the Reader's study?"

He shook his head. He shouldn't have been in the study without Shenol being there.

"Did you talk to him? Rax, can you just tell me what it was about? Without all the questions."

"I didn't say nothing to him. He looked like a policeman," he explained. "I just ran to get you."

"Thank you, Rax. I will go find out what he wants."

"Can I come? I wanna watch," he said eagerly.

"You're not the Next Reader yet, Rax. This is Reader business. Thank you for coming to get me. You did the right thing. It shows you will be ready to be the Next Reader soon."

Rax sulked. "OK, I guess." He turned, pouting and wandered back down the rows of the Hive, one dramatic, disappointed step after another.

He was still too young. He had just turned ten and every Next Reader had been at least eleven when they were appointed. Shenol had been twelve when she was appointed. He would be her choice, however. He only saw himself as Reader, didn't care about his gender, and was used to not having friends. He picked up the material fast and had a great memory. He would be a great Reader if Sumatta returned. *No,* when *Sumatta returns*, she thought.

She turned, heading back to the Reader's study. What could a policeman want here? He was still standing at the study, but waiting idly. He must have figured out that Shenol wasn't in the study. The man turned around as she approached. He was in formal attire and wore a name badge, but he was not a police officer. Perhaps an investigator.

"How can I help you?"

"I represent Governor Spratee's office. This is for you," he said, handing over a small envelope.

"Thank you," she said, taking the envelope and slipping it into her robe. "Does the governor need anything else?"

The man just turned and walked past Shenol, brushing carelessly against her as he did. What was up with such little respect?

She walked into the study, closed the door behind her, and opened the letter.

Shenol laughed as she read. The governor wanted the Bahnderia closed. Didn't he know that only the Reader could close the Bahnderia and only if ordered by Sumatta itself? She threw the paper on her desk as she plopped down in her chair.

What was she going to do? Fight him? She looked up at the needle in the center of the room and wished it would move.

The needle moved. It inched upward until it pierced the sphere, causing it to burst with a blinding light. Shenol screamed, squinching her eyes. That wasn't a wish! The needle actually moved!

Shenol got up and ran over to the device, holding her hands up to shield herself from the light. Even before her eyes could fully see again, she was there, touching the sphere. How did Alia do it? She cursed and just pinched the whole ball with an aggressive push, turning it back and forth. It did nothing. It stayed bright. She didn't remember it staying bright for so long last time. "Work!" she yelled at it.

Finally, the light died and one of her twists actually made

the sphere move. It burst with a little shock of electricity that shot down the needle and electrified the pool.

She'd confirmed the message. Now, now... She remembered her training. *Now I seal the Bahnderia.*

The irony was too funny. Shenol's laugh was maniacal.

Only Sumatta commands the Reader, governor. The Bahnderia will be closed. It will definitely be closed, she thought as she folded up the governor's order to close the Bahnderia. *And you're not going to like why.*

Press Conference

If the fools filling his office now had been the fools he'd worked with seventeen years ago, Sumatta would still be alive. It was amazing that Arterians like this managed to figure out how to breathe, much less the basics of their jobs. He was fairly certain they had enacted a secret law banning sense.

"Listen, the Sumattan cult now makes up less than one tenth of one tenth of the voting population. I can deal with that much of a loss of the vote. I want the Bahnderia shut down. You can find any reason you want, but no more excuses. Shut it down by the end of day," said, leaning back in his plush chair.

His cabinet understood the tone. No one would object and no one would see fit to offer counsel contrary to his wishes. They quietly nodded, scribbling notes, and left his office.

He was done for the day. It was amazing how they had come up with so many obstacles for him, even when he had emergency war powers. Then, when he finally enacted every bit of legislation necessary to overcome all of their objections— an act he had signed moments before his order—they had come back and said it was politically dangerous.

Everything is politically dangerous.

The weekend was coming, so he hopped in his transport and headed to his Hydrona home. Noselar and Noal would be there this weekend. Noal had some news to share, so they were all meeting there. He was probably going to say he would be going into the military. Spratee had been sure it would be academics, just like Noal's real parent, but the kid liked the hands-on approach and his mentor reported an increased focus on history and combat tactics. It would be a longer route to true success; Noal should choose politics. He would be riding on great shoulders and find himself on an accelerated path to success.

He set his transport on coast, put on some music, and leaned back, relaxing for the short trip. It lifted up, turned southwest and angled upward, giving a remarkable view of the Living Rainbow in an array of pinks and yellows, despite the three security craft flanking his ship as it accelerated toward Hydrona. He dozed off as the comforting light filled the transport's cockpit.

The trip seemed like 15 minutes, not three times that as he woke during the landing. He rubbed his eyes and yawned as the transport set down, the security craft zipping off toward a private landing pad.

Today had taken more out of him than he thought. He checked his touchpad and grinned. The Reader should be throwing a fit about now. One way or another, Spratee had made sure Sumatta would come to its end. Completely.

Noselar came out of their cylindrical house huffing and stomping along the long balcony between the front door and the landing pad. "Well, now you've done it. Just couldn't leave it alone, could you?"

"What is it?" Spratee said, groaning.

"What have you been doing? Sleeping? I'll bet that's exactly what you've been doing. You launch an attack on religion, then go take a nap." Her disgust was palpable, infuriating. "If you were as calculating now as you were when you first got elected, you would have known this was going to happen. Riots! Check your touchpad. For Sumatta's sake, Spratee!"

Noselar looked at him, debated for a moment, then finally gave him a kiss. She shook her head with a mix of apathy and disgust as she turned and left him to his panic.

It was true. The Reader had closed the Bahnderia, and almost immediately rioting broke out. Why hadn't anyone called? He pulled up his chief of staff on his touchpad and tried to open a communication channel. No answer. His secretary.

No answer. His... He stopped as the headline scrolled across the bottom of the screen: Governor's staff reportedly resigns amidst attack on religion.

By Sumat—no, by Arter itself (he needed to make new swear words). Those fools hadn't even taken the time to tell him they were resigning? He threw his touchpad against the wall and ignored it as it flipped through the air and bounced off the platform into the brush below. His security detail raised an eye, but didn't take action. He headed for his war room.

"I'm going to the Room. Stay here," he said to them.

The war room was his basement. It had one main entrance and one secret entrance. Only his high-ranking officials—now resigned—and himself were allowed in this room. He didn't even permit his security detail here. *Maybe*, he thought, *I should have let the security detail in and not those fools.*

That was an issue for another day. For the moment, he needed to show Arter that he was in command of things, that his cabinet resigning was only a minor inconvenience, that everything was still going smoothly.

He sealed the room to keep that nosy bonded of his out, then contacted Dise. She answered, laughing.

"Now you call? You're joking, right?"

"I need a new cabinet. Have any candidates?"

"You're joking, right?"

"I can take care of the press, but betray me once and you're out. I'll need a new cabinet. I'm not asking you again."

"I can get you a cabinet, but first you need to stop the riots. You can do that by rescinding your order."

"I'm not rescinding the order. I'm going to re—"

"For Sumatta's sake, Spratee. You are going to rescind that order. You don't get it do you? You're so used to going by the numbers that you forgot Arterians matter, not numbers. Listen, just because someone doesn't go to services, doesn't mean they don't believe. Even those who don't believe, believe in the freedom to choose. You've just gone out and attacked eighty percent of your electorate. If you don't rescind that order, your successor will, and it will be before the end of your term. You'll get a cabinet when you can show me you'll finish your term, and that happens only if you rescind that order."

She disconnected. Dise disconnected on him! Even she felt like she didn't have to respect him now.

An alert popped up on the main screen. General Byelt connected a moment later. "Governor Spratee. I know you're short on time. I needed to notify you that Oxyahyd has joined the resistance and is attacking Attatar. They attacked from the west shortly after your cabinet resigned. Someone gave them a head's up. We will be able to handle this in short order, but there will be casualties."

Spratee was not in the mood. "The casualties are on them. Make that known. We were not attacking them. Crush them, General."

"Yes, sir," he said, then dropped the connection.

Spratee opened his press release software and sent an announcement. At the top of the hour, he'd give a live press conference from his home in Hydrona.

* * *

Trellia rubbed the railing as she looked across Attatar's night sky. Fires and smoke peppered the city, overshadowing the pink and yellow of the aurora with the orange of fires below. Both the attack from Oxyahyd and the riots were tearing the city apart while Governor Spratee hid in Hydrona. She'd come here as much to get away from the memories she had of Unel in Sumna as she had to stay away from Noal. However, tonight she wished they were both with her, Unel so she would feel safe and Noal so she could keep him safe.

Noal didn't really need her to keep him safe. According to her last update from Unel's parent, Strypan, Noal was joining the military. He was strong and could take care of himself. She was still his birth parent, however, and she felt an obligation to protect him even if he didn't know who she was. He was her shame in so many regards that she doubted she could ever face him. It was better for him to think that an idiot governor was his parent.

She really needed Unel. She hadn't seen him since he disappeared. She refused to believe he was dead. She couldn't rectify his absence with his passion for her and the pain was so great that she opted to just stare at it with a foggy mind, drawing no conclusions, hoping desperately that one day he would appear and explain everything. That it would all make sense and all her pain was for nothing. Seventeen years had gone by and that day, that explanation, had not come, but she still hoped and she still carried on his dream, if for no reason other than it was the only way she would be able to find him.

Moving to Attatar had seemed like a good move. It would still seem like a good move except for the riots breaking out because their idiot governor—the one she'd given her son to— had banned religion. He didn't say it that way, of course, but forcing the Bahnderia shut was the same. The Reader always had unilateral control over the Bahnderia. When the news had come, she and Gemtra had locked themselves in their house.

If that wasn't enough, they were now under attack from Oxyahyd who saw the governor's weakness as an irresistible opportunity. Who knew what they were thinking? Attatar was larger and more well-fortified. Maybe they thought that in the weakness of their governor, their city would be weak too.

Something needed to be done to stop the mayhem.

"The Reader is going to send a message," Gemtra said, holding out a cup of tea for Trellia.

"I hope it's a call for peace. We need to end these riots," she said, taking the cup.

"Me too, dear. Me too. Really, they should let me close to the governor. I have a tea to help his hate of religion."

Trellia laughed. "Gemmy, you have a tea for everything."

"That I do... Oh, there's the Reader," she said, holding up her touchpad.

The Reader stood in front of the closed Bahnderia, a notice posted on the door. She stood there in full garb, hands folded before her, patiently waiting. As soon as the hour changed, she held up her hand and waited for quiet.

"Sumatta calls for calm and quiet in Attatar and across Arter. Sumatta, Giver of Life, Protector of Arter, Guardian of the Ages, is not an agent of destruction. Arterians must not be either."

She turned around, grabbed the notice from the door, and held it up.

"Governor Spratee, take notice that your laws have no hold on Sumatta nor Sumatta's home. The Bahnderia has *not* been closed by your order."

She tore the notice in half and let the pages flutter to the ground.

"The Bahnderia has been closed by order of Sumatta itself. Sumatta's law applies to the Bahnderia, not any other law."

She turned around, ignoring pleas and questions from the media, and walked into the Bahnderia, bolting it closed behind her.

The touchpad screen switched to Governor Spratee speaking, but they'd heard what they needed. That windbag of a politician could say whatever he wanted... Sumatta was coming! If only Unel were here to witness this.

"I want to try and reach him again," Trellia said. "Can I have some avak, Gemmy?"

Gemtra gave her a solemn nod. She was all too aware of Trellia's pain—they'd both lost their bonded on that day. She went to the kitchen and brought back a steaming cup, handing it to Trellia. "Still no luck?"

"Not yet. I can see him and interact with him, but it's not him. Something happened that day, and I need to replicate it. It had to be the solar storm, but I've adjusted all the energies as best I can and I'm still not getting anywhere. Sometimes I just go to see him again. You know, you could..." She trailed off, not willing to fully say that Gemtra could visit Xarat in her dreams. Trellia took a sip of the tea. It wasn't too hot, so she downed the whole cup. She wanted to see him now.

Gemtra shook her head. "I'm afraid I'll see him shot again. It's bad enough as a fading memory, dear."

Trellia yawned, kissed her birth parent, then went to her room to lay down. The avak root tea had settled in. She grabbed the latest version of the *draumr* and hung it on her forehead, then lay back. The projector would transmit a dream world to her now—the Dreamoria was no longer needed for anything except a workshop; the *draumr* was fully portable. She was really just lucid dreaming in a dream world projected from outside of her. She dozed off as the projector began.

Cleaning House

Spratee flipped through screen after screen of news on his touchpad. The riots had quieted down and fires were being put out. Oxyahyd had retreated. He expected an entreaty to rejoin the alliance soon.

Not only had the fighting and looting been quashed by news of Sumatta's return, but Arterians took to the streets in droves, partying. It was like a grand celebration with streamers, musicians, dancing, and parades.

There was one thing missing from the news: him. Sure, he was there, but as an afterthought when included at all, even then like a bitter aftertaste to blame for all the bad that was a precursor to the current celebratory spirit.

He sighed, long and hard. Oxyahyd's retreat was a coward's retreat. They might not be able to wage a war in the face of Sumatta, but he was a real leader, an Arterian of purpose. He had the skills and experience to do what that city-state could not. It was time to take action.

The first thing he needed was a support team. His cabinet had abandoned him. It was time to replace them. He opened a communication channel to Dise. She answered immediately. Dise was more faithful than his cabinet.

"The riots have ended. You have what you want," he said.

Dise snorted and started laughing obnoxiously. More faithful than his cabinet didn't mean she was a wholehearted supporter. She could be quite dangerous, in fact. He was sure she'd gotten wind of the assassination attempt and how close it had come to including her.

"Spratee, you're a joke if you believe you had anything to do with stopping the riots. Don't try politicking with me. I was around before you tasted your first hint of an office."

"Regardless, you offered a cabinet if I could prove I would finish my term. Arterians are celebrating in the streets. Whether they're celebrating because someone pissed from a rooftop and called it rain during a drought or because they love me doesn't matter. I'll finish my term."

Dise leaned forward, putting her hand to her chin as if considering the idea.

She was thinking about it? He'd just given her the chance to pick an entire cabinet, seeding her group at the highest level of government and...she was pondering!

It was that Reader. The beast-loving insurrectionist had held a press conference announcing Sumatta's return at the same time as Spratee's. The beast was supposed to be dead, not returning from the dead! That didn't sound better; returning from the dead was far worse. Now, they doubted him and hesitated, those like Dise. Others, like his cabinet and the media, were just ignoring him.

"Dise!" he yelled. "I'm not offering this again!" he said, almost apoplectic.

"Fine. You'll have your cabinet, but it's going to cost you."

"Whatev—" He choked himself off. Was he about to really just offer Dise anything she wanted? He was a fool. "Whatever you need, send me a list and I'll see what I can do."

"These aren't needs, Spratee. They're demands. And you will do them. Remember they will be your cabinet, but they're my team. You just asked me to grab you by the balls and squeeze tight. Don't think of complaining about my grip."

It was both a blessing and a curse that Dise hadn't died during the Cycle of Ages. She was supposed to be on the ship that blew up with Governor Muaske, but it had gone over the edge and somehow the two of them had survived. He'd been sure as he watched her go over the edge in the transport and the roof of the building collapse that they had died. He'd also been sure Sumatta had died. The only good thing to come out of that day was that he won the election. Governor Muaske couldn't lead from intensive care, so Spratee was the natural selection. And the best thing about being governor was that he could finish the job he'd started. Dise thought she had him in her grip, but the truth was he just bound her closer to him.

True, he'd just bound a wild animal ready to bite him at a moment's notice to him. But Dise wasn't the same strategic planner as he was. She too often went with the flow when it seemed to be going in her direction. It had worked for her up until now, but Spratee was a great strategic planner. Dise would find something unexpected if she tried to bite him.

It was time to come up with a new plan. One that would get Sumatta out of his life forever and one that would take Dise with it.

* * *

The Bahnderia was surrounded by the faithful. Arterians who had not come in years had returned, new acolytes were coming in droves. They brought money, food, and supplications for Sumatta's blessing. Donations were pouring in. They had been badly needed for some time and were especially needed now. Shenol had been living on a pittance of donations and a reserve since the Cycle of Ages and it was going to take some work to get the Bahnderia ready for its owner.

Huol stood before her in the Reader's study as full of energy as Rax. The old man walked with a crutch now, but seemed to have caught a new lease on life with the news of Sumatta's coming.

"Huol, I'm putting you in charge of the donations and getting a team together to clean the Bahnderia. I don't need to tell you that the Bahnderia isn't what it used to be. We must be ready for Sumatta."

"Yes, Reader," he said, his voice raspy and aged, but eager. "How long do we have?"

"Twenty minutes or twenty days. I don't know," she said. Hesitating, she added, "Don't repeat that, please."

Leaning on his cane with both hands in front of him, Huol gave the Reader a wink of acknowledgment.

"Four times in one life," he said, shaking his head. "Sumatta has honored me more than most men. You honor me by giving me this task, Reader. Thank you."

He tapped his cane on the ground a couple of times and headed out, giving Rax a razz on the head as he quickly hobbled out of the study.

"Rax, I need you to take some of the donations and go to the market. Pick us up some food. I am starving."

"You honor me, Reader," he said, beaming with pride and mirroring Huol's speech.

"Only a little candy, Rax." His eyes opened wide at the thought that he could get any candy and he bobbed his head vigorously.

"Only a little. I promise." He turned to run off toward the market.

"Rax, take a bag with you," Shenol called out and he flipped around, grabbed a bag, and flew out the door.

Shenol got up and went to the rooms of the Complete Histories. She needed to find out how to read the glowing needle light ball. It wouldn't hurt to know its name either.

She'd watched all of the Age Histories, but they started with the message from Sumatta. Maybe one from just before would help interpret the glowing needle light ball.

A rap of a cane on the Reader's study came too suddenly. Was he having problems? Shenol made her way out of the Complete Histories, sealed the door behind her and answered the door to the study.

"Is something wrong, Huol? You were only gone for ten minutes." She looked behind him and a group of roughly forty stood behind him, eager.

"So many? I don't think we should spend every donation on

this task."

"You won't spend anything, Reader," Huol said. "They are volunteers."

Overhearing them, an Arterian cheered, "For Sumatta!" The rest of the volunteers erupted with the cheer, chanting it.

Shenol raised a hand and they quieted.

"Sumatta thanks you. The Bahnderia has not been maintained as well as it should have been in recent years. No one is allowed in the Bahnderia when it is closed, but I am making an exception for you. I need you to clean every inch of the building from top to bottom."

The group acknowledged her, large smiles on their faces.

"However," Shenol continued. "If I command you out, you must leave immediately. If you see the pool in the middle shake even the slightest, you must run."

Still smiling, the group nodded soberly. They would take her seriously. They very much needed to take her seriously. Never in the history of Arter had anyone else been in the Bahnderia when Sumatta arrived.

"Get them what they need," she said to the faithful man. He grabbed a few volunteers and ran off to get supplies.

"I will take you to the Bahnderia," she said to the volunteers.

She took them there and Huol's supplies group joined them shortly after. Everyone got to cleaning, thanking Shenol for the opportunity.

She had no idea how long she had until Sumatta arrived. Somehow Alia had known it was thirty minutes, but it had never shown Shenol how to figure that out and thirty minutes had passed hours ago. It could be minutes, hours, or days. Shenol didn't know and didn't know how to find out.

She went back to her study to review the replays on every meeting with Sumatta. It must have been recorded.

The part that made her nervous was that regular visits were for the change of Reader, but this was not a regular visit;

however, since there had not been a change of Reader, there technically was no Reader. Would Sumatta insist on the ceremony—one that would take Shenol's gender from her—or be willing to consider her plea? She loved being the Reader as much as she loved being a woman. Alia had been convinced Shenol would have to make a choice. Couldn't she be two things?

A woman was a special thing on Arter. The only gender capable of being a birth parent was nothing compared to what it meant. It meant eloquence of a magnitude far above what men could achieve, being more socially intelligent, wearing clothes which fit the weather, ... No, Shenol could do that if she was any gender. Yet she felt like a woman, identified as a woman, and enjoyed being a woman. Your gender didn't make you any of the things she listed, but did that really matter?

She would have to come back to that. Her time was better spent figuring out when Sumatta would show up. She returned to the Complete Histories, picked a couple of replay disks from just before Sumatta showed up and placed one in the replay core. She sat back and was disappointed. It was about the past age, not just before Sumatta had arrived. She sighed. This was going to take some work.

The fourth replay discarded, Rax peeked in the rooms. "Reader," he said nervously. "Where do I put it?"

"Put what, Rax?" she said, standing and heading to the doors. "And you know you're not allowed in here."

He swallowed nervously. "The food."

"In the kitchen."

"There's too much."

"How much did you spend, Rax?"

"Nothing. They gave it to me. And I got *lots* of candy," he said grinning as only a ten-year-old boy could at such a statement.

"What do you mean nothing?"

"They gave it to us. We need more kitchens. There's two

transports outside. They think you're going to feed Sumatta. I tried to tell them, but—"

"It's ok, Rax," she said, sealing the door to the histories. "I'll take care of this."

Feast or famine, she thought. Either could be a problem when you didn't know how much time you had.

Everyone else seemed so energized by Sumatta's arrival, but the more it went on, the more trepidatious Shenol became. She didn't know the time and she might have to make a choice she'd been happy to avoid for the last two decades. Still, her god was back. She could deal with the nervousness.

New Hunt

Tanseor walked up the path to Noal's old school. It had taken time to find Noal, but like a spatiatta never far from the Swarm, Strypan kept Noal close to him. Too often and too close. It had made it easy to guess that he was the other one he'd been looking for. Two decades ago, when he'd been searching and had given up, choosing to strike down Strypan alone, Noal was just being born. There was no one to find. Noal had missed the Cycle of Ages. It wouldn't even be a memory for him. In that regard, Tanseor had mis-estimated his timing. He would not make a similar error again.

The round school building was painted a light yellow that took on a green tone under the day's aurora. He'd come when the children were at class to avoid the young Arterians running around jostling him. If Noal was actually the one, then he would have started showing signs of it in school. Tanseor was hoping to find the proof he needed.

In full regalia, a little worn and wrinkled, Tanseor opened the door and entered the school's main office. He approached the receptionist desk and stood there with a strong posture, arms straight, hands out backward. "I'm Commander Tanseor. I need to check the records of one of your former students. His name is Noal."

"I know Noal, commander," said a friendly receptionist, "but we can only turn records over if you have the paperwork. I assume you have that?"

Tanseor pulled out a package of authorizations and sifted through them. He wouldn't need the one from the Reader for this. He found the one Noal filled out when he joined the military and handed it over. "Sorry. It took a minute. I'm not as spry as these youth," he said, motioning at the kids sitting in the lobby waiting. Some of them snickered and the receptionist turned a glare toward them. They quickly silenced.

"Ah, yes. This is in order. Thank you. Let me get those records for you."

"I'm actually not looking for his school record," Tanseor said with his aged voice. "I need to know about his science projects. He's into science, right?"

"Oh yes," she said. "He won a prize. Most innovative or something. Let me see if I can find out what it was for."

She tapped at the screen in front of her for a minute. "Ah, yes. It was in the news. I'm sure you could have found that."

He looked at her blankly as if using technology were a young person's endeavor.

"Anyway, he made something he called a spacetime continuum progressionist. It..." she hesitated and frowned. "I actually don't understand what it says. I can send you the article, if you'd like."

"No, thank you. I'd like his actual report for that project. Can you get that?"

"Let me ask the instructor."

He waited while she contacted the instructor.

So, Noal was studying the spacetime continuum? While still in school. It wouldn't be long before he deciphered the necessary bifurcation of concepts and saw past that. He couldn't help but be himself. Tanseor had definitely found his other Arterian. He would have proof now. He smiled. Not just any Arterian, either. Noal was the one. He had waited to capture Noal for longer than the boy had been alive. He had searched for him on other planets. He had vetted thousands upon thousands in his search for him. And now he'd found him.

Now Noal would die. Noal would die in a way that told others the Torhe had done it. They would all know the Torhe would no longer accept being excluded from their elite group. The Torhe would have to become igri tufuers.

"Commander?" the receptionist said, holding out a stack of papers. "Here's a copy for you. Do you need anything else?"

"No, thank you. This is exactly what I needed. It's my bet," he said, curling the papers up and rapping them against his hand, "that he's the best asset we've got. This will prove it. Thank you for your time."

"Sure thing. Anytime, commander."

He bowed his head in a civilian-like salute and turned about, marching out of the office with the report in his hand. As he stepped outside, he uncurled the report and began to read it.

Noal had been looking at moving forward on the spacetime continuum. That wasn't possible and he'd discovered that, so he'd looked to go backward. *That* was possible in a way. In fact, his theory was almost complete. His teachers hadn't caught what was wrong, why it hadn't worked when the experiment had been conducted, but Noal would have figured it out by now. Yes, Noal was definitely the one.

There was going to be a trick to this. He couldn't just come out and shoot Noal. Strypan would catch wind and punish him. He had to get them both together at once and take them out at the same time. He was going to have to find an opportunity to do that.

He got in his transport and lifted up, heading to Si'inth. He needed to prepare an away bag. He was going to be gone a long time. It was time to study his prey, find their patterns, discover their weakness, then wait for the right moment when both of them were vulnerable.

Approval

They were arguing again. Adults always told kids not to
fight, but they tended to fight more often than kids. Maybe the
irony was part of Life's harmony. Like a symphony being
played and one dissonant thread. Now would be a good time to
interrupt their melody, maybe give them something else to
focus on. He sighed and headed out to the living room.

Sure enough, Noselar was standing between the living
room and the kitchen and Spratee was in the living room,
pointing and shouting.

"It's a dead religion with a little uptick since the order was
put in place. There's no Sumatta—that's just that un-Reader's
ploy to draw more attention. Haven't you seen all those
running there in hopes that monster will return?"

"Spratee, you're a fool. You keep pitting your party against
Sumatta and when that thing shows up, you'll be lucky to
escape with your neck. Your governorship is gone."

"Fool?" he said, turning to Noal. "There's a fool. Go ahead
and tell us that you're going to waste years of your life in a job
that won't lead you anywhere. Go ahead. Come on. Spit it out.
You're going to the military, right?"

The shock on Noselar's face turned to anger. "You leave
him out of this! How dare you involve our son in your
argument? You petty, weak man."

Noal was a fool for going to the military? The more he
understood their arguments, the more he saw things from
Noselar's perspective. His other parent was a fool. Noal decided
to expose the fool.

"We have religious opponents—not zealots, just religious—
controlling whether the city is sacked or celebrating. Your
supporters deserted you. All advisors tell you you're doing it

wrong. Do I have that about right?" Noal continued without stopping, just a presumptive nod. "That leaves only one recourse. Fall back. Your pride is your folly. You'll keep marching forward hoping that somewhere you'll be right.

Let me tell you this, parent. The military has more to teach you in five minutes than you seem to have learned in your entire lifetime. If that's being a fool, well look at the decisions you're making."

Noal could almost smell Spratee's fury at being challenged. Spratee marched right up to Noal, who stayed calm, and leaned in to talk to him face to face.

"Let me tell you this, *child*," Spratee said between clenched teeth, spit foaming between his teeth. "Assuming you know all there is to know is dangerous. You have no idea what I can do, what I have done. So, before you say one more word, remember whose house you're under."

Noal felt a huge weight evaporate from his shoulders. Spratee had just crossed the line. Noal shook his head with condescending sadness, then turned and walked over to Noselar. He gave her a small kiss and whispered in her ear. "I'm not leaving you. Just say the word and I'm here. I love you, Nos."

She kissed him back and whispered in his ear. "Go now. I'll be ok. I love you, son."

Noal stood up, took a deep breath, accepting that he was leaving his Nos with a very angry, borderline violent man, then walked out the front door, leaving everything except the clothes on his back in the house, hopped in his transport and lifted off.

Before he said one more word to that sorry excuse for a parent, he had left the roof of the one whose it was. Would Spratee even catch that? The man's arrogance was only outshone by his ego.

It had been hard. He had anticipated something close to this, but it was still hard. He had only one place he could go, so he set the destination to his mentor's house.

Strypan answered when Noal tried a connection. He spoke first. "See you soon."

"Huh?" Noal was thrown off. How did he know? Who would have told him? Who could have told him?

"Happy news means you're spending time with your family. Calling me means you're not. That means you're alone. It went bad, so you're coming over."

Noal laughed. "Yes, mentor. I'm coming over."

"Good. I can give you your last lesson for now. But you were supposed to wait three days. I guess I can make an exception. I'll have to check. This is highly unorthodox. See you soon," he said, then abruptly cut off the transmission.

Noal ignored the odd ending to the call. He hoped the last lesson was some hand-to-hand combat moves. He needed to get out some aggression he'd really wanted to get out on Spratee. Strypan's style wasn't like the other hand fighting Noal had seen. It flowed, pulled you with it, was like a dance, and was very effective at clearing you of your emotions and directing you to find balance in the universe.

It was a four-hour trip over mostly ocean to get to Strypan's house in Sumna. Strypan looked out the window over Attatar, watching as the fires died, being put out by Arterians whose energy had been redirected to saving the city instead of tearing it down. As the transport headed over the ocean, he turned his eyes to the waves of blue and yellow aurora sparking with electricity as they fed the Living Rainbow. It was a meditative journey that ended all too soon as he passed over the Falls of Attadore as they crashed down into the ocean from high cliffs on the eastern shore, then his ship started descending as it sought Strypan's house.

He set down at Strypan's and went looking for him. Strypan was in his alphabet soup. Noal smiled as he thought of the name. Three rows of three columns three deep showing every letter of the alphabet. Noal had asked what he did when a word required two of the same letter. Strypan had just grinned and said to wait and see. Noal got the impression that Strypan didn't fully know the answer, but didn't know enough Sumattan to test him.

Noal greeted Strypan and only half listened as Strypan talked about the words he was working with today.

"Noal? If you don't talk, I'll keep talking. Sleeping on your feet is bad for your health."

"It is?"

"Yes, you're more likely to fall down and bump your head," Strypan said with all seriousness. He left his letters and headed for the door. "Come on."

Strypan took them to the combat circle. It had been cleared of the normal dummies and replaced with weapon racks. Swords, knives, quarterstaffs, and more... in triplicate. Large candles flickered against the evening sky with enough light for a small campfire.

Noal's excitement was uncontainable. That last lesson was fighting!

"We've never used weapons before," Noal said.

"The biggest one is not around you, it's in you."

The mind. Noal understood. His mind was his biggest weapon. He bowed, acknowledging the admonishment. He'd always used his biggest weapon.

"When your opponent is determined to fight you, remember your biggest weapon."

Strypan reached out, palm up, and lifted Noal's chin, pausing for just a second, then lunged forward.

Noal almost jumped when Strypan's fingers got to his chin, but quickly gained his focus and flipped his palms to hit Strypan's wrist, deflecting the lunge to his right. He lowered his arms creating a right angle and prepared to thrust forward and punch Strypan's sternum, but Strypan held a finger up and stepped backward. He drew a beautiful quarterstaff with swirls of Sumattan letters streaming down its length and came at

Noal.

Noal froze. He couldn't reach a weapon in time and his mentor was armed. He couldn't figure out what to do, how to balance the situation.

Strypan leaped forward the last few feet landing parallel to Noal, then swung the staff around and against Noal's back. It cracked against his spine. Noal stumbled and begged in a confused voice, "What do I do?"

Strypan tumbled forward and rolled into a standing position, then turned around. "Fight. It's a fight, after all. Does my big stick scare you? It's just a stick."

Noal didn't take the bait. He swept his foot around, bent his knee, raised his arms to protect his face, and held his fighting stance.

"Very good," Strypan said. "How is a stick different than my arm? It's just another attachment. A sword? A gun? Where is the energy? Don't forget your biggest weapon."

Noal looked back at his mentor and smiled. He closed his eyes and tried to erase the bias of knowing it was a weapon. He wanted to see the energy. He opened his eyes and flipped his head up, challenging Strypan.

Strypan hadn't waited for Noal to focus, his quarterstaff was overhead, almost smacking down directly in Noal's face when Noal saw it and rotated around, spinning forward and ending up behind Strypan. Strypan began to correct, turning around, but Noal reached around Strypan, his arms matching Strypan's in a hug from behind. He grabbed Strypan's hand and pushed down, driving the quarterstaff into the ground.

Strypan went with the momentum and tumbled forward, abandoning the quarterstaff. He turned around, the quarterstaff laying at their feet. Noal kicked upwards against the stick to fling it into the air and caught it as it came waist high.

Strypan did a three-sixty spin and came back, gun in hand, aiming at Noal's head. Noal instinctively thrust upward toward

Strypan's wrist with the end of the quarterstaff, forcing the gun away from his face as it went off.

"Enough," called Strypan.

Noal was enraged. He had actually shot the gun! At Noal. The nerve! Noal pulled the stick around, dead aiming for Strypan's chest.

Strypan yelled, "Enough! No!" and thrust his hand out, palm first, the base of his palm hitting the stick with such force that it cracked, peeling up the edges along the grain of the ancient letters.

Noal watched the stick shatter and froze with shock for a moment. Strypan had understood the energy of the moment that well? What had Noal missed?

"What is the final lesson, mentor?"

"It was a blank. I know you want to know that. It shouldn't matter. What is the lesson?" Strypan asked as he paced around Noal. "I never needed the weapon and neither do you. Come, let's go again."

Strypan reached around and grabbed two disks with *aten* sewn in. He threw one to Noal. "*Atenases* harness the energy of *atens*. These weapons are outlawed. They're too dangerous. You think a gun is something? Look at the *aten*. What does yours do?"

Noal studied the disk. On one half were an array of *aten* on the other half, a different *aten*.

"*Na'aten* and *ca'aten* are bound to the strong and weak forces, to land and water. I don't know what it does."

"It breaks things down and builds them up. Hit this with the *ca'aten* side," he said and threw a small metal ball at Noal.

Noal swatted it away with the *atenase*, taking it with the side with the *ca'atens*. It disintegrated.

"Now, swipe through its trail," Strypan ordered.

Trail? What trail? It disintegrated. Following orders he did not understand, Noal hit where the metal ball disintegrated and the metal reformed as a thin, prickly metal plate with sharp needles poking up all over. It flew at Strypan.

Strypan swung his *atenase*, catching the metal plate with one side. It crushed into itself and fell to the ground.

"That's the uncontrolled. Now, if you control it, watch."

Strypan stepped forward slowly and gently put his *atenase* on Noal's sternum. "As I apply greater force on the pad, more energy is applied. Do you feel it?"

A tension in Noal's chest began to build up that made his sternum feel heavier, as if just that part of his body were gaining mass.

"Oh, Sumatta. That's intense. Stop, please," he begged.

Strypan pulled his hand back and Noal's chest instantly relaxed. He gasped for air.

"With your *atenase*, you can disintegrate me or make me compress into a small ball. With mine, I can give you the gravity of a star or convert your cells to electricity."

This was too much. How do you fight with such weapons? No wonder they were outlawed.

"No," Noal said. "I can't."

"You will," Strypan said and swung his *atenase*-wielding hand toward Noal. Strypan was focusing on the other side of his *atenase*, the part that would turn Noal's cells into electricity.

Noal did not flinch. He would not allow this. He lifted his hand and caught Strypan's hand with the *ca'aten* side of his *atenase*. He squeezed causing the *aten* in Strypan's *atenase* to burst, then the device evaporated.

"I said no!" he yelled, then threw his *atenase* on the ground and charged Strypan.

Noal could sense the energy of his environment. Somehow the super lethal threat of the *atenase* made the more mundane that much easier to understand. As he approached Strypan, he leaped up into the air, thrusting a foot forward at face level with Strypan.

Strypan swatted Noal's foot to the right, but Noal sensed

that was the natural course and turned his body, spinning with the swat and bringing his other foot around. It clipped Strypan's head as Noal rotated around and fell to the ground.

Strypan's head jerked to the side, almost causing the old man to go tumbling over.

Noal pushed himself up as Strypan held his head. He went in to attack. He had shot a gun at him and tried to kill him with an *atenase*! He ran just to Strypan's left as he threw out his arm in a throat punch at Strypan's neck.

Strypan leaned his head back, but again, Noal had seen that flow of energy and brought his run to a halt just past Strypan, dropped his extended arm down, formed a right angle with his elbow, and pulled it back, smacking into Strypan's spine.

Strypan stumbled forward, grabbing his back, spun about and looked at Noal.

"I will defeat you this time, mentor," Noal said, then took a step forward. He could feel the flow of the energy. He could see where it was going before it went there. He understood the energy of the situation. *He* was master of the flow of energy now.

Strypan held up a finger and Noal stopped. Noal was not out of control; he was very much in control. Strypan's energy broke. He was surrendering, calling the fight to a stop.

"The difference is not in your environment, the difference is in you," Strypan said

"I don't think I understand this lesson, mentor."

"The last lesson is how to find your own lessons. What do you see inside yourself now? A man able to stand on his own, capable of anything, and who knows his values? Know yourself and approval from others is not necessary."

Noal didn't fully understand, but understood a lot more than moments before. He needed to get a better grip on his mind, better understand himself, then he would better understand his environment, the energy around him.

"Again?" Noal asked.

Strypan stood up, hobbling slightly from the knock to the back, face red and scraped from the kick.

"One more," he said, then grabbed a sword.

Noal didn't take a weapon, he just swept his foot back, brought his hands up in a fighting stance, and motioned for Strypan to come forward. The flow of energy was back. He could see it, feel it, sense it. It gave him a sublime sense of self and situation. Noal was ready.

Strypan swung the sword at an angle, targeting Noal's neck. Noal followed the flow of the motion, the flow of the energy, Strypan's momentum. He leaped forward and interrupted the flow of energy, coming in and grabbing Strypan's elbows, locking them in place as he pushed and created a new flow of energy, his elbows coming up and striking Strypan in the face as the sword scraped into the dirt.

Strypan dropped the sword, stepped back, and drew a gun from off the table behind him, swinging it around and aiming toward Noal, but Noal sensed this balance of energies and ran forward. He placed his right foot on Strypan's left knee, then pushed up, placing his left foot on Strypan's right hip, then jumped, spinning around, landing on his shoulders. He tightened his legs around Strypan's neck and leaned hard to the side as a surprised Strypan was still swinging the gun. The twist brought them both falling to the ground, Noal's legs still wrapped around Strypan's neck. Strypan dropped the gun and laughed.

"Let's get some tea," Strypan said.

"Do you see the energy like I just did? If you did, how did I win?" Noal asked as they got up off the ground.

"Yes. I did not try to change the flow of energy."

"You let me hit you."

"I gave you a chance to find yourself. One day, Noal, you will know exactly who you are on so many levels that you will understand there is more to the universe than what I have taught you. There is more than balance."

"What is that?"

"You already know. You just have to accept what you knew from the beginning."

Noal knew that would be the end of the conversation. He dusted himself off, then said, "Actually, I think I need to shower and get some rest. Do you mind?"

"Not at all. I have some things to take care of myself," he said, rubbing his face gently with one hand and pressing against his back with the other. "I feel like I just got in a fight."

Sumatta Returns

Trellia woke into her dream in darkness. As her eyes adjusted, she made out the shadows of distant walls and a twinkling glow in the distance. The room was very large. It was a place she'd never been in before. She tapped her eyes twice, then envisioned herself close to the twinkling glow. The vision blurred and appeared there.

Sumatta itself was before her, a majestic forty-foot-tall god. She stood at the foot of its tentacles as they hovered over the ground and bent her head to look up, taking in its magnificence. Tendrils dangled from Sumatta's four wings, twinkling with electric sparks. Its pearlescent skin reflected the sparkling tendrils as its body undulated in time with its heavy breath. Its head glowed softly with a bright energy as its gills swayed back and forth taking in deep, powerful breaths.

It was hovering over a metallic plate in the floor. Energy of a slightly brighter hue than she'd seen in an *attaten* flowed in a stream up into Sumatta's tentacles, being absorbed into its body.

A tentacle suddenly unfurled and reached out, wrapping around her waist, its flow of energy fading as it gripped Trellia.

"You are safe with me," a voice said in her head. She saw three three dimensional letters appear in her mind to accompany the words.

Sumatta opened its outer skin and the tentacle curled, setting Trellia inside its inner cavity. The skin folded around her and oozed a thick green liquid that surrounded her, then Sumatta floated over to a nearby pool. Its deep, dark waters reflecting the darkness of the cavern. The giant creature's head became cone shaped, then Sumatta turned, flipping upside down and dove into the pool. The vertigo overwhelmed Trellia as she was turned over, head down, and they plunged into the water.

Sumatta swam like a tornado. She could hear its tentacles—thankfully not still holding Trellia—spinning like a drill from the back. Water filled Sumatta's inner cavity, dowsing Trellia. Sumatta seemed to be trying to give her air through the gel surrounding her, but Trellia couldn't understand how to breathe through the gel. She tried to breathe, but only swallowed some of the gel. She gagged, then stopped trying to breathe. She felt like she was suffocating.

This isn't real, she thought. She was in a dream. She had lost control of the dream. Sumatta seemed to be in control. She tried to reach up and tap her eyelids so she could take control of the dream back, but Sumatta burst up out of the water. Its skin unfolded and ejected Trellia. She rolled out onto the ground, the thick ooze splattering away and evaporating as it touched the ground, while Sumatta melded with a tree and erected a dome around the building.

It was the tree. The tree was the answer to everything. It was made of the same metal as the plate. They were linked together. That was Sumatta's power source of some kind, the source of her life giving? Either way, Unel would have been close to the highly charged plate during the Cycle of Ages. That kind of energy would cause a massive shift, a massive change in behavior. It had to be good. If it was bad, then it killed Unel, and she refused to believe he was dead.

Sumatta lifted its tentacles out of the water and used them to hover over the pond. A fair looking woman in regal garb was standing by the edge of the pool. It was the Reader and she was reading while Sumatta talked. The song was jerky, stressed, sad, resigned, encouraged, then agreeable. The Reader kept speaking back, but Trellia couldn't make out the words. Trellia couldn't read Sumatta's words either, but if the tone of the song meant anything, then this had ended well.

The Reader also periodically turned to Trellia as if she could see her, but ignored her. Trellia stood quietly, looking back and forth at the two of them as they talked.

Sumatta reached out with a tentacle and surprised Trellia as it lifted her up. She looked around and found herself at eye level with Sumatta. Its head had taken the shape of a bubble, the print of a mouth and eyes on the skin.

"You coming here is good," it thought at her, casting two more three dimensional letters into her mind.

She could only take that to mean that she was allowed there and supposed to come back. Sumatta had understood her, but... this is a dream, not real.

"Your dream is real; it has happened. Come again. You will see," Sumatta answered her thoughts, showing a different array of letters.

If the claim might be half true, it was worth trying. Worth trying now. Trellia tapped the side of her eyes twice, then woke.

A loud buzzing permeated the air, making the building vibrate. It took a minute for her to realize what the sound was. It was like dozens of songs all being played at once, but sounding like a persistent buzz. The Swarm was back. She'd heard it this loud once before when Sumatta had come. Somehow it was all true.

She got in her transport and rushed over to the Bahnderia.

* * *

Sumatta launched up out of the pool, its pearlescent body gleaming, threw something to the side, became one with the Bahnder Tree, formed its shield around the Bahnderia, and lifted up out of the pool, hovering above it.

Shenol stood on the Reader's pedestal, wet and shrouded in the mist of the arrival, marveling at her living god hovering before her. Sumatta was a glory to behold.

She looked to her left. The thing that had been thrown to the side was a woman. The woman stood up and shook herself off, quietly staring at them. She seemed as surprised as Shenol that she was there. The woman was translucent, like a ghost. Shenol had never heard of Sumatta bringing a guest, but this was Sumatta's home and if Sumatta wanted to bring someone, it could. She was just glad the cleaning crew had cleared out in time. An uninvited guest would have been a different story.

"We have been worried about you, Sumatta," Shenol said.

Sumatta began singing and moving its tentacles in sync to the song. It said, "The Igri Tufuer protected me from death. The healing took a generation of your kind."

"He did! I had almost given up hope that Tanseor had saved you."

"Tanseor? The Igri Tufuer saved me."

"Tanseor is not the Igri Tufuer? If he's not, who is?" She looked at the ghostly woman. Was she the Igri Tufuer?

Sumatta's song took a deeper, regretful tone. It didn't want to say what it was about to say. "The Igri Tufuer tells of itself to those who are to know of it. It is not something for my words."

So, the woman was also not the Igri Tufuer, she was simply a mystery.

Sumatta firmed its body, standing straighter, taller, more commanding. "Next Reader, it is time."

Shenol's skin suddenly felt clammy, her palms sweaty. This was it. The time for her to make a choice. She had made her choice. It was not a choice to Sumatta, it was a matter of fact. The same had been true of every Reader until now. She took a deep breath, then spoke confidently. "I am ready, but I want to keep my gender."

"I am without gender," Sumatta started, but Shenol cut it off, raising her confident voice with a touch of nervousness.

"I am not without gender. Sumatta is Giver of Life, Protector of Arter, Guardian of the Ages. I ask you to protect me. I am of Arter, and I want to keep my gender."

"Generations of the same blood become about the blood.

Readers cannot be of the same blood; it cannot be about the Reader. The Reader does not have heirs."

"Then I won't have children. That is a choice I can make. It is a choice I do make. Sumatta," she said, her voice pleading, but still confidently strong. "I *am* female. That is who I am. If you change my body, you won't change who I am. How could you take away who I am?"

Sumatta was silent. Was it thinking? Was it going to force her? Had it worked? The silence was almost too much. Should Shenol try to argue her case differently?

Sumatta answered, it's song resolute, inspiring, confident. "You will become the first Reader with gender. Now." It waited for a moment. Was it letting that sink in? She was going to get to keep her gender! If only Alia could see this moment.

"Thank you, Sumatta. I am ready to be your voice."

Sumatta grabbed the ghostly woman with a tentacle, raised her up to its head, then the woman disappeared. It brought its tentacle down and grabbed Shenol, pulling her into its body, wrapping her in its folds.

What had the woman meant? Was she the ghost of a previous Reader? Was she part of the ceremony? She didn't have time to think about that now.

The inner body began to coat her with a green liquid, forming a protective shield, then Sumatta lifted into the air, leaving the tree behind and burst into the security shield, flying up into the Swarm. The swarm of spatiatta were little replicas of Sumatta the size of an Arterian. They zipped through the air and off toward Mount Sumat.

Sumatta dove down and into an opening in the mountain, wove its way into the heart of the mountain and came into a huge cavern where it set down. It reached into its fold, freeing Shenol of the coating and pulling her out, then set her down in front of it. Shenol was dripping in the goo, but it was light and airy and evaporated quickly. It left her hair a tangled mess and she tried to brush it with her fingers.

She looked around the dark cavern and noticed only a shiny metal plate in the floor. It looked like the metal that made up the Bahnder Tree. "I'm here, right? The base of your ship?"

"The Foothold is the source of life. On my coming, it brought me here. The mountain formed over the years, building up a shield. It was here before Arterians."

Sumatta moved over the plate and opened its body, exposing its inner cavity. Held in an inner pouch was a large *na'aten*.

Sumatta began to dance over the plate in specific patterns while singing a melody. The plate began to mirror Sumatta's electromagnetic patterns. It came to life, teaming with twice as many electromagnetic patterns, then three times as many before it started to slow again, in time with its song. Suddenly all of the energy flooded to a single point, then broke free of the plate and oozed out into space.

"Recipe for canine and *aten* to fuse," Sumatta said, then lifted the large *na'aten* which was actually a pouch containing other *aten*. It moved the *na'aten* pouch into the energy sludge, being careful not to touch it.

The *aten* sludge blended together, then shrunk down to the size of a small bead.

"A canine egg. This is how Sumatta brings life," it said.

Shenol marveled. The egg of a canine made in front of her from scratch. She had just witnessed the creation of life itself. The most sacred act on Arter, perhaps the most sacred act in the whole universe.

"Amazing," she whispered to herself. Had Alia seen this? Or was this part of the process of becoming Reader? Alia had died performing its duties. Died reading the Cycle of Ages, something no other reader would ever do again now that it was destroyed.

"What was the message from the Cycle of Ages?" she asked.

Sumatta groaned, its body hunching with what appeared to

be sadness. The full-bodied reaction was atypical for it.

It reached out and wrapped four tentacles around each arm and the other around Shenol's waist just like it had done to Alia, then turned its head toward the metal plate. Energy flowed from Sumatta through Shenol and she began to see through Sumatta's eyes. Sumatta didn't have eyes. It was more like through Sumatta's mind's eye. Shenol could see the words. There were so many of them all at once and changing rapidly. The words organized themselves, stacking like a replay showing frames of a scene after each other. She was able to understand them. It was like speed reading, but she could now say the prophecy in everyday Arterian:

The Final Age for Arterians is here. Hope is in all that changes. Salvation is for everyone. Do not fear, we have come.

"Who is 'we'?" she asked.

"That was not the whole message. I was attacked before it finished. That is the beginning."

That was frustrating. Not nearly enough for the message to have any meaning. Shenol had figured out more than the message had delivered. It still left the question of the Arterians in the Hive. Now was her chance to get answers.

"How can we get them out of the pods?"

"Not a pod, a capsule of life. Must hatch to get out."

"A part of your ship? Those?"

"No, they are capsules of life. They protect things. Like eight-legged crawlers."

Eight-legged crawlers? The kind that wove a cocoon around its food to store it. Capsule of life meant...

"By Sumatta itself, you mean cocoon." She blushed. "Sorry for using your name like that."

"Yes, that is your word. They are safe; they will hatch."

There was more to it. Maybe not to the cocoons Arterians were in, but to the history where Shenol had first heard about the capsules of life. She needed to find out what it meant. This new definition of the word was significant, but it had been too long since she had watched that replay. She needed to watch it again.

"I need to go back to the Bahnderia. Can I do that now?"

"Yes. I will take you through the water and come back that way, Reader, you who have witnessed life's creation."

So, that's what it was. When the Next Reader became Reader, Sumatta made them genderless—until now—and showed them how life is created. For the first time in seventeen years, Sumatta now had a Reader.

Shenol beamed with pride, standing taller than she'd ever stood. She had made the choice to be herself and it was accepted. She had done it. The Reader, for the first time, was a she.

Sumatta coiled its tentacles into its body and folded Shenol inside, coating her with the gooey substance again, then dove into the pool and barreled through the water to the Bahnderia.

Losing

Spratee watched with horror as the bright white dome over the Bahnderia broke into shards and Sumatta burst out of the building. Billions of spatiatta surrounded the murderous beast as it flew through the sky toward Mount Sumat. In the street, crowds cheered, waving as Sumatta flew over. Scrolling across the bottom of his touchpad was a news flash: Sumatta Returns!

Spratee swore as he slammed his touchpad against the wall. The device tumbled to the ground and he kicked it again. He kicked it repeatedly, swearing louder and louder, smashing the thing until it was in so many parts, there was nothing to kick.

Sumatta was back. The Swarm was back. That murderous creature *had* returned.

"You had everything, you fool. Everything and you threw it away," Noselar chided as she tapped him on the chest. She looked him in the eyes and asked, "For what?" She shrugged. "So, you could go," she said, "after... a... god," she finished, tapping his chest after each word. "Did you really think you could take on Sumatta?" She turned her back to him in disgust.

That woman had no idea what she was talking about. If she knew what was best, she'd shut that mouth of hers. And what was she doing poking him in the chest? Who did she think she was? His anger welled up and burst. He reached out, grabbed her by the shoulders and flipped her around, backhanding her as her head spun. It was an awkward hit, but it would sting and maybe she'd shut her hole. Maybe she'd learn her place.

Noselar's head jerked to the side as his hand slammed against her face. Her eyes watered as she grabbed her mouth.

Her hurt quickly changed to anger, her face grew red with fury, and she huffed like a wild animal. Noselar pulled her right arm back and launched her fist forward, slamming into his nose with more force than had come from the back of his hand.

Spratee felt his nose snap under the force of the hit. He leaned forward, grabbing his nose.

Noselar had hit him! Who did she think she was? No one hit Spratee. No one. "Woman!" he growled.

He stood upright, abandoning his nose and threw a solid fist forward, ramming it into her jaw. He heard her jaw snap at the same time he felt it. She fell to her knees, holding her jaw and crying. "Who do you think you are? You can't just do whatever you want. I am the President of Arter!" he screamed.

From the window, he saw Commander Chier nod at another of his security detail and they turned away. He marched over to the door, pressed the button and drew the shades down. It was time to put Noselar in her place. He should have done this a long time ago. The woman just had no respect. He would teach her.

He stomped over to her, looking at her pathetic crumpled body and ignored the moment's hesitation he felt at hurting his bonded. As he got to her, he pulled his right foot back and thrust it forward, taking her in the side. "Why do you make me do this?" he asked, then kicked again. It hit below her ribs and he thought he could feel one snap. "You're supposed to be a good bonded," he added, kicking her directly in the stomach. She hunched over and his next kick landed alongside her right ear. "I swear by that infernal beast!"

Noselar toppled to the side, barricading herself with her knees and arms. He kicked at her fetal-like body. Right foot hitting over and over. Head, arms, then legs. *Why can't you learn your place?* he thought.

Spratee felt powerful. Ruler of his domain. Fury seemed like too small a word to contain his feelings. He reached down, grabbed her by the hair and pulled her up.

Noselar clawed at his hands and arms, trying to free herself from his grip on her hair. She screamed a sloppy scream that came out as mostly a gargle of her own blood. In her wild defenselessness, she tried to swing for his face as he brought her up face to face, but his arms were longer. He pinned her against the wall, feet dangling, holding her by her hair alone and slapped her.

"Stop it! Just stop it!" he said, slapping her again.

"Why can't you just learn your place?" He slapped her again, his hand slipping and taking her in the eye. Her eye immediately reddened and swelled up.

He spit in her face, then unhanded her, letting her crumple to the ground. She had stopped trying to talk. She was just crying. Maybe he had beat some sense into her. At least she knew to shut up. She was a pathetic bonded, though. No aspirations. Weak.

Spratee turned his back to her.

"Get out," he ordered. "Now."

Crying and bloodied, Noselar started to crawl toward her room, a trail of bright blood dripping from her chin.

"No," Spratee said, stopping her. "*Now*. I told you to listen, woman!" He raised his foot, readying it to kick her in the side as she crawled.

"I'm sorry," Noselar pleaded almost unintelligibly through a swollen broken face. "Please don't." She swallowed and with a look of hopeless defeat crawled to the door. She climbed up the door, smearing blood on the curtain and a man from the security detail opened it, offered her an arm and helped her hobble to the transport. Noselar got in and tried to set the destination by speaking. Frustrated at choking on her own blood and saliva, she punched in the destination with her broken, bloody fingers. The transport lifted off.

Spratee peered out the window as the transport took her away. He didn't care where she went. Probably her parents'.

She had served her purpose. He was still Governor Spratee, President of Arter.

He wiped his bloody hand on a towel, threw it into a corner, then went back to his chair in the living room study. He needed to come up with a plan.

It's a bad situation, he admitted to himself, focusing on the moment at hand and discarding Noselar as an old thought. *Outlawed a religion that came back the same day, lost your cabinet, lost your family, but might still have Dise. Now what do I do?* he thought

No, what do I have? I have a potential cabinet. I have a strong following. I have my strength and I'm a great politician. Whatever it is, everything must lead to that beast's death...

* * *

Trellia banged on the Bahnderia's door like a law enforcement officer getting ready to kick down the door. "Hello! I'm here!"

The door opened and a shorter blonde woman with hair past her shoulders and slightly out of breath answered. It was the Reader.

"You were real," the Reader said, surprised. "Come in," she said and pulled the door open for Trellia.

Trellia stepped in and the Reader closed the door behind them. "Let's go to my study," the Reader said.

The Reader extended her hand to the left. "This way."

They walked down a growing spiral toward an array of doors. "Why did Sumatta send you to me?" the Reader asked.

"I need to use the Bahnder Tree, Reader."

"*Use?* The Bahnder Tree is only *used* by Sumatta," the Reader said, stopping to look at Trellia. "How can an Arterian even *use* the Bahnder Tree?"

Trellia took a deep breath. This was going to take some

explaining. "My bonded made this," she said, pulling a *draumr* from her pocket and holding it up. "It connects dreams to things. Others' dreams, artificial projections, and apparently the real world. Until today, it hadn't crossed the line into the real world. Sumatta showed me that when it brought me here. It also showed me that the Bahnder Tree is the next step in making it fully functioning."

"And why is that?"

"This device was my bonded's dream. He thought that one day it would let everyone communicate from mind to mind. He started with dreams. During the Cycle of Ages, he was using one. He disappeared, vanished.

"The Bahnder Tree is connected to the metal plate in Mount Sumat. I think that metal connected him to the real world in some way and that's what made him disappear. I need," she replied, breaking up with a teary cough. "I need to know he's still alive."

"Sumatta showed you the metal plate in Mount Sumat?" Shenol seemed so surprised that she hadn't heard anything about Unel. That metal plate was apparently very secretive.

"Yes, it showed it to me. I thought I was dreaming, but it called me to it using the metal plate. I saw it inside Mount Sumat. A big dark cavern with a metal plate in the middle and a pool it uses to come here. Sumatta brought me here through that tunnel in the pool."

"I see," Shenol said.

"Can I at least try?"

"This is Sumatta's home. Sumatta has invited you. I am the voice of Sumatta. I cannot say anything other than what Sumatta would say. Yes, you can try," the Reader said. The Reader turned around and pointed back the way they had come. "The Bahnder Tree is this way," she said.

They walked around the curved spiral until they came to the pearlescent Bahnder Tree. This was the first time Trellia had seen the tree while awake. She took in the majesty and awe of it for only a brief moment, too focused on how close she was to finding her Unel to be properly enraptured.

She carefully stepped through the pool to the center of the Bahnder Tree, its hollow trunk more than three times her size. She ran her hands against the smooth, crystalline bark marveling at the magic within and leaned back against the trunk. She put the *draumr* on her forehead, then waited, trying to relax and fall toward sleep.

She entered that moment just before falling asleep, when the mind is half aware of the world and half dreaming. She was able to hold herself there, not falling fully asleep.

The world around her was still the Bahnder Tree, the Reader standing at its pedestal, stands surrounding the tree for the crowd to sit around and worship. She could see clearly, but the haze of the dreaming mind was there giving the world a vividness beyond the real world.

I didn't choose a place to be. Where would I find him? she thought.

"Where do I find you, Unel? Unel!" she said as a mumble in the real world and a shout in the dream.

Unel did not answer.

She wished she could look everywhere, see everything, hear everything. It was a dream. Why couldn't she? Is that what the tree did? Did it give her that much range?

Trellia envisioned being above Arter and looking down on the entire planet. The world blurred as her consciousness zoomed out. She could see all of Arter. She could even see the Bhander Tree as her viewpoint changed, but at a certain distance, she was no longer visible. She wasn't just a small dot, she wasn't there. It was as if her consciousness and existence had followed her. Is that what had happened to Unel?

She took in the full continent of Arter, the whole world, including the oceans, in one single sweeping look that stretched from Photania in the west to the edge of Sumna in the east to the Isle of Lights to the south and the depths of the ocean in the north. She could sense inside buildings and under the surface; she could smell the slightest scent; she could hear every breath.

She turned her view to the space around her and scanned it. She realized she could go enormous distances from Arter. Unreal distances. She quickly scanned the entire solar system, zipping from planet to planet and even went inside the sun.

She did not sense Unel. He was gone. Where had he gone to?

She envisioned zooming back to the tree, barely noticing herself appear back at the tree before she arrived. She took off the *draumr* and woke completely.

The Reader looked like she was staring at an apparition. She walked up to Trellia, an arm extended with a wary finger, and touched her on the cheek in disbelief.

"You're real again. You disappeared," she said, unbelieving. "You just disappeared, then a few minutes later you were just back. Where did—"

"I did? My whole body?"

Nod.

"Then that's it. He is alive. I just have to find wh—"

"Where did you go?"

That was a good question. She had been above Arter. God sized. But she wasn't really there. She couldn't be. "Above Arter," she said. "Can I come back? I need to get some tools. Don't worry, they're for the *draumr*, not the tree."

"If you bring a second *draumr*, yes," Shenol said thoughtfully.

"Yes, I will," Trellia said. "I'll be back soon." Trellia ran through the spiral hallway and out of the Bahnderia. She was out of breath when she got to her transport and lifted off, setting the destination to the Dreamoria.

"Go! Go! Go!" she said. She was tempted to take over the controls and speed her way there, but that wouldn't help. She'd get caught and that would just slow her down.

Balance

Noal grabbed letters from the pool of letters and spelled out the word for continuum. In the letters of Sumattan, the word was symmetric, a small harmony to itself. It gave the feeling of never ending. He worked the second one into the first, then added the third until he had all nine letters as one three-dimensional shape. He smiled at himself as he finally solved the puzzle, getting the letters to all mesh together. The next thing was—

"Noal, come. Remember that good can be found in your darkest hours," Strypan said interrupting, then held up a touchpad.

"Hi," a woman he didn't recognize said. Her voice was hard to understand, as if her jaw were broken. Her eyes were swelled up and bruised in so many places that her skin looked dark and red, not Arterian white. She was crying. She looked almost like his...

"Nos?" he said slowly.

She bowed her head. "Don't go after him, Noal."

Noal ground his teeth. His birth parent was unrecognizable, attacked by that foul excuse for an Arterian, Spratee. Spratee was a fool to think anyone could touch Noal's birth parent.

"Never touch my birth parent," he growled. He softened his voice, addressing Noselar again as he reached out and touched the screen. "I love you," he said, then closed the connection and handed the touchpad back to Strypan with hands shaking with rage.

"You're being tested, Noal. What will you do?"

It would be like Strypan to not even hint at what Noal should do. No, he'd just ask the question with naive simplicity. Noal gave his answer just as simply: "Don't try to stop me."

Strypan simply stared at Noal almost as a curious parent would while Noal marched to his transport and hopped in, quiet, foreboding, and watching a child make a huge mistake. Noal didn't give in. *No one touches my birth parent*, he thought. *Not even the great president of Arter.* "Home," he said with a foreboding tone. The navigation system registered the location and set in course. The transport lifted off and headed to Hydrona.

The flight over was a mix of emotions. For a while, Noal was afraid of what he would do, but that fear turned into resolution. Four hours gave him some time to think and plan. Strypan had taught him the world was about balance, that there was a harmony to it. He needed to understand exactly what had happened to Nos to find that balance.

He opened a connection to the perfect friend of his for this job. Aulot answered looking as harried as ever.

"What's up, Noal?" she asked.

"I was going to ask if you still interned as a med student, but from the looks of it you're there now. You know my birth parent, right?"

"Yes, what's this about?"

"I need her medical scan. The one from when she just came in."

"Wait, she was here? Let me look."

Aulot tapped at her touchpad, then looked up with disbelief, a soft tear falling from one eye. "By Sumatta itself, what happened to her?"

"He did. Can you send that to me?"

"No. You know these are confidential. She wasn't even at this facility. It would require her direct request."

"I'm her son, Aulot. I'm asking on her behalf. Please. You can say I faked the request. I'll take the blame."

"If it were my birth parent," Aulot whispered, then bobbed her head. "Yeah. I got the request from her. It's right here. Thanks for forwarding that, Noal. I'll transmit to you now."

"Thanks, Aulot. I owe you one."

"Not for this, you don't." She wiped her eyes and looked at him with hopeless resignation. "As a friend, I should tell you—"

"I promise. I'll only do what's right," Noal said. "Balance needs to be restored to the universe."

Aulot bobbed her head, looked at her touchpad, and said, "There you go, my friend. Send Noselar my best. I've got to go." She closed the connection.

Noal called up the scan and had it replayed in full three-dimensional color. Noselar lay there in front of him, nude. Bones and flesh displaying the entirety of her abuse. Normally, he would be embarrassed to see his birth parent nude, but embarrassment was not in the mix of emotions vying for his attention.

Noal studied the replay with tears rolling down his cheeks. He memorized every wound. He studied it until he felt he was there, could see the flow of energy, could see every punch, every kick, every aspect of the attack.

He studied it until he had a sense of detachment from the scan, as if he were simply a musician studying notes on a sheet of paper. He came to a calm sense of resolution. Albeit, a dangerous calm, but one that didn't control him.

His parent was finished. His political world had just come crashing down as if Sumatta had fallen on him personally. No one had the staying power to survive that. He didn't even have a cabinet, not even a public relations person to help him.

If that wasn't enough to finish him, his parent had attacked his birth parent. Noal was going to do what politics couldn't. He was going to finish him, once and for all. Striking a little balance in the universe would be a good idea, it would be like a little harmony played with Spratee's face.

By the time the transport started to descend, Noal was ready. It twisted and turned, planting itself in his old spot. Noal lifted his touchpad and sent a brief message, pitching himself as a member of Spratee's new cabinet and offering a press conference in fifteen minutes. That would be all he needed. He pocketed the touchpad and opened the door.

Spratee didn't come out. Noal could see him sitting behind his desk in the living room study acting as if he were looking through reports.

Noal stepped out of the transport as a calm, decisive man. He'd never thought of himself as a man until now. Not this kind of man, the one who puts himself in harm's way to protect his family.

Spratee's personal guard hadn't abandoned him. They were positioned all around the house in their usual spots. Commander Chier walked up to Noal, catching him halfway to the door. "I can't let you go in there, son," he said, holding his hand up.

Noal looked at the commander in the eyes with peaceful resolution, then caught a trail of blood in his peripheral vision. He looked at the trail as it led away from the house, then faced Commander Chier again. "You—"

"Let him in," called Spratee.

That was your second biggest mistake, governor, Noal thought. He took the opportunity and walked past the commander without another word. When he opened the door, he saw the blood on the handle from the other side and swallowed. His birth parent's blood.

Noal reached over and pressed the curtain button on the wall. The shades lowered. He saw the blood on the other side of the shades and almost growled with angst. The shades had been closed? They had turned a blind eye to Nos' suffering? He would remember that. He pressed another button to lock the door.

He walked toward his parent's desk and stopped five feet away. The Arterian actively ignored Noal, continuing to flip through reports.

"Who do you think you are?" Noal demanded.

"That is not how you address me, kid," Spratee

commanded.

Noal leapt forward, throwing his foot out and kicking the desk toward Spratee. Spratee tried to jump up, but Noal moved too quickly. The desk caught him just below his waist. He fell back in his chair, swearing.

"Are you here for revenge? Going to beat me up?"

"Yes," Noal said, leaping up on top of the desk. He lifted his foot and swiped his foot at a precise angle across Spratee's face. Every kick would mirror Spratee's kicks at Noselar. Every hit would mirror Spratee's hit. Every wound would find its mirror. There was about to be a balance restored to the universe.

Spratee groaned, cursed, and curled up as if he'd been kicked three times as hard. The Arterian was not that weak. Noal was not surprised when Spratee used the faux pain to pull a gun from an ankle holster.

Noal had just swung his foot for a kick to the ear. It was over Spratee's hands as the fool drew the gun. He saw the flow of energy and harnessed it, redirecting the power of his kick and aiming deep into the ground below Spratee's wrists. He brought his foot down through the man's wrists. They snapped and Spratee screamed, his fingers dropping the gun as his hands fell limp.

Noal kneeled down, then pushed forward, ramming his knee into Spratee's jaw as he dropped his fist straight into Spratee's face, pummeling his eye.

Noal could see her, his Nos, spinning about in front of him in the transport. He could see her wounds becoming his. No, it wouldn't heal her wounds. He wasn't here for healing.

Noal reached down and drug Spratee from behind the desk, throwing him against the wall and kicked him. A foot to the ribs cracked a rib on the left side, just like Noselar's left side. A foot to the stomach made him groan in agony. A bruise would show up there, just like on Noselar. He kicked at his arms as Spratee raised them to protect himself, his legs as he curled up. Noal kicked repeatedly, returning bruise for bruise, wound for wound, the image of his birth mother fresh in his mind.

"Guards!" Spratee called. The door began shaking almost immediately.

Noal reached down, picked the coward up by the hair and slammed him against the wall. Noal slapped the man with carefully timed strikes, bruising his face as solidly as Noselar had been beaten.

Now, Spratee looked like Noselar. Noal stopped, dropping the man. The guards fired shots into the door and burst in.

"Don't move, Noal," Commander Chier said, aiming a weapon at Noal.

"You're done? What's that? Tired? You're worthless, you know. Not even our kid. You're adopted. Someone else's trash," Spratee said.

Noal had not planned to hit Spratee again, but he saw all the flows of energy, saw the commander's hesitation and spun around in a flurry of a roundhouse and kicked Spratee's jaw hard. The bone snapping made one want to cringe.

Come to think of it, his birth parent's jaw had been broken. Technically that meant that except for the wrists, he had only returned blow for blow. He could face his mentor's judgment on that.

It was the next part his mentor wouldn't like.

"I said not to move, Noal," Commander Chier said. His hesitation was gone. He would shoot again.

Noal lifted his hands. "I won't hit him again," he said. "I just want to show him something."

Noal didn't wait for permission. Commander Chier's hesitation was gone, but his charge was directly behind Noal. He wouldn't fire if it meant he could hurt his charge. Noal reached into his pocket and slowly pulled his touchpad out of his pocket. He tapped at the screen. "I just happened to fulfill your cabinet position of public relations for a minute. In my new role, I scheduled a live broadcast for you. It starts now..."

Noal held up the touchpad, turning its camera to capture

the entire room, and loudly said, "Governor Spratee, can you tell us what's happened here?"

"Bye," Noal said as he set the touchpad down in front of Spratee. Noal turned away from the crying, bloody mess that was his parent and looked at Commander Chier.

"If you want a job after this, I suggest you leave now," Noal said. "That's what I'm going to do." Noal walked over and Commander Chier kept his aim on Noal.

"No," the commander said and shook his gun at Noal. "Get on the ground. I'm arresting you for assaulting the governor."

Energy, beautiful energy. Noal could see the flows in the room. The rest of the security detail were already over tending Spratee, but Commander Chier had stayed focused. Noal spun to the commander's strong side and kneeled, then swung his foot around as he locked the man's kneecap in place. The commander fired his shot as Noal went down, but Noal moved too quickly and the shot went over his head. The commander fell forward as Noal's foot hit. Noal reached up and grabbed the commander's gun hand, slipping his fingers inside his grip and freeing the gun. The man's kneecap cracked just as Noal stole his gun. Noal stood up and threw the gun to the side as the others spun on him, weapons drawn. "I'm unarmed," he said. "I will not forget what you let him do to my birth parent," Noal said.

Their energy was confused, reactive. They were supposed to have been better trained than that.

"You're a disappointment, Commander Chier," Noal said looking at the man as he cradled his broken knee. "I thought all this time you were good, but you're as pathetic as Spratee."

Still calm, still collected, and still in control, Noal walked through the broken door and headed to his transport. He climbed in and lifted off. Looking out the window at the chaos below and smiled.

"I just ended your career, governor. Never touch my birth parent."

Survival

Shenol had barely made it to the Bahnderia when that woman from Sumatta knocked. She hadn't even got the woman's name. Now that she had left, it was time to find out exactly what Sumatta had meant about the cocoons. She hurriedly walked to the library, as close to running as she could get while maintaining her feminine poise. She burst into the Reader's study and threw open the doors to the library. *Where is that replay?* she thought. She closed her eyes and thought for a moment, trying to remember where she had last grabbed that disk. It came to her as a vague memory, but enough that she knew where to look. She went over to the cases of replays and picked out the disk. She stumbled with excitement as she slid it into the device.

The little three-foot version of Sumatta popped up and started speaking.

"I fled my dying Space and was given here. On my coming, capsules of my life I saw put on the land as towers to last a hundred thousand years."

They weren't capsules. They were cocoons. Arter's mountains were all cocoons. Of what? She played it again and caught it. Sumatta had said "my life" which could also mean "parts of me". They were cocoons of Sumatta!

All this time she had felt that something was different about that word and now she found out that it was the secret to everything. This was phenomenal. She wanted to scream it from the rooftops. But the Reader knew she could tell no one except another Reader. At the moment, there wasn't even a Next Reader to tell. There was Rax, but he was young. He would be the Next Reader, but not for another year. Still, she could safely tell him. But she wanted to tell everyone, yet

Sumatta had kept this secret for a hundred thousand years. It was not Shenol's to tell the world. Arter would have to wait.

She put the replay away and flopped back on the couch.

All this time, she thought. *And you're just waiting for them to hatch...* What would happen if the mountains hatched? It would be a catastrophe. *The Last Age. I get it. Your children are coming. That's why you're here.*

If that was the case, then what could Shenol do? What could anyone do? Just the amount of gas released into the air would make it toxic to Arterians. We're all going to die so that they can be born. It was a harsh thought, one that questioned her faith. Sumatta was the Giver of Life, Protector of Arter, Guardian of Ages. There was nothing there that said Sumatta was protector of Arterians. Would Sumatta let Arterians be wiped off the face of the planet?

Right now was a horrible time to doubt her faith. Her god had just returned and she had news of even more gods. It should be a time to rejoice, but the truth made it hard to find joy.

Someone was knocking again. Why did they knock when the door was open? It's the Bahnderia, for Sumatta's sake. The door is always unlocked during the day. It only gets fixed open when the weather is good. Didn't everyone know that?

* * *

Trellia burst into the Dreamoria and started gathering supplies. She grabbed two *draumrs* and energy emitters, which she used to mirror the solar storm energy waves from the Cycle of Ages, and a projector. She was at the door before she remembered to grab *aten* for the energy emitters. She went to the shelf, selected an array of *aten*, then headed back out.

She rushed to her transport and threw everything in the passenger seat, then hopped in. She set course for the Bahnderia and the transport lifted off, turning south. It took an hour and a half to get back to the Bahnderia after she'd left, much longer than Trellia wanted. Unel could be out there waiting for her and she didn't want to miss one second with her bonded.

She pounded on the door as vigorously as she had the last time and waited. After too long, the Reader opened the door and let her in.

"The door is unloc—" the Reader started, but Trellia was too excited.

"I brought two, just like you asked," Trellia said, holding up a *draumr*.

"Good. No, great. Sorry, I was doing something and I'm a bit distracted." The Reader straightened her dress, regaining her demeanor. "I am eager to see this work. Will you explain it to me?" she said and motioned for Trellia to enter.

"Of course," Trellia agreed. She followed the Reader to the Bahnder Tree and set out the energy emitters.

"These emit energy based on the *aten* inside," she said as she set one down and grabbed a brown, flaky *aten*. "This one will use *na'aten*. It binds things to Arter," she said and dropped the flaky ball into a slot of just the right size. "This one," she said, setting up another emitter exactly three feet away, "uses *siaten*. I'm not sure why it works, but it does. I tested every combination to make sure."

Measuring out another three feet, she set the last emitter down and dropped a purple *phoaten* inside. "And a *phoaten* for light. That was an easy guess since the message came from the sun."

She set a small black oblong box down at the edge to the pool around the tree. "This is the projector. It sends a dream world into our minds."

"You did not use that last time. Why do you need it now?"

"When we go to sleep, we never know what we'll dream of. The projector sets our dream. Some dreams can be bad to fall asleep into."

"Can we not use that today? I am not worried about our dreams. I want to see what you did to vanish."

"What exactly do you mean by vanish? What happened?"

"You just disappeared. Got fuzzy, then vanished. Your whole body was gone."

That didn't make much sense to Trellia, but little did right now. Showing the Reader how it worked would help her understand it better too. Unel had to be there somewhere and helping the Reader was the only way to find him.

"No projector," Trellia agreed.

She gave everything a final inspection, then turned to the Reader and held out a *draumr*. "We're ready. Place this over your forehead like this," she said, placing her *draumr* on.

The Reader put on the *draumr* and Trellia adjusted it slightly to sit dead center at even rotation. Being off too much could cause things not to work well. The *draumr* was a fine balance between the energies of the universe. Anything slightly off and it wouldn't work the same. It could even be dangerous. She knew that all too well.

She turned on the energy emitters. "We didn't use these last time. I don't fully understand the effect, but they mirror the energy from the storm during the Cycle of Ages. I think that's why I couldn't find my bonded. Sumatta would not have brought me to this tree if it wouldn't have helped."

The Reader nodded, then leaned back against the Bahnder Tree just as Trellia did. They were both pulled into sleep.

Trellia reached up and tapped her eyelids. She envisioned them on a cloud above Arter. The world blurred, but did not change. "We're asleep," she said. "Where we go, we go together."

The Reader stepped out and touched her arm. "How do you know we're asleep? I feel real."

"We have tells we create while awake that help us when we're asleep. For me, I tap my eyelids twice to take control of a dream. Unel would reach out and touch the sun. Everyone's is different. You choose your own." Trellia thought about what a good tell would be for the Reader, then it came to her. "Tug on your dress," she said. "You're always primping on your dress, so imagine giving a command and tugging on your dress makes it come real. When I tap my eyelids twice, I always follow it with thinking of a setting."

The Reader nodded and straightened her dress. She shook her head. "Nothing. The world just got fuzzy for a second."

"That fuzziness is because we're here together. Where we go, we go together. Do you want to try going to a cloud above Arter?" she asked, looking up and pointing at one. "Let's think about going there together."

They both closed their eyes, then when a cool breeze tickled their ankles, they opened them to find themselves on the cloud. They looked at each other with eager excitement.

"The moon?" the Reader said.

"Beyond," Trellia encouraged.

The Reader nodded and in the blink of an eye they were in the darkness of space, all of Arter in their view.

"What I did when you saw me appear and disappear is this," Trellia said, holding her fingers up as if zooming in and out on a touchpad. It worked again, so she made the adjustment smaller after she zoomed too far and left the Reader alone in space.

"That's interesting," Trellia said. "We only have to start in the same place. After that, we can move around, but not change the world. I didn't know that."

"My turn," the Reader said and used her fingers to zoom. She disappeared for a bit, then zipped too far back before finally working her way back to Trellia.

"Together?" Trellia suggested.

"Yes."

They held their hands up and zoomed in and out slowly while they watched their bodies at the Bahnder tree until they found the exact point at which the body ceased to exist. It was halfway between Arter and its moon.

"What does it mean, Reader? If we don't have bodies, where are we?"

"I read an old book from the Journal of Thought that talked about this. It was an old religion before this age began. They would meditate and, at some point, ascend, leaving their physical bodies behind. As far as I remember, it never spoke of them coming back."

The Reader looked at her with all seriousness. "What if we could survive the coming of the next age?

"By... ascending?"

"Yes."

"How would we get everyone around the Bahnder Tree?"

"Cocoons," the Reader said. "The pods that hold the Arterians who attacked Sumatta are not pods, they're cocoons. If we could get into their minds and guide their dreams, we could help them escape the cocoons and ascend. They could live here through the coming of the next age."

"I don't know how long we can stay here," Trellia objected.

"So long as there is energy," the Reader explained.

"Energy from where?"

"Their inherent energy. We are not nothing right now. We are energy. So long as we do not lose our energy, we can stay here."

It sounded like a great plan. Except it didn't give her the one thing she wanted: Unel. Where was that man?

"I need to find Unel," Trellia said. "If you'll help me find Unel, then I'll help you get them ascended."

"Agreed," the Reader replied. "Let me check something first," she said, then concentrated, closing her eyes. She opened them with a wide smile on her face. "Yes, it will work. They're all alive in the pods. I can sense them. This will work. Let's go back."

"You go ahead. I want to see if I can find Unel."

With that, the Reader vanished, waking up back on Arter at the tree.

Trellia reached out with her senses to Arter.

"Come on. I have the tree, the solar storm, the device. You have to be there, Unel," she said to herself. She couldn't sense him anywhere on the planet.

"Unel!" she screamed into space. "Unel, I need you. Where are you, energy of my life?"

She zoomed back and took in the galaxy. Still no Unel.

"By Sumatta itself, I swear I will find you, my love," she said. She was missing something, but she didn't know what. Maybe the Reader would have some knowledge of that day back during the Cycle of Ages which would help. She envisioned herself back at the tree and woke up.

Answers

Noal's transport set down on Strypan's landing pad and he stepped out. He walked into the house, but Strypan wasn't there. He went out one of the back doors and found Strypan meditating in the center of the training ring.

"He now looks like her," Noal said. "I returned punch for punch, kick for kick, wound for wound. No, it doesn't make me feel better. Nothing will. No, it doesn't heal her. I accept that. I brought balance to this."

Noal took a deep breath, drawing a silent shape in the air with his arms. It looked like a rough version of the symbol his parents had shown him for his name: all things.

"Not completely, mentor. I added to it. I destroyed his career. I ruined him as punishment.

"He was defenseless compared to me. The only thing he could do was cry out like a child and throw out lies at the end. He said I was adopted. He was a weaker man than I anticipated."

Noal swallowed as Strypan remained silent. He'd never felt so nervous in his life. He wasn't afraid of Strypan, but his disapproval gave Noal great angst.

"I have disappointed you, mentor," Noal said.

"How did you disappoint me?" Strypan said calmly, opening his eyes and standing.

"I took an unnecessary action just to inflict mental harm for the sole purpose of punishing him. Spratee was already finished. He knew that, and I knew that. I rubbed it in his face out of pure vengeance."

"There is a balance in all things, Noal. You must find this balance, or you'll be unbalanced," Strypan said. He paused for a moment, reflecting on what he just said, then winced, perhaps because it was not as philosophical as he'd intended, but a mundane statement of the obvious.

"Balance is the natural order of things, Noal. You assume an added punishment disappointed me. When your opponent rises up against you—or your family—they become your enemy and you must put them down in a way that prevents them from seeking retribution. Do not confuse the choice to use a weapon as a last resort as a sign of pacifism. When your enemy attacks you, everything else has failed to prevent that, and you must respond with force. Your goal should be to prevent it if you can, but do not shirk yourself by failing to attack."

Noal looked reflective, then summed it up. "So, you're saying by beating him up worse, I was achieving balance?"

"Yes," Strypan said. "You were restoring balance by dissuading him from doing it again."

Noal shook his head and laughed. "You should never be a parent. You're not supposed to tell your kids to beat someone up."

Noal must have hit a nerve. Strypan looked hurt.

"Sorry, I didn't know you had ki—"

"*You* are my kid as much as you are not."

Noal bowed his head, giving Strypan the point.

"Noal, you are adopted. What he said there was true."

Noal took a moment. He took a few moments. Adopted? Spratee's angry lies were true? They had hidden that from him all these years? Noselar? Strypan? Why? No, it didn't matter why. But then...

"Who are my parents?"

"We lost one at the Cycle of Ages. His name was Unel. Unel is my son. You are my grandson."

"And my birth parent?"

"She felt guilty when she saw you. She thinks what happened with Unel was her fault. She put you up for adoption and Spratee was chosen. I stayed in the distance, serving as your mentor. Training you as I trained my own son. I give her monthly reports." Strypan paused for a moment, rubbed his chin, then asked in an encouraging tone, "Do you want to go to the next one?"

Yes. No. Why? Maybe. Should I? What if I don't like her? What if she doesn't like me? He's not even talking in philosophical riddles!

Noal collected his thoughts and replied coolly. "Yes. If I don't, I will never know her. Do you... do you see any balance in this?"

"A balance is the result of highs and lows, some greater than others. So, yes, I do. I also see your hurt."

Noal fell to his knees, hands over his eyes and cried. "Teach me how to handle this, mentor," he begged. He didn't know his parents, he loved the wrong birth parent, he'd been abandoned as a baby, and he couldn't know one of his parents. How do you handle that? How do you handle your whole life being a lie? Can you handle that?

"You already know how to handle this. You just haven't accepted the decision you've already made," Strypan said. "Remember who you are, Noal. That is where your strength comes from."

Noal jumped to his feet, landing in a fighting stance. "Tell me what my fight tells you today," he said, his voice half begging, half commanding.

Strypan nodded and took on a lethal stance. "Every stance can be weak," he said, then lunged forward in a clockwise spin to kick at Noal's right side.

Noal spun with Strypan's kick and lifted his leg, knee up and sweeping to the left. He knocked Strypan's leg forward faster so that it completely missed Noal and threw Strypan off balance.

Strypan spun around, his feet landing next to each other and stood there, knees locked, like someone who'd never fought before. "Every stance can be strong," he said. He rolled himself forward like a barrel through the air, catching himself on his hands as his legs spun toward Noal's knees. He pulled one leg in, extending it again to behind Noal, catching him as if he were in the middle of scissors, then twisted his legs backward.

Noal tumbled backward into the take down, then rolled to a standing position, swinging his foot forward to catch Strypan's arm.

It hit.

Strypan's arm flung out on the path of the foot and he tumbled face first into the ground. Flopping down flat.

Noal arched downward and wrapped his legs around Strypan's like Strypan had just done to him, pinning Strypan down as he placed a hand on his back, holding him firmly in place.

"Every strength can be a weakness, and every weakness can be a strength. Sometimes they can be both."

"What's the point?"

"Why do we ask questions we know the answers to?"

"Because we might not get the answer we expect," Noal answered readily.

"Strength and weakness come from accepting them and using them, but without you, they cannot help. Who you are is what matters more than your strengths and weaknesses. You have a new last lesson. Your last lesson is that you have not found yourself yet. Now, go find yourself, grandson."

Noal stood up and dusted himself off. "I'm going to Attatar tonight. Let's do dinner. I'll cook."

"Oh, no! Why?" Strypan said in a serious tone, his body showing playfulness.

"Why ask questions..."

"Because I might get an answer I want to hear!"

Noal laughed, but he did need to find himself. Strypan was right. He'd just had his world turned upside down and needed to figure out what kind of balance there was in a universe where you couldn't trust anyone you'd ever known.

* * *

Shenol slipped the *draumr* over her forehead and checked herself in the mirror. She looked stunning with the *draumr*. She'd suggested some cosmetic changes that really made it look more like jewelry and less like a scientific device. Working with Trellia over the last three days had not only made the *draumr* look better, but she was now very comfortable using it in the wake-dream world.

It was too bad Trellia had not found Unel. Shenol wasn't sure Trellia would ever find Unel. You could see, hear, and sense everything in the wake-dream world. If he were to be found, they'd have found him, but Trellia wouldn't give up hope, so Shenol wouldn't give up helping. She'd given her word and, just as importantly, Trellia was like a friend now.

Today Trellia had to take a break and deal with some family issues, but this was the first time they'd been apart in three days. They had spent every waking moment working on the *draumr* and mastering the wake-dream. So far, they had figured out how to harness the Bahnder Tree's metal up to a mile away. It was nowhere near what they needed to save all of Arter, but it was a good start.

While Trellia was off dealing with her parent-in-law, who seemed to be a handful at the least, Shenol planned to visit Sumatta. She had more questions.

She reached out and turned the energy emitters on her desk on. They had been adjusted for this distance from the Bahnder Tree and worked like a charm. She leaned back in her chair and focused on the Cycle of Ages as she entered the world of half-reality, half-dream.

She quickly entered the wake-dream state and was standing in the pool at the base of the Cycle of Ages, or at least where it had been before it exploded. Off in the corner to the right was a small waterfall. She swam over to the rocks of the

Readers platform and climbed up. It was just rock behind the waterfall where the hallway for the Reader had been during the Cycle of Ages. How was she going to get in? Sumatta hadn't mentioned that it had been sealed. Was it normally sealed between ages?

She turned around, looking for another way in. There was a rock missing just below the surface of the pool edge. Was it missing in the dream world or the real world? Had it always been missing? It couldn't have been. The opening below was large enough for Sumatta. They would have noticed it on the expeditions to find Sumatta.

She hopped into the pool and swam over to the opening. Holding her breath, she dove down. Hopefully she would find an air pocket soon; she was not a good swimmer. As she swam into the opening, a large rock rolled in place behind her sealing her inside. She felt a surge of panic at having no way out.

She looked around at the large opening. It was large enough for Sumatta. Exactly large enough. *Sumatta's secret escape*, Shenol thought. *This is how it survived.*

She swam quickly, feeling short of breath already. Luckily, the tunnel was shorter than Sumatta's biggest wings, so Shenol made it through quickly.

She climbed up out of the pool and onto the ledge, gasping as she caught her breath. Looking up, Sumatta stood before her.

"You took the long way," Sumatta sang.

"I don't know another way."

"The same way you got to the door."

Sumatta had a point. If Shenol could wish herself a fourth of the way around the planet to get here, why not a few more feet?

"Next time," she replied, blushing slightly. "I have some questions."

"From my energy to yours, from my knowledge to yours," it promised.

"The Final Age is when your children will come, right?"

"Yes. They are coming."

"You are Giver of Life, Protector of Arter, Guardian of Ages. Are you a protector of Arterians? Will you let us all die?"

"You are my children. I will protect you. I brought you the woman. You have the capsules of life. Saving all life is not Sumatta. Sumatta saves those it can."

"What else do I need to know? What other secrets?"

"Since my coming I have told you all I can. Some secrets are of the Igri Tufuer. It will tell you what it wants. The history is complete."

"It is not complete, Sumatta. You hid your children."

"You did not understand the word. I said the truth."

That was true. It had been mistranslated by the only Arterians able to translate it.

"How does it start?"

"Capsules of my life break."

"What causes that?"

"Birth."

"How do we know when?"

"Capsules of my life break."

Great, she thought. *We don't know when.*

"Thank you, Sumatta. It is comforting to know you will protect Arterians. I was worried."

"Your feelings are not what I understand. Sumatta is Bringer of Life, Protector of Arterian Life, Guardian of Arter through the Ages. The Reader reads much, but does not read all. More meaning is inside my words than your words understand. I give my life to protect your life. 'Sumatta' means 'all life'."

"I doubted you only because I'm afraid, Sumatta. Thank you for answering my questions."

She had come to a conclusion different than what she anticipated. For as much faith as she had in Sumatta, killing Arterians off would be too much. Sumatta promised to give its life protecting Arter. Shenol believed that.

She motioned to zoom out. She had another thing she wanted to check tonight. She found her point, then zoomed in, landing herself inside a hidden cave, just at the inner opening.

She looked up through the opening and saw a giant green capsule. Inside of it was a giant clone of Sumatta. Not technically a clone, like the smaller spatiatta, but another of its race. *An infant?* she wondered. The infant looked very close to Sumatta. It had wings with tendrils still glued to its husk and scaly skin and was just as tall as Sumatta. Its head did not appear fully developed, but was close, and the speaking tentacles were curled up in a bunch at the bottom. This could hatch any time. Shenol wasn't sure if it was a month, a year, or a few years—she didn't know anything about their reproductive cycle. It would be soon, though. They looked too much like Sumatta.

A broken voice twilled behind her. "You must—" She spun around and stared at the spatiatta standing before her, hovering on its tentacles. It adopted a look of recognition and switched to speaking in Sumattan.

"Danger to Reader here. Swarm protects capsule of Sumatta's life." It opened its outer skin, exposing a flap to hold her. It was offering her a ride.

"I was just looking. I will leave," she said and zoomed out.

She didn't know the animals in the Swarm could talk. By Sumatta itself, she would have sworn they were animals of pure instinct until now.

She zoomed into her room, then zoomed in close enough to solidify.

She now knew Sumatta would save Arter. She had a lot of work to do.

* * *

Noal. Her Noal. She'd heard the descriptions of him, but

seeing his tall, strong body, almost-white hair, and gray eyes with his cute smile was not the same. She had refused to get involved until she saw the governor with Noal in the background demanding an answer. Now he was without a parent. That's why she'd always listened to the reports—he might need her one day.

And there he was. She realized they were just staring at each other. He must have been waiting for her to say something.

"I'm sorry to tell you now, but you deserve the full truth. There's more to tell you."

Noal closed his eyes for a moment. He was acting strong, but he didn't feel it. Still, he should know.

"What is it?" he asked.

"When my bonded, Unel, asked to have a baby, he didn't know that he was sterile. *Attaten* do not work on males. I wanted so badly to give that to him, I wanted so badly for us to have a baby, that I asked his friend, Col, if he would help," she said.

"He agreed and I impregnated myself after a night with Unel. He was never supposed to know," she said, defending her actions. "Then the Cycle of Ages happened and you were born. He just disappeared. When I saw you, I saw Col. I saw my shame. I saw my lost bonded. I put you up for adoption because I couldn't handle the constant reminders. I put you up for adoption because I'm weak."

She stopped and looked Noal in the eyes. "Seeing you reminds me of everything about my bonded."

"Not so good at greetings, are you? Let me show you," Noal said and stuck out his hand. "Hi birth parent, I'm your child, Noal."

She reached out gently and shook his hand.

"Won't have a relationship like if you had kept me, but if I learn about you and Col, I learn about me."

She nodded. The kid was right, but he missed one thing.

"And Unel. Without him, you would not exist. He is my energy's source."

"And Unel," Noal said, smiling. "We came to an agreement. My mentor says that if a relationship starts with agreement, it rests on a foothold not easily shaken."

"Your grandparent is wise. A little rough on the humor, but wise."

"I'm right here and wise enough to listen to what I hear," Strypan added.

"Then smart enough to know it's true," Trellia retorted.

Strypan laughed.

"I'm going into the military," Noal said as if sharing a secret surprise.

"I know," Trellia said. She looked at Strypan with a telling eye.

"Oh, yeah. Well, would Col or Unel have gone into the military? I mean, did they?"

"Both. They were—no, are—best friends. They have been since school and... all the way through the military," she said smiling as she drew out the last part.

Noal took that very well. He came to life.

"Were they scientists?"

"Unel is."

"What about Col?"

"Unel's assistant. Mostly the strong guy in the military."

"I am both of them. And more. There's pure me, too."

"Then you are your own man, Noal. Always remember who you are. When you forget, you regret."

He nodded, then looked at his touchpad, turning off an alarm tone. "I have to head out now. Time for me to report in. Will you contact me?"

"Yes. I would love to," she said. She'd expected to be berated. Instead, she'd received a warm welcome.

She took a risk when he reached out his hand to shake hers again and stepped forward, wrapping her arms around him and giving him a hug. It was the first time she'd touched him as a birth parent since the night he was born. He was strong, grown, almost a man; he was her baby. She held him tight until she started to shake as she cried.

"I'm sorry," she said.

"Let's just move forward from here, Trelly," he said, giving her an affectionate name as he patted her on the back.

He was right. She'd gotten caught up in the moment. She let him go, smiled and wiped the tears from her eyes. "We have an agreement," she replied.

He laughed, got in his transport, and lifted off for Attatar, waving as the craft turned before accelerating.

Her baby had grown up, and she'd missed every step. Quite literally.

Advanced Technology

Noal laid back on his bed, arms behind his head, thinking. A little over five years in the military had taught him quite a bit about life, pushing his limits, self-control, and science. It was like a fast-track education. The classes pushed you, but as soon as you took the class, you could start using the science. Noal had invented a couple of things. He loved creating things.

He didn't think much about his inventions, but his superiors thought very highly of them. He'd been promoted twice and was under consideration for another promotion. His term in the military was also almost up. He still hadn't decided which route he was going to go. He'd taken a week's leave of absence to think.

The building shook. It was a small quake. About a three and a half grade. They were getting more frequent. Arterians were starting to panic, fearing for their life at the end of the world.

To Noal, that was naive thinking. There's no balance, no harmony, in an unpopulated planet. How could the creator of all life on the planet not have something in mind? It did, of course, and they were signing up, but signing up to have a spatiatta coat you in goo and turned into a cocoon wasn't enticing just yet. Complaining, it seemed, was very enticing.

Rumors had it that a scientist had discovered something, but he hadn't heard any more details on that. If Sumatta was saving them, why did they need another method?

"Noal?" Noselar said, peeking in his room.

"I'm awake. Just thinking about things. There's a lot of bad stuff going on out there now, Nos."

"Can I talk to you?" she asked.

Noal flipped his legs over the edge of his bed and sat up.

"Any time, Nos." He scooted over and she sat down next to him, placing her hand on his knee.

"I've signed up for a cocoon," she said. "It's getting worse. I don't think it's safe to wait any longer. I," she said, hesitating. "I think you should too."

He had called her his birth parent most of his life. The truth was she was his honor parent, a parent who assumed the honor of raising another person's child. She didn't see herself as an honor parent; she treated him as her son, her biological son. He had to answer her with care. He didn't want to hurt her by being as blunt as his thoughts.

"Strypan says there's a balance to the universe, Nos. I think there's more to it. I don't know what it is, but I believe that what I'm doing at the military will help. Arterians shouldn't be fighting now—they shouldn't have been fighting since the Cycle of Ages—they should be coming together and helping each other. I think my role is to bring them together."

"How, son, do you expect to achieve something so big as that? You can't make everyone cooperate."

"That's true. I don't want to try and make everyone cooperate, but how many lives could I save? How many would be lost if I did nothing?" His face showed a level of affection deeper than that of just a man talking with his birth parent, it showed the love of a son. "Weak positions can be strong, Nos. Strypan told me that too. I might be just like every other Arterian, but I believe I'm stronger than my position; I believe I can help."

Tears welled in Noselar's eyes. She thought she was losing him.

"You won't lose me. I will be safe. I need you to trust my mentor's training. I need you to trust in me as much as you do in Sumatta. I will be ok. I promise you."

Someone knocked at the door.

"I'll get it," he said and went to answer the door as she wiped the tears from her eyes.

There were two officers at the door holding an envelope.

"Noal?" asked one of the officers.

"Yes," he replied, saluting.

The officer extended the envelope and Noal took it. They stood as if waiting for him to read the letter. That was a silent order to read the letter now.

He opened the envelope, slipped out the letter, and unfolded it. It was a summons. He was to leave immediately.

"It was a one week leave, guys. You couldn't give me a week?" he said. The officers didn't respond.

"Let me get my stuff," he said.

He went back to his room. Noselar was still sitting on the bed, quietly reflecting.

"They're calling me back to base," he said.

"Now I lose my baby boy and the world gains you," she said, quoting herself. She stood up, adopting a solidness to her that bespoke birth parentage and with a stronger voice said, "Except you're not a baby anymore. You're a young man. Noal, I trust you."

She said that, but she didn't mean it. She trusted him, but she didn't trust that he'd be safe. She said that because she supported him even when she didn't agree with him. Noal couldn't expect more.

"Thank you, Nos. I love you," he said, giving her a hug.

He grabbed his duffle bag and slung it on his shoulder.

"Love you too, son," Noselar said. He could see the hurt in her eyes, but it was not something he could affect. He couldn't do what he needed to do and make everyone happy. He was just trying to play his part in what was a messy symphony.

He joined the officers in their transport and headed for Sumna Military Base.

"OK, what's this about?" he said after the transport took off.

"Do you know anything about reverse electromagnetic resonance?"

"Yes, sir. Of course. You know my work on that. Why?"

"We need you to make a big one. One big enough to cover the city."

The problem, they should know, is that the process was not controlled. Anything which collided with the resonance field was crushed by the force. Now they were ordering him to make it. They were ordering him to make a killing machine. He wasn't sure he agreed with them. Agreeing wasn't an option.

"Of course, sir. I'll follow orders," he said. He knew he'd just lied to them.

* * *

Spratee sat on a dirty seat in a militant installation. The fenced-in installation housed about a dozen different buildings. The red and orange afternoon aurora gave the place an ominous feel. He shifted in his seat and sighed as Dise met with some agents. It used to be that when he came, Dise dropped everything. Now he had to pay for the privilege of her presence. It was one of the disadvantages of being a regular citizen. He still wasn't used to it and resented being forced out of his governorship.

One of the agents was discussing attacking Sumatta head on and hoping for the best. He shut up after she slammed her fist on the table and pointed at him, demanding he give up the idea. Another agent wanted to poison the waters around Mount Sumat. A third came up with something even worse.

She finally stopped blathering with those idiots. None of their plans would work anyway. None of his plans had worked, so what made them think they could do better? Especially with what they were coming up with now. They were quick to judge him, but the truth was that he had more strategic skill in his afterthoughts than they'd be able to muster in their prime.

"Dise will see you now," some peon said to him.

Spratee groaned and followed the peon to Dise. He took a

seat across from her desk, noting it was also a dirty, foul piece of furniture, just like their operation. It was their dirtiness that brought him here. He was going to have to get dirty to get the job done. He didn't have the same resources as he'd once had and money couldn't buy a job like this, not since the religious fervor following that beast's return.

Dise, former Director of Education, sat behind the grimy table in worn and equally-dirty clothes. Her hair was a mess and she looked to be in a foul mood. That was not much of a shock given the fool plans she'd just had to entertain. She looked less happy to see Spratee.

"Dise, I need something," he said.

"What's that?"

"A phonahyd bomb."

"What are you going to do with it? Blow yourself up?"

"What I plan to do with it is my business. I'll pay."

Dise eyed him and shook her head. "No, you're lying to me. You're far too self-centered for a suicide mission. What are your plans?"

"What do you care? Give me this and I'll be out of your hair. You won't hear from me again."

Dise shrugged. "If you go and kill yourself, *governor*," she said condescendingly, "make sure you leave your money to the cause."

Spratee smiled wryly. "Then we have a deal. Good. I am off to take care of some things before I leave. When will you have it?"

Dise shrugged. "This afternoon. Tomorrow at the latest."

"The sooner the better," he said.

"Have a hot date with Sumatta?"

He didn't rise to her taunt, he just stared at her.

"Fine. I'll contact you. And Spratee? I expect you to keep your word. This is it for us. I have other plans and they don't involve you anymore."

Spratee stood. He felt like skipping as he turned and walked out. He didn't skip, he walked. He didn't want her to see how happy she'd just made him or she'd reconsider getting the bomb just to deflate his happiness.

Killing himself had never been in the plans, though truth be told, he'd go down if it meant ending that murderous beast. Phonahyd bombs were always supplied in jackets for suicide missions, but that didn't need to be what they were used for. He just needed a few modifications to it.

The Philosophy Of Repetition

The building shook. It started as a low rolling rumble. Shenol looked around. It seemed to be a grade four quake. She'd have to check for minor damage later, but for now she ignored the disruption. They were too frequent to stir much activity unless they got up to at least a grade five.

Shenol wondered what it would take to get Arterians to take up Sumatta's offer. Only a couple million had reserved slots and some of the early slots had had no takers. She didn't know if they had time for everyone even if all the remaining slots were filled. Too many Arterians would die.

When a spatiatta made a cocoon, it filled its inner cavity with a green gel. It took a few hours to fill a single spatiatta. To seal an Arterian, the spatiatta pulled them into their folds and wrapped them in the liquid. The liquid solidified when exposed to air, so only so many could be made at a time and they couldn't be created ahead of time. This limited supply was a problem.

That's where she hoped the *draumr* would come in, but they had still not extended the field. No change in wavelength or power helped extend the field. They had reached its theoretical and practical limits. Waves simply expanded until they were no longer powerful enough. They'd have to have a Bahnder Tree every few miles through all twenty-four million square miles of Arter. There was only one Bahnder Tree and making more was technically impossible—the metal just didn't exist elsewhere on Arter.

The quake rolled on and so did Shenol's thoughts. She wasn't willing to accept that there wasn't a way. She had, after all, found a way to get the Cycle of Ages to all of Arter—repeaters... Repeaters! It might not be possible since this was a different type of wave, but it was a new solution and they could give it a try.

She grabbed her touchpad and opened a channel to Trellia. Their friendship had developed as much as the *draumr* over the last few years. They were like old friends now, and she loved having a friend, especially one as driven as she was.

Trellia answered quickly. "Hey girl! What do you have for me?"

"Can you make a repeater?" Shenol asked.

"That depends. What does it need to repeat... Oh!" Trellia's surprise quickly shifted into consideration. She tapped her fingers against her chin as she pondered. "I don't know, but it's worth a try. I'm going to come over," she said. "Let's talk on the way."

That meant Trellia would talk to herself and work out the problem. Shenol would be a good ear and ask questions at the right time—she was not the scientist, Trellia was. She hadn't always been a scientist, but had earned a degree after losing her bonded. It was then that she took over his project. She still hadn't found him.

Trellia grabbed her bag, slipped it over her shoulder, and hopped in her transport. It was only a ten minute flight to the Bahnderia, but every minute of brainstorming was valuable.

Shenol watched as Trellia sat back and closed her eyes as she started to talk, the soft yellow and blue lights of the aurora made her face look sickly, but she was far from it.

"We know that it harnesses life and is made of metal. That gives us the *attaten* and *ca'aten*. It'll be traveling through air and be bound to our saltwater-like bodies, giving us *oxaten* and *na'aten*. Those four cover the forces, except for gravity and we've figured out that's what the tree covers."

She took a deep breath. Shenol nodded.

"Since a repeater captures a signal and forwards it on, we need something which captures energy. That gives us *phoaten* since light contains energy. That's a lot of *aten* for one device.

But it doesn't tell us how it should be shaped."

"Like a lens?" Shenol suggested.

Trellia shook her head, discarding the idea. "We're not actually capturing light. We need something that captures waves of energy. How are we going to come up with something which uses an ancient energy source?" she said, then abruptly stopped brainstorming with herself.

"Strypan. We need Strypan. He knows the ancient ways."

"Your parent-in-law? The one you say is more than a little off and has his head in the clouds as much as it's in philosophy?"

"Yes," she said, giving a small laugh. "Exactly. Hold on."

Trellia put Shenol on hold, then came back after a couple minutes.

"He's happy to help. He's getting on his transport and heading over," she said. Behind her the aurora fell from sight as her transport descended. "I'm here. Looks like you're in the study. I'll meet you there."

Shenol sat back and smiled. After years of work, there was hope. Hopefully there was more than hope, there was a solution.

Trellia walked in, the only Arterian who did not knock on the Reader's door before entering. "I made it," she said.

A knock came at the door. It was soft and small. "Come in, Rax," Shenol called.

He peeked in the door with wide eyes. "I saw Trellia was here! Hi!" he said, running up to her and giving her a hug. "What's going on? Can I help? I'll be good. I promise."

"Do you ever repeat what I say?" asked Trellia, hunching over as if telling a secret.

"No," he said seriously, shaking his head vigorously.

"Well, today we are going to make a repeater. It's going to repeat everything the Bahnder Tree says to everyone on Arter. Doesn't that sound like fun?"

"Yeah!" he said, bobbing his head with equal vigor.

Growing perplexed, he added, "But the Bahnder Tree doesn't talk."

"It helps us talk, right?"

"Oh!" he said, faking comprehension. "Can I watch? I'll be quiet while the tree talks."

Trellia turned to Shenol, who smiled, giving assent. She turned back to Rax and gave him a big grin. "The Reader says yes."

"Yes! I get to be included. I am so going to be Next Reader when I get older. I just know it!"

"Show me the energy," Strypan said, appearing at the door. It was unusual for him to skip a friendly greeting. They looked at him surprised by his demeanor, he just stared back blankly. How could the man be so smart and yet be so oblivious?

Shenol stood up. "It's this way," she said and led them down the spiral path to the Bhander Tree.

Strypan seemed to light up like a kid as they circled around to the tree. He looked at Shenol and Trellia and quite solemnly said, "From my energy to yours, from my knowledge to yours. It has been a long time since I have seen this."

"You've seen the Bahnder Tree before?" Shenol asked. "I don't remember you coming."

"It's not a tree," Strypan said. "It's an energy fractal. I saw this generations ago. It's as magnificent today as it was then. Changed very little."

Shenol looked at Trellia when Strypan corrected her about the tree, but Trellia shook her head, signaling her not to address the correction. He was wrong on two accounts. It was a tree and it did not change, even after it housed Sumatta it returned to its exact shape. The Arterian was definitely more than a little off.

"What are you trying to do with it?" Strypan asked.

"Communicate," Trellia said. "Its connection with gravitational force allows us to communicate through our minds." She hesitated in her explanation as Strypan walked over to the tree and traced patterns on its bark. "It does more," she said.

"Show me," Strypan said, turning away from the tree. "It does a lot more than you can imagine."

Trellia handed a *draumr* to Strypan and put one on her head. He mirrored her action and waited for instructions.

"Try to rest," she instructed. "That point between sleep and waking. That's where you want to be. It will take over then."

Strypan put his hands behind his back, closed his eyes, and meditated. Shenol leaned against the tree and relaxed.

Shenol looked around as she entered the wake-dream. Strypan was already there. They were standing on a large pearly box.

"What's this?" she asked.

"The energy fractal. We're on a small piece."

"How did you—"

"It's a dream. Our imagination is the limit. I wanted to see it close up."

"Um, okay. Draw your fingers like this," she said, zooming out.

Strypan zoomed out and followed her like an expert.

"Do you see our bodies?"

He nodded.

"Go a little farther out."

They did and their bodies disappeared.

"We can ascend here. Our bodies actually stop existing on Arter. We're safe here."

"For energy's sake, we're safe," he said. The statement seemed to have a different meaning when he said it, as if energy were the reason they were safe. She smiled at the thought. He knew exactly what it meant. So long as they had energy, they were safe here.

"Now you know how it works," she said.

He acquiesced with a head bow.

"Let's go back."

They zoomed in, putting themselves where they were standing.

"To wake—"

He cut her off. "Open your eyes. Yes, I know."

Strypan opened his eyes and Trellia broke from the wake-dream, stepping away from the tree.

"One belief, two paths. Science unites with faith to strike a balance between the last end and the last beginning."

"What?" Shenol asked.

"I said I like it," Strypan explained. "Hold on," he added.

Strypan jaunted off toward his transport and came back with an array of wind chimes. One for each letter of the alphabet.

"'Bahnder' means 'a thing which binds.' We need a word which binds the Bahnder." He tapped the fingers of one hand against his leg, the fingers of the other against his temple. "No, more than that. We need a word which repeats the thing which is bound. Extends it."

"The Bahnder Tree binds life, not just anything. Does that help?" Shenol offered.

"Yes, it does. The word you want will mean extending or magnifying the binding of life. The closest word I can think of is 'enliven'. Except, in Sumattan, it has a letter repeated three times."

"Is that a problem?"

He held up the bag of letters. "When you only have one of each, yes. I'll need to go back to my place. Why don't you come with me? Unel needed to rework the metal when it was done. My guess is that you'll have to work to get all those *aten* in one piece."

"Can I go?" an eager Rax chimed in from the benches surrounding the tree.

"We'll all go," Shenol said.

"Can I go with him? He's funny," he said, pointing to Strypan.

"Only if you'll be funnier than me," Strypan said and winked at Shenol.

They all headed to the transports. Strypan and Rax headed off first, Trellia and Shenol following closely.

Shenol looked at Strypan's house and marveled. A wall of *aten*? An algae door? ... there were so many unbelievable things in the Arterian's home that she couldn't take it all in. Most amazing was the array of letters in his letter room. Did he know that Sumatta made these shapes when talking? Was he a Reader? He couldn't be—he had gender and she was the first to keep her gender.

Strypan grabbed the letters for his word and started twisting them into each other.

"It doesn't work? That's the wrong word?" Shenol asked.

"Not the wrong word. I just don't see the pattern. Every word can be formed from letters, but only if the letters are arranged in the right order. This word has eight letters."

"That's a lot of combinations!" Rax said.

"Permutations, my dear boy," Strypan said, roughing up Rax's hair.

Rax smoothed his hair and giggled. "See, he's funny."

Strypan put his hands on his hips and glared at Rax. "I thought you were supposed to be the funnier one."

"I was laughing funnier than you. That's the same," Rax said defensively.

"Can I try?" Shenol interrupted.

"Sure. I love unexpected results," he said, handing her the letters.

Shenol folded them together in three tries. The final shape was like a tower with four wings coming down the side. In each wing, there was a small section just big enough for an *aten* and a larger gap in the middle. It looked sharp, aware, poised.

"How did you do that so easily?" Strypan asked as he took the device and studied it.

"I read Sumattan, Strypan."

"Oh, yes. I imagine that helps. I only know a few words from chats with Readers over the years. It would be helpful to know how to do that, but nonetheless, here you go," he said, handing the device to Trellia.

An earthquake shook the house jarringly. His wind chimes rattled in a storm of sound and sparkles. Strypan abruptly turned and walked into his main room. It would have been a living room to most, but, well, Strypan was always a little different about what things were used for. The living room was more like a complex study and research center.

Shenol and Trellia followed. Rax ran behind him at his ankles.

On the wall was a map of Arter. A very old map drawn by a master artist. Strypan had drawn circles all over the map and pieces of yarn hung from pins spread throughout the map. He looked at his touchpad, measured two strands of yarn from a skein laying on the ground below the map, cut them, then put two pins on the map to hold the yarn. He added a third, the pin affixed to where his house would be on the map, then drew circles using the yarn as a radius.

He shook his head and turned to them, worry in his eyes. "We have two years at most. The epicenter is moving down the mountains and faster."

"What happens then?" Trellia asked.

"The mountains erupt," Strypan said plainly. "What else would happen?"

"Then this had better work," Shenol said, holding up the repeater prototype.

Strypan's touchpad sounded off. He looked at the message and said, "I need to be going now. You have what you need."

"Thank you. We need to get to the Dreamoria. I need to get this prototype working."

Noal's Test

Strypan always said that there was a balance to life. For every action, an equal and opposite. For every force, an equal and opposite. For every life, an equal and opposite. The reverse electromagnetic resonance shield had never been finished, it had been discovered about a year ago, before Noal had finished it when the force of reversing ripped the poor fool who'd collided with it in shreds. Noal had been working on actually finishing it while he lied to his superiors about the difficulty of scaling the weapon. Was that truth with an equal and opposite lie? Noal chuckled at the thought.

Strypan had always taught him to be true to himself, to know himself. Strypan had warned Noal that the military would try to change him and that the only way to handle that was to be himself. The truth was that Noal was not a murderer, he was a creator and being a creator necessarily meant he was not a murderer. That meant that a little lie brought a balance to the universe—his universe if nothing else.

It had worked. The lie, that is. His resonance shield followed suit. Now it was a gravioelectromagnetic resonance field and when someone collided with it, they weren't killed, but they also could not get through. Whatever force hit it was repelled equally and opposite.

Noal thought of it as an artistic weapon. Every bit of energy left a trace through spacetime. That tracer could be seen as a phantom trail. That phantom trail could be followed backwards by following the gravitational signature of the object. The effect was that the object moved back along its own time trail.

He couldn't have it work exactly that way. They would test it and that didn't provide the solution they were looking for; it didn't kill everything. So, he changed the frequencies, making the device more responsive up to the size of an Arterian. Below that size, the object would have its trail reversed so rapidly that the object was destroyed. Above that and his commanders would not be happy as it followed its own course back its time trail.

Tough for them. It was his invention, so it'd work the way he wanted. He would face the backlash of upsetting his commanders, but he could not face the backlash of failing to be true to himself.

Now, he was ready to make it big enough to cover the entire city.

"Are you done yet?" someone said from behind him. He jumped and turned around, then saluted. The man was an officer of some rank, but he didn't have a name tag or rank insignia. He was an older man with wizened eyes whose unsettling look said that he held a grudge against Noal.

"No, sir. I have one more thing to do."

"It will have to wait. We need it now."

"But—"

"Cut it, Noal. We're going to end this war in seventy-two hours and your invention is going to win it for us. You're done tinkering with it. We've been watching and you haven't made any progress in a month. Show us what it can do."

That was going to be hard. He hadn't solved the one problem they'd wanted solved. They wanted it to go city wide. That was the last problem he was working on and the last unsolved problem.

Is this a lie with an equal and opposite truth? he thought.

"That's an order, Noal. Follow me," the man said, turning and marching off. Noal raced to follow the man, who quite curiously never referred to Noal by rank. The man rounded a bunker and led him to the Attatar Military Base's airport field. It had been cleared of all aircraft.

"Set it up in the middle," the man ordered, pointing at what he defined as the middle. "There's a power supply there for you."

Noal jogged out to the power supply, set his device down next to it and hooked it up to the generator. It had the correct power cables already set up. They had been watching him carefully.

He flipped the switch on the generator. As soon as the generator turned on, the air around him glimmered and wobbled. A force field appeared around thirty feet from the generator. It wasn't really a force field—it was the light seen bending from the gravitational force exerted by the resonance field that they saw. The field itself permeated the entire area, but only at its outer limit was it weaponized.

"It's ready," Noal yelled.

The man had not followed Noal and was outside the field. He pulled out his gun and fired a single shot at Noal. The bullet hit the field and exploded. Technically, it hit the field and accelerated backwards on its own time trace so quickly that it shredded itself into pieces. The man just saw the bullet explode.

The man looked pleased. He yelled at Noal. "Come out."

"I can't. I have to turn it off to come out. I haven't finished that."

The man cocked his head to the side as General Byelt approached. The general stood to the man's right, whispered something to him, and they both bobbed their heads concurring.

The general gave a signal with his hand and they both turned their attention to the sky. Three aircraft changed course and headed toward the strip. They were coming in too fast to land. They were coming in for a run, and they were targeting Noal.

Noal shook his head with disbelief. This man was crazy. Thank Sumatta Noal knew this would work. But how much heat would come through? Theoretically the heat would be affected the same, but heat was a messy energy in nature—

almost everything generated heat, quite often due to friction.

Noal held his breath as a dozen missiles shot through the air and slammed into the resonance shield and exploded. The aircraft turned sharply after releasing their payloads.

It didn't get hot! It looked like the flames were riding the magnetic field and being propelled back out into space. It looked like that to Noal, who knew how it worked, but to the general and the man, it would just look like an explosion on the surface of the shield. This was working better than he had expected.

"Make it bigger," the man commanded.

"I need a bigger generator," Noal called back. That had been his problem. The device harnessed an energy source to create its protective field, but getting a large enough supply had been a problem Noal couldn't work around, so he'd been working on increasing the output of the device relative to the same energy input.

The general gave another hand signal and a tractor trailer pulled around a bunker.

Noal turned off the smaller generator, and the tractor trailer pulled up next to him. The huge truck was filled with a massive generator in the back. Noal hooked up his device to the generator and waited for the driver to leave the area.

By his estimate, this would cover the entire airfield. It would surround the general and the man. He hopped up on the truck and pushed the power button. The generator started up. The lights on the device indicated all was operational, that it was generating a field from the power being supplied by the generator.

"It's working," Noal yelled.

No one saw the force field boundary.

General Byelt looked at his touchpad for a moment, said something to the man, then signaled to end the demonstration.

Noal was sure they'd caught his lie. The field must have gone too far and someone walked into it. This could get very bad. He powered off the generator and the lights went off on the device.

General Byelt waved for him to approach. Noal obeyed and jogged up to the two officers. General Byelt greeted him. "That went four city blocks in every direction. We can get enough generators to power your shield all over Attatar or any other city in the alliance. You've changed the course of the war, boy."

Noal nodded. "Noone told me we had larger power supplies I could use, sir. That would have helped a lot. What do I do next, general, sir?"

"That depends. Is this your only one?"

"No, sir. I have five more just like it in my workshop."

"Different makes and models? That's what we assumed they were."

"No, sir. They're the same. They'll work the same as this one."

"Why did you waste your time making them?"

Because I was wasting time, Noal thought. The general seemed to read his mind.

"Nevermind, son. I don't want to know. We're just lucky you have one for every city-state in the alliance. It was good thinking, even if you didn't intend it."

"Thank you, sir," Noal said, happy to let the general feign ignorance.

"Take the week off. The war will be over by the time you get back. Everyone else has had home rest, go get yours. Great work, sergeant."

Sumatta as his witness, Noal never ran so fast in his life. He got off the base and was on a transport to see Noselar before they could figure out how he'd tricked them.

* * *

Firing a shot at Noal had been sublime perfection. It didn't matter that Noal was in a protective bubble. Tanseor had been aching to do that for decades. His weapon showed a lot of promise except it wasn't what Noal claimed it would be. Tanseor could see that, but General Byelt had believed. There was no need to dissuade him of his beliefs. Sooner or later the truth would come out and Noal would do one of two things: face the general's wrath or run. If he ran, he'd run to his mentor and that would be a perfect time to catch them both.

"What do you think?" General Byelt asked.

"We haven't tested a sustained attack on it. I must use energy to rebuff the attack. We'll have to be able to ensure the power supply doesn't run out during an attack."

"Good point. A backup?"

"Why not hook it up to the main power grid?"

"Too risky. If it takes that down, then the whole city will be without power. Attatar would fall to the enemy in a heartbeat."

It was a good point. Not likely to happen, but if you didn't understand how a weapon worked, you had to consider every possible ramification. Arterians could be rather dull. You had to break things down for them, give them small chunks that they could take in.

"Could we section off part of the grid. Insulate it from the rest of them?" Tanseor suggested.

General Byelt pointed at Tanseor. "Yes, sir. That's a great idea!" He pointed at someone else standing nearby. "You there, soldier. I want a portion of the grid partitioned off for our use. Find the people who can do it and get it done. I want it done within the hour. And get one of these devices to every city-state in the alliance. I want them there on the fastest craft we have. This war is going to end."

The soldier ran off and the general looked back to Tanseor.

"Why was he delaying?"

"He doesn't want to kill."

"He's in the military, for Sumatta's sake. What did he think was going to happen? I swear, if he delayed for that, I'm going to lay into that boy. Doesn't he know that every delay meant more deaths? He's been working on that project for a year. You can't save everyone, but you sure as Sumatta can get off your ass and save as many as you can."

"He's only twenty-two. We were idealists at that age too," Tanseor said, then chuckled. "I even used to believe in gods. Now if I ever found one, I'd kill it."

"The only god I know is myself," General Byelt replied.

"I think we're all gods in some way. I just wish some weren't," Tanseor said and laughed again.

General Byelt had no clue what was in store for him. He was one of those arrogant types who was more interested in getting his way than finding out what was right. Tanseor had seen that type when he was twenty-two, too. He'd kill them now if he found those pretentious fools. There were quite a few he'd kill if given the chance. Right now, though, he was looking for a chance at just two: Noal and Strypan.

That chance was here. He was sure of it. Noal would go home for his leave, but he'd contact his mentor and confess. They would be together. He had to be there too.

"I'm going off base for a bit. I have something to do," Tanseor said.

"Fine. I'll contact you if I need anything," General Byelt said.

Solutions

"Are we there yet?" Rax asked.

Trellia groaned. "Yes, Rax. That's it," she said pointing at a building in the dark obsidian cavern in front of them.

"Really? I want to see," Rax said, tilting his head left and right, trying to peek between Trellia and Shenol's shoulders. "I can't see it. I'm too short."

"Feel that? We're descending," she said as the transport descended towards its target landing pad.

"Finally," Rax said of the twenty-minute flight. "It took forever." He flopped back in his chair throwing his arms to the sides, as dramatic as ever.

Trellia and Shenol laughed, much to Rax's consternation, as the ship slowed and came to a rest on the landing on the pad. Rax's door was open in a flash, and he leaped out.

"What is this place?" he asked, looking around and arching his head back to look up at the obsidian cavern's walls.

"I'll take care of him," Shenol said to Trellia. "You just do your thing. I'm so excited."

"Thank you," Trellia said. She opened the door to the Dreamoria and went to a table in the back of the room. She pulled the enlivening device out of her pocket, set it on the table, then grabbed some bits of metal used for the *draumr* and began replicating the prototype.

The letters might have fit together, but the repeater, like the *draumr* needed to be one piece. Just like Unel had done when Strypan gave him the word for the *draumr*, Trellia formed the letters, then started to meld them together until she had one continuous piece.

"This is where you started, right?" Shenol asked as she came up behind Trellia, her voice soft.

Trellia looked around as she considered the question. It was a simple building with much of the metal taken out, replaced by different synthetics which would not conduct electricity. This wasn't the first Dreamoria, but it was the Dreamoria. It was the one where he had perfected the device before his disappearance.

She looked behind her and smiled affectionately. Rax had curled up on a couch and fallen asleep. It would be a boring place to him. It was a lab with very little, if anything, to play with. In all these years, she had never brought her best friend to the Dreamoria. This was the first time Shenol had seen the place.

"Where he started, yes," Trellia answered.

"Right. This is a really important location."

"What do you mean?" Trellia asked.

"You chose this spot after the lightning accident, right? Inside the largest obsidian cavern on Arter? Because glass isn't a strong conductor of electricity. That's true, but..."

She stopped for a moment as if she could barely contain herself. She took a deep breath before giving up her secret discovery.

"Can't it be used to broadcast a signal? To repeat? Like an energy source or something?"

Yes, Trellia thought. Its earthiness needed *ca'aten*, its strength, *na'aten*, its translucency, *phoaten*, its brittleness, *oxaten*, but that left *attaten* of the *aten* needed for the enlivening repeater. Maybe *attaten* was just a necessary ingredient. Either way, that meant she could use it and, more specifically, use it as a massive repeater.

An air raid siren sounded. Trellia ran to the window and peered out through the open end of the cavern. As she looked on, the ground began to shake and flakes of obsidian came falling down like a heavy rain pounding the roof. She lost her footing and held onto the wall to keep her balance.

Off in the distance, battlecraft were flying toward the city from the south. The siren and shaking of the quake woke Rax, and he started crying. Buildings erupted in fire, some collapsing, others dropping downward a bit. They weren't under attack from whoever was attacking the city yet, so the other damage must have been from the quake. This quake would grade out at at least a six, she was sure. It might make a seven.

"Air raid," Trellia said. "Get down!"

Shenol ran to the couch and jumped on it, grabbing Rax and pulling him close to her.

The wall on the left side of the window dropped a foot, shattering the glass and tearing the wall into two parts. Trellia fell backwards as the house screeched with the agony of being torn. She held onto the floor, gripping tightly as the quake rolled to a calm.

Trellia got to her knees, then stood up and walked slowly toward the split wall and looked out across Attatar through the window opening.

The raid had not stopped. Aircraft were approaching faster. They were almost to Attatar's borders. The quake might be over, but the attack was about to begin. She moved back a distance from the window, got down on her knees, and waited as she watched the imminent attack approach.

At first, she didn't believe what she saw. She blinked with disbelief, trying to reset her eyes and correct her vision. The airships started to go back home. But they were flying backward, almost as if they'd run into a bouncing wall. They kept going, too, flying backward as fast as they had come.

"Shenol, come look at this! They're flying backward."

Shenol was on the couch comforting Rax. He'd stopped crying, but was still shaking and pointing at the sundered wall as he crouched up against Shenol. She patted him on the head, gave him a kiss on his cheek, and walked over to look, motioning for him to stay put.

They both watched speechlessly as the aircraft returned

home, flying backward. None changed course—they just kept going backward until they vanished out of sight.

The siren stopped.

"What just happened?" she whispered.

"I don't know, but I'd love to know who did it."

Figuring out who did it was easy. The military had just diverted an attack with no loss of life using a new shielding weapon. There was only one who had the knowledge and the principles to do that. It had to be him.

"Noal," Trellia answered. "Strypan will be proud."

An entire city surrounded by a force field like that. That meant they had a huge central power supply. They might be able to use that to power a larger enlivening repeater.

"I need to talk with him," she said.

"I need to get Rax back to the Bahnderia. I'll come back afterwards. He's had too much excitement for one day. Mind if I take your transport?"

"Nope. Go ahead," Trellia said.

Shenol picked up Rax and carried him to the transport.

* * *

Sometimes the simple solution was the best solution. Spratee didn't believe that was always the case in war. Sometimes you could use a simple solution to hide a much bigger solution. This was just such a time. Dise had delivered on time for the first time he could remember. He had the bomb.

The phonahyd bomb was about the size of a seat cushion, the shape of a box with two buttons on the top which had to be pressed at the same time to start the timer. The timer was set for ten minutes. He wasn't actually sure how to change it from the default time, but that didn't matter. Ten seconds or ten minutes and it would blow up. It didn't matter which of those it was.

The trick had been the trigger. He didn't want to be anywhere near when the device was triggered, and he didn't know in advance when it would have to be triggered, so he needed a way to remotely activate it. He had had to consult someone on the basis of needing an adjustment to a game controller. The man hadn't fully believed Spratee, but it didn't matter, he'd built the device.

The last step, getting the bomb into the Bahnderia, should have been the hardest, but the Reader had taken a sudden trip, leaving almost no one in the Bahnderia. She had suddenly come back, but then left again. That should give Spratee plenty of time.

Spratee walked in with a backpack, dressed in street clothes, acting like one of the faithful, and took a seat in front of the Bahnder Tree.

He took his backpack off, carefully nudged it under his seat, then looked at the tree.

The tree looked like it was made of crystals the color of a pearl, crystal that seemed metallic. Its branches bent around in smooth curves and the hollow trunk was almost perfectly round on the inside. The sky lights reflected against the inner facets of whatever it was made of, making it twinkle. It wasn't really tall for a tree, but not short either. It was a little shorter than the monster that called this place home.

He wondered if it would withstand the explosion. Despite everything he believed about Sumatta, the Bahnder Tree had been the celebration of couples' binding for as long as he or anyone else remembered. He had been bound in ceremony here to Noselar. He couldn't help but feel Arter would lose a part of itself with this, but it was part of Sumatta and everything Sumatta had to go. Its time had come and it was time to share the power with the world, find a balance that didn't involve the control of a murderous tyrant.

"Hi. I haven't seen you here before," a young boy said, plopping down next to Spratee. The boy must have been ten or eleven years old. He was tall for his age, but his youthful naiveté betrayed him as younger. Except for the height and hair color, he looked a little like Noal at that age. Noal had always been average, except for his almost white hair and gray eyes. This boy had dark muddy brown hair and brown eyes. He looked tired, as if he had been crying, but had that youthful resilient energy that moved beyond bad times into the good with little thought.

"It's been a long time since I have been here," Spratee said. "What are you doing here? Where are you parents?"

"They gave me up," he said nonchalantly. "When I'm old enough, I'm going to be the Next Reader."

"Why would you want to do that?"

The kid looked genuinely confused. "Who wouldn't?"

"I wouldn't. They don't even let you stay a boy."

The boy blushed and shook his head. "I don't care about my gender. Never felt like a boy or a girl or anything else. I just feel like me. But that," he said, pointing to the Bahnder Tree. "I always felt like I should be a Reader."

"Will there be a Reader in the next age?"

The kid blinked disbelievingly at what he clearly perceived to be a dumb question. "When the cocoons open, there will be even more Sumatta! The Reader will be the most important Arterian ever."

"Cocoons?" Spratee asked as perplexed by the statement as the kid made his question seem stupid. "You mean Arterians? They're going to be changed into sumattas?" The mere idea was horrific. That beast was turning Arterians into copies of itself? Spratee shivered.

"Huh? No. I don't know what is gonna happen with them. I mean the mount—" the boy stopped abruptly, his eyes growing wide, fearful. "I mean, I am not supposed to say. I'm going to be in so much trouble. Please don't tell."

"How about we make a deal," Spratee said. "You don't tell anyone you saw me and I won't tell anyone I saw you."

The kid nodded appreciatively.

"So, tell me about the mountains."

The kid bowed his head, sad that he'd told a secret he shouldn't. He gave in, likely assuming he'd already said too much anyway. "The mountains are baby sumattas. They're cocoons. They're gonna hatch and blow up the mountains, but we'll have more sumattas. It's going to be great."

By Sumatta itself, he thought, cursing. Nine more of sumattas. No, eight. Mount Sumat couldn't be a cocoon—that's where Sumatta lived. There would be nine sumattas. Not one, nine. His response to the boy was lackluster. "Yeah, great."

"I gotta go or I'm gonna be in more trouble. I wasn't supposed to tell. Don't tell. You promised!" the boy said, then ran off.

Spratee had a much bigger problem than being told on. He'd just planted a bomb to kill Sumatta, but Sumatta was going to make more sumattas—it already had—and his problem would skyrocket to all of them.

He wasn't sure how he felt about the sumattas. Only one was guilty of letting his mother die, but wouldn't all sumattas be the same as one? What was he going to do? Would he do anything? He'd have to think about it.

He got up, leaving the backpack snug under the chair, and headed out, deeper in thought than he had been in decades. Nine sumattas? Well, eight after that bomb went off.

Noal's Answer

"I'm home," Noal called.

"Yes, you are," Noselar said, getting up from the couch and giving him a hug. "It's so good to see you. There's some food on the counter."

"Thanks. Let me set my stuff down," he said, then headed to his room. She'd kept a room for him with a bed and a desk even though he'd never fully lived in the house. It wasn't much, but it felt like home. He tossed his duffle bag in a corner, then headed back out to the living room.

"There's a load off your back. Now get some food. I can't have you starving."

Noal grabbed a sandwich off the plate and took a bite.

"It's not like the military to just give someone a week's leave. Are they sure it's for a week this time?"

"They like my invention," Noal said as he chewed. Noselar frowned at him and he wiped his mouth leaving behind a smile. She never liked him talking with his mouth full. "The thing is, Nos, it doesn't work the way they think. It's not a weapon of death."

"You're in the military, Noal. *Everything* is a weapon of death."

"It doesn't have to be. They're going to see that soon enough. Sometimes you can win a war without killing everyone. Didn't Sumatta show us that? All those pods?"

Noselar took a deep breath and sighed with approval. "Noal, you have to be yourself. Whatever you do, never forget who you are. I love you."

Noal's touchpad sounded off. Incoming transmission. He groaned.

"It's General Byelt," he said, looking at Noselar. "They've

found out."

"Well, answer him," Noselar said.

Noal opened the connection.

"Anything else I should know, *sergeant*?" he demanded, the emphasis on Noal's rank coming across more as a threat than any degree of respect.

"No, sir. I stabilized the field to be harmless at certain masses. That was all. It reverses their momentum by applying a gravioelectromagnetic force to their spacetime wave equal and opposite to what they hit the shield with. It puts the agent out of play."

"That's what took you so long to build it, isn't it?"

"Yes, sir," he confessed.

"Son, you're in the military. You don't make plans and you don't change them," he began. He closed his eyes and recited. "Arsk, Paterntia, Tramex, Saerth, ..." He recited so many names that Noal lost count. When General Byelt stopped, he opened his eyes and looked at Noal. "Those are the names of Arterians who died while you took your time saving our enemy's lives. Son, when you get orders, you follow them. You don't modify them."

"Sir, yes sir," Noal said. The general was right. Those deaths were on him. He recognized some of the names. Those who'd gone out on missions and not come back. He'd been to their funerals. He'd killed them while delaying his device so that he could save lives. He knew it was part of the balance—some would die and some would live—but, it didn't make it easier to accept those who died.

"I thought the war would be over after this, son. I don't think it will be now. The enemy suffered no casualties. They won't think twice about trying to attack again. I'm calling you back. I want the weapon you were commanded to build, and I want it before the day is out."

General Byelt closed the connection leaving Noal with a deep hollowness. Was this part of the balance of the universe too? He had to make a device to kill as penance for making a device that didn't? He had to kill others as penance for killing his friends?

"Be yourself, Noal. If you don't, then who are you?" a surprise voice counseled.

Noal turned around and smiled. "Mentor! How'd you—"

"Noselar told me you were coming. Noal," he said, growing far too serious for Strypan. "I have taught you about the balance in life, but you have taught me about the harmony in life. It is time you teach yourself."

"What?"

"'Everyone seeks balance as if it is the natural order of things. Balance is not natural, imbalance is natural. Art brings imbalances together in a harmonious way. Do not seek balance, seek harmony.' You told me that."

"I never said that. I can understand it. I feel it, but I never said it."

Strypan took two steps forward, closed his eyes, and pressed something against Noal's head. "You're ready, my friend," Strypan said, then a burst of light and energy flashed in front of Noal. Both of them crumpled to the floor.

"Noal!" Noselar screamed, running for Noal.

There was a knock at the door.

She screamed again as she got to Noal, lifting him into her arms as she cried. "Noal!"

Another knock at the door.

"Not now!" she screamed.

"I'm sorry to disturb you," a man called through the door. "Is there something wrong? My name is Tanseor. I'm with the military. Can I help?"

"No! Leave me alone!"

"I'm here for Noal," he said.

She rested her sleeping Noal on the ground and opened the door, tears and fury in her eyes, her body shaking.

The man from the military was a little old man. They sent

him for Noal? Last time they sent two officers. Young and strong. He'd just done something to upset them. Why would they send this man?

"No, he left already. Some general wanted him," she lied.

"I see," the man said. "Thank you. Are you sure everything's ok?" he said, peeking around her body.

Another quake rippled through the building, shaking everything in its wake. A window in the front of the house shattered and a streak of lightning shot out from the sky, tearing through a tree dangerously close to Tanseor. He seemed to take that as a hint and turned around, leaving rapidly.

Lightning Strikes

Tanseor trailed Noal toward his home at a more than safe distance. When they were a few miles out, he took manual control of his transport and turned as if he were headed elsewhere, then rounded about and set down between Noal's house and another. They were a distance from each other, so no one would see his transport and he could approach unseen.

Noal's house had been secured. He had scoped it out after he identified Noal as his primary target and discovered security hidden throughout the house and a distance down the property. Approaching in any threatening fashion would trigger the alarms. Bringing any standard weapons would trigger the alarms. And since the Cycle of Ages, Strypan had erected a security screen around the perimeter to prevent sharpshooter attacks. Strypan was so ready for Tanseor that he'd even secured Noal's house.

That just meant that Tanseor needed to be ready for Strypan. He reached into his bag and pulled out a mechanical weapon with his special *attaten* ammunition and checked the chamber. This one was meant for close up. It had six shots and automatically reloaded. If he fired fast enough, he'd be able to get both of them before they had a chance to do anything.

Now he just needed to wait. Noal should be contacting Strypan at any moment. A bit later, Strypan would show up and...

Strypan's transport came into view traveling fast. He landed it adeptly on the landing pad and hopped out, moving quickly inside. He had anticipated Noal would be there. Tanseor could hear the surprise of those inside as Strypan entered.

Tanseor didn't have much time.

He got out of his transport and ran to within a few lengths of the door. He stopped to catch his breath. The body was too old to keep up with the spirit, though he was in better shape than he appeared, he just quite often played up his age to gain cooperation from others.

"Noal!" the woman screamed as Tanseor got to the door.

Tanseor knocked. It had to be now.

He knocked again. She told him to go away.

"I'm sorry to disturb you," he called through the door. "Is there something wrong? My name is Tanseor. I'm with the military. Can I help?"

He was going to have to shoot through the door. He didn't have much time. Strypan wasn't saying anything and she was screaming Noal's name.

The door opened. Tanseor spoke with her, but he wasn't focusing on what he said or what she said. He peeked around and noticed his two targets laying on the floor. He was too late.

It was time to get out of there. Fast.

A quake rumbled the ground and a bolt of lightning struck down from the sky, tearing into a tree next to him. He wasn't moving fast enough. Tanseor turned and scurried away, heading back to his transport.

He'd missed his opportunity. They had found him. He wouldn't have another opportunity. He had failed.

Pure Energy

Shenol sat on a couch across from Trellia in the Dreamoria. Trellia was in a stupor after receiving word that Noal and Strypan were in a coma like Col. She hadn't even asked to go see them. She was useless trying to figure out how to use the obsidian cavern to broadcast.

"You can only put it together in so many ways," Trellia said dejectedly.

"I know, but I have to believe there is a way."

"Only Sumatta knows," Trellia said, laughing wryly.

That was a great point. She hadn't meant it seriously, but it was true. "That's it. I'll ask Sumatta. Why wouldn't it help?"

Trellia shrugged. "It doesn't know where Unel is and doesn't know how to get Noal or Strypan or even Col back. Sumatta doesn't know everything."

"It knows Arter and it knows the *aten*. I'm going in."

Trellia grew quiet, reflective. Shenol placed the *draumr* on her forehead, set the *aten* in the energy emitter, and dropped into a wake-sleep. As always, she envisioned herself in the Bahnderia. She appeared there at the center of the Bahnder Tree.

She envisioned herself sinking into the water under the Bahnder Tree, traveling across Arter to Mount Sumat, and appearing at the pool beside Sumatta. In a moment, she was next to Sumatta.

The inside of the dark cavern showed a lot of wear and tear. Apparently, the devastation of the hatching cocoons hit Sumatta too.

"There are not enough capsules of life," Sumatta said.

"You're going to let everyone else die?" a shocked Shenol said.

Sumatta scowled. It squished its head down, aiming it forward, and hunched a little. It was very weird and very unnerving to be scowled at like that.

"Arterians not coming for them."

That was true. Shenol had misunderstood again and questioned her god. She was not being a good Reader.

"I am sorry, Sumatta," she said. "We have a chance to save lives. We have a device that can help. It uses the Bahnder Tree to connect minds and ascend to the skies. We will be safe there, but it doesn't go far enough. We need to make something that repeats the signal to save all of Arter."

Sumatta nodded. It perked its head up and hunched a little to lean forward.

"You need more Pure Energy. I can give you more."

"Pure Energy? *Attaten*? How many do you have?"

"Not *attaten*. *Attaten* have Pure Energy, they are not Pure Energy. Few *attaten* have been made on coming from the Cycle of Ages. I have Pure Energy."

"Can you show me?"

"Yes," Sumatta said, doing its bowing nod movement again. "We will go to the Bahnderia."

Sumatta wrapped around Shenol and carried her through the waterway to the Bahnder Tree, lifted up into the tree, melded with it and formed the shield around the building, then lifted up, its tentacles keeping it hovering above the pool.

"Go to obsidian. Activate device."

Shenol half woke from the wake-dream, enough to say, "Turn it on."

Trellia heard her and turned on the device even though it was not connected to the obsidian cavern. When she turned on the device, all of Arter was visible. As if the device had magnified it to cover the entire planet. Shenol went back into the wake-dream completely. "What was I not doing?"

"You are not Sumatta. The Bahnder Tree draws Pure Energy to Arter. I use the Bahnder Tree. I can be your repeater."

Shenol laughed. "So, I don't even need my device, huh?"

Sumatta's wings seemed to shrug. "Maybe not. It works."

"We can save them all," Shenol said.

"I told you. Sumatta is bringer of life, protector of life."

A bright flash lit up the Bahnderia and Sumatta disappeared in a puff of light. The whole dream disappeared in the light and Shenol was kicked out into space. She righted her body, stopping it from tumbling backwards, then took control by changing the zoom. Shenol ascended and looked into the Bahnderia. Sumatta was in the waterway. It hadn't made it out. It was in trouble.

Shenol zoomed back in on Mount Sumat, envisioning herself going through the walls, then appearing before the Swarm. She descended, showing her wake-dream existence and yelled into the cavern. "To the waterway! Sumatta needs you!"

The Swarm erupted in song, a song of different forms of the word Sumatta. The Song of Sumatta sounded like a war cry. The Swarm took flight. Billions of them from every mount as the song carried across Arter. They formed a series of moving sheets across Arter, all headed to Attatar, all headed to Sumatta.

City governments sounded their own alarms as the Swarm took to the sky. Sumna raised its new shield, but it was too far north; none of the Swarm would cross it. Skycraft were scrambled into the air, armed and ready. The Swarm quickly overcame the aircraft, ripping them apart and leaving the cocooned body of its crew on the ground below.

The waterway swarm was the first to get to Sumatta. It began to spin around it faster and faster until they became like a spinning blade growing in radius, cutting through the rock. The swarm ate through the rock to the surface, then lifted Sumatta into the air. The arriving Swarm enveloped Sumatta as its body was brought up, surrounding it completely.

The Swarm of billions blotted out the aurora and formed layered spheres around Sumatta. The land grew dark. The Swarm carried its hive mother back to Mount Sumat and continued swarming around it as if giving part of their energy to the hive mother. Some of the swarm started to drop. Dead. They were giving their energy to Sumatta and dying to do it.

After far too long, Sumatta pressed its wings to the ground and pushed, lifting itself up. It arched its body as it was finally able to stand. It was weak, out of energy. Scales had been blown off of its skin. A thin, viscous fluid leaked out of its body from its wings to its skin. Sumatta was bleeding. Shenol's eyes watered as she looked at the tatteredness that was her god, the suffering that was her god.

Sumatta collapsed on its tentacles, slouched down heavily, then toppled over. The electricity lighting its body stopped. All movement stopped, then it gave a final song with its last breath, a soft melody. The Swarm picked it up, repeating it. They circled around Sumatta's body in a spiral as they mastered the melody, then burst out through the tunnels of Mount Sumat and into the sky. They flew across Arter in every direction singing Sumatta's last song. A peaceful melody of hope, forgiveness, and agony spread across the land. No Arterians could escape it, no small creature did not feel it, no sleeping babe was not woken by its touch. The Mounts of Arter echoed with its tone.

The tops of the Mounts of Arter—all of them except Sumatta's—exploded. The cocoons had heard.

Shenol zoomed back to existence in the Dreamoria and leaped up.

"We have to go! Now," she screamed. "It's happening."

Bits of lava, rocks, ash, and other debris that shot up into the atmosphere was starting to fall. The aurora electrified the volcanic mass as it hit the sky, blanketing the land with tentacle-sized lightning.

She didn't give Trellia time to question or argue. She

grabbed her and pulled her to her transport. When she turned the ship on, the news reported that the Falls of Attadore had collapsed, dragging half the city into the ocean. *The Swarm would have cocooned Arterians*, she thought. It all seemed like a horrible nightmare come to life through Sumatta's death.

"What's going on?" Trellia said, her voice hollow and dispassionate.

"Sumatta is dead. The mountains are hatching. They're going to hatch more sumattas. We have to get out of here. We're going to the Isle of Lights."

"That's on an island in the south. How's that going to help us?"

"It's as far as we can go away from all the mountains."

"They won't let us in. There's the war."

"We're refugees. They have to let us in. It's all over the news."

"Why can't the swarm put us in cocoons? Why do we have to run?"

"We still have work to do. Our job is to help the Swarm save as many Arterians as it can."

"Then we go to Attatar. We go to Noal and save my son and parent-by-bonding. We can tell the Swarm to save them first."

Shenol nodded and changed trajectory, turning northwest. She lifted higher to fly over the debris from the volcanic explosion and took in the sight as they passed over the top of one of the mounts. Lava rolled down the sides of the mountain, the bowl of which was bubbling with pure liquid fire. She wasn't sure how the cocoons survived the lava. Forests were burning and rivers were boiling away under the heat.

The Swarm had a small honor guard around each mountain, others were scouring the cities, cocooning Arterians. A small, angry contingent zipped up to Shenol's transport, but recognized her and left them alone.

When they got to Noal's house, Noselar greeted them. She

was infuriated. "Where did they go? How can you come into my house and take my son?"

"You're saying Noal's gone. Like he vanished?" Trellia asked.

"Yes, and you were the only one who knew he was still here. Well, you and that old guy."

"Old guy?"

"Yes. Name was can-see-or or something. Tanseor, yes, that's it. Very old and—"

"The man who said he was the Igri Tufuer? He was here looking for Noal? What did you do," Shenol interrupted, wholly excited.

"I told him to leave. He said he was with the military and had come to get Noal. No general is going to send an old man to retrieve a boy. Something was wrong with him."

Noselar was smart. Something was wrong with that man. Sumatta had said he was not the Igri Tufuer.

"Where is he now?" Shenol asked.

Noselar shrugged. "He left. Almost got hit by lightning. Serves him right," Noselar said. "He was walking. You might be able to catch him," she said, pointing toward the door.

Shenol thanked Noselar, went to her transport, and took manual control, heading out along the Tanseor's path.

The Sumattas Must Die

"Dise!" Spratee yelled from the edge of the compound. A guard's hand on his chest prevented him from getting in. "Dise! I have info you need," he pleaded.

The guard pushed him back.

"Give it up, old man," he said. "She's said she doesn't want to see you."

"Tell her there are more sumattas," Spratee said growling through gritted teeth. "Tell her now!"

The guard whispered something to another guard and the guard jogged off into the compound.

"Just wait here," the remaining guard said.

Dise had come a long way from her role as principal and leader of an underground rebellion. She had moved up quickly even from the last dirty hovel he'd seen her in a few weeks ago. This compound was huge, housing thousands of Arterians who looked well trained. They were preparing for something big. It had to be an assault on Sumatta. *That won't be necessary*, he thought, quite pleased with himself. He had a new mission for them. The sumattas must die. The species needed to be wiped from the face of Arter for Arterians to be truly free.

Dise did come. The other guard trailing behind her along with three more guards.

"What is it, Spratee?" she said, exasperated.

"Let me in. We need to talk. The mountains. They have cocoons in them. Cocoons filled with sumattas. We're going to have eight of them on our hands."

She laughed at him. "You've lost your mind."

"I have a plan," he said. "We can be rid of sumattas forever. Let me in and we'll talk about it."

Dise sighed. "I'll tell you what, Spratee. I'll waste the fuel on you to have you take a transport and show them where these cocoons are. If you can show me a cocoon, I'll consider your plan." She paused then sneered at him. "You had better be able to show me a cocoon."

She wasn't as dumb as he thought. Proof? Anyone would want proof. He wasn't sure how to get into a mountain was the only problem. It couldn't be that hard. He'd just have them fly around until he saw an entrance.

"You three take him," she said, pointing to the three new guards who accompanied her to the gate. Two of them stepped forward, turning and taking him by the upper arms and dragging him forward. He stumbled and they kept walking, not giving him a chance to gain his footing.

"Hey, show some respect. I was your governor," he pleaded.

The men snorted as they followed the third guard to a transport and shoved Spratee inside.

"Where to?" the third guard asked as if humoring Spratee.

"Mount Sumat," Spratee said. It was far enough away that he would have some time to think about how to find an opening.

"No," the man said. "We'll go there," he said, pointing to the nearest mountain. "It's closer."

The transport lifted up and turned, heading toward the mountain.

By Sumatta itself, Spratee thought. *They don't want me to show them the cocoons. They don't believe. They're taking me to my death.*

The men were watching him carefully, so he pretended to doze off and turned his body like he was trying to get a better positioned. He was trying to get a better position, but not to sleep. The fools hadn't buckled up in the open-air transport. Spratee suddenly lunged forward and pushed one of the men out of the transport. The surprised man flailed as he went over the edge, trying to grab whatever he could while the other man tackled Spratee.

Spratee leaned down and reached into the holster at his ankle and pulled out his gun, turning it backwards and firing into the man's abdomen.

"You are not going to kill me," he screamed, then turned to aim at the pilot as the man on Spratee's back rolled off, grabbing his abdomen. The pilot's gun was already at Spratee's head.

"You're wrong," the pilot said, then fired.

Journey To The Isle Of Lights

Trellia watched Shenol lift off, then turned to Noselar. How could the woman think she would take Noal and Strypan? Where would she hide them? What purpose would she have? The whole exchange seemed a weird and an unnecessarily rude interruption.

"I did not take them. I think they ascended. Maybe some of Noal's military research helped them do it without me. He was always so bright and creative. I'll have to check when I get back to the Dreamoria, if I can. I wonder why they didn't take me. Tell me what happened."

Another quake roiled the ground and the main living room window shattered. They both screamed. "Maybe tell me later. We need to get out of here. Can we use your transport? Grab what you can hold. Let's go. I'll get it started," she said, racing to the transport.

A couple of minutes later, Noselar returned. She hadn't grabbed many things. It looked like she'd brought mostly memory trinkets or family heirlooms. She got in the transport and they lifted off, setting course for the Isle of Lights.

Trellia opened a communication line to Shenol.

"I found his transport," Shenol said.

"And?"

"He was gone. I'm on my way back to the house."

"We left the house. Let's rendezvous at the Isle of Lights."

"Sounds good. See you there. Stay safe."

Soon, everyone in her life that hadn't ascended and still mattered would be in one place. None of them her family. Maybe she deserved that. She'd done so much wrong in her life. Maybe when they ascended, they had decided not to include her. It would be a fitting punishment.

What was she really doing now? Trying to escape the end of the world by going to an island. The island would get hit hard by the weather. She doubted anyone on the Isle of Lights would survive.

They needed to ascend or get into cocoons. She abruptly tapped the controls and instructed the transport to set course for the Dreamoria.

Maybe it wasn't time to ascend or get in a cocoon.

She opened the line back to Shenol.

"Meet me at the Bahnderia," she said. "I know how we can do the most good."

"On my way," Shenol said and dropped the connection.

The flight there was not as easy as it was with Shenol. The Swarm approached more than once, and she had to take manual control a few times to avoid the heat and lightning in the air. She made it and the transport set down still in one piece.

"I need to get some *draumrs*," she said to Noselar. "Just wait here."

She had four *draumrs* ready for use. She picked them up. There had been one for Trellia and Shenol, and a backup just in case for each of those. This time there was Noselar, so she would need one. They only needed three, but since there were four, she grabbed them all and put them in a bag with the energy emitters and some extra *aten*.

She hopped in the transport and set the bag on Noselar's lap, then set in course for the Bahnderia.

Shenol was already there when they landed. "Here, let's go to the tree. We can do a lot in the wake-dream state and when we're done, we can just ascend. The only thing is..." She took a deep breath. "If the Bahnder Tree is destroyed, I don't know if we can come back."

"I've lost Sumatta," Shenol said. "I will take the risk for what Sumatta stood for."

"I've lost my son. He was a good man," Noselar said,

whimpering. "I'll do what good I can in his name."

"I've lost my bonded, my child, and my parent-by-bonding. I just want to see them," Trellia said. "I'll do what I can."

Trellia thought she heard Noselar whimpering again, but she wasn't, she was smiling, comforted. It wasn't Noselar who was whimpering. Trellia arched her head to the side to peer behind Noselar at the source of the sound. Under a bench in the background was a little leg, bloody and scratched. It was shaking.

"By Sumatta itself. Are you ok?" she said, running over to the boy.

He shirked back from her touch.

"Rax?" Shenol asked as she ran up. "Rax, come here," she said, taking a commanding voice.

He shook his head. He must have been very near when the explosion happened.

"Next Reader," Shenol pronounced. "Next Reader, you must be as strong as Sumatta is strong. Come here and be Next Reader."

Rax twisted his head, peeking out wide-eyed, his expression asking if what he'd just heard was real. He came to life and started squirming out in between oohs and ouches. "Really? Really for real? I'm the Next Reader?" he said. His voice was scratchy from smoke inhalation.

Shenol maintained her grace, keeping an air of authority. "Since you've shown the strength to come out, yes. Welcome, Next Reader. Sumatta has a task for us. You will join us, but you must listen to me."

Rax bobbed his head rapidly in agreement, wiping away his tears and leaving smudges on his face.

Trellia handed the fourth *draumr* to Shenol. It was probably best that his mentor give it to him so she could give instructions.

Shenol handed the *draumr* to Rax who received it with an air of dignity befitting the Next Reader and listened attentively.

"When you lean against the tree, you will go into the wake-dream state. Listen for my voice."

He nodded and they all leaned against the tree and entered the wake-dream.

Out Of Time

Shenol entered the wake dream first. She was ready when Rax appeared. He didn't appear with her. She sensed him and focused on him. He was in his room picking up his toys. It seemed to be a memory from years ago. It was not the Bahnderia and he looked about half his age.

"Rax? It's time to stop playing. Put your fingers in front of you and act like you're pushing away space by pulling your fingers apart. That's zooming in and out. Zoom out until you can see Arter."

A moment later, he was back to his ten-year-old self and zipped past her, laughing. He came back. "Sorry. It goes fast," he said.

"The Swarm is dying," she said, pointing at the planet. They were able to sense the spatiatta falling, their energy spent as they used it to generate the green liquid faster. At the rate they were going, the Swarm would be gone by the end of the day.

"Your job is to bring them *attaten*. They need it to—"

"Make babies," Rax blurted out.

"No. Not make babies. To live. *Attaten* is the life *aten*, not the baby *aten*."

Rax blushed. "So, you want me to get the *attaten* to the Swarm?"

"Yes, do you..." She stopped abruptly; he didn't wait. He was suddenly down by the Swarm. She zoomed in to watch. He had somehow mastered the wake-dream within minutes of entering it. He zipped around, walking through things, skipping to distances far apart, and seeming to do all of that while maintaining an overhead view. How he'd managed to do that was remarkable, and it was just what they needed. He would zip to one area where an *attaten* was at that Shenol hadn't sensed, then would be at a spatiatta who was about to fall, pressing it to their head. As soon as the energy was consumed, he was out at another. He would save the lives of thousands today.

She zoomed back out. Trellia was coaching Noselar on how to navigate around. She was still practicing, taking time to adjust and learn the ropes just like Shenol and Trellia had on their first trip. Maybe kids were just plain better at dreams than adults.

"Rax is saving the Swarm. He's amazing..." She trailed off as they saw one of the mountains drop a number of feet. Actually fall down as if something under it had given way. A ripple like a sound wave emanated from it, tearing through the land and the land cracked like a lightning bolt streaking through the soil. Buildings toppled under the force, rivers sank into it, the ocean poured into the crack. Losing her sentence altogether, she zoomed in on the mountain.

A cocoon about four times the size of Sumatta was in a large cavern, much like Sumatta's. It had tumbled to the side and was beginning to crack. Streaks of lava steamed over the cracks like fire opening a tree cone. Lava dripped from the top in splatters and streams, pouring into the base. It flowed over a large plate made of the same kind of metal as Sumatta's Foothold. It flowed over it and off into the pool of water surrounding it.

The sumatta started to push open its cocoon. Shenol zoomed back immediately.

"We're out of time," she said. "I don't know how we're going to get everyone out where the Swarm can cocoon them."

"We don't have to," Trellia said. "We need to convince that one to use the Bahnder Tree." She nodded to the mountain Shenol had just zoomed out from.

The hatchling burst out of the mountain, flying above it, and let out an enormous roaring song while the force of the mountain crashing down into itself continued to ripple across the land. The quake had to be more than a grade nine. She could see buildings collapsing, rivers sinking, trees being thrown as if dust on a shaken cloth. And flying around the sumatta were tens of millions of the Swarm.

Shenol zoomed in on the creature, moving herself to near it. *I hope it understands me*, she thought.

"We need your help," she said. "Sumatta would help us."

"Sum atta," it said, correcting Shenol's pronunciation. "It means the negative word for all life. It means killer. Why would a killer help you?"

"How do you know what it means? You were just born."

"Sumattia sings to us," it said. Its tone suggested Shenol should have known that.

"Sumattia is dead. It would help us. It was the giver of all life here. Will you help?"

"I know. I will," the creature said.

"Please follow me," Shenol said, guiding the creature to the Bahnder Tree. "We will descend and reappear. Then we can start."

"You will," Trellia said. "You have what you need. Now I am going to find what I need, my family."

Shenol bowed her head respectfully to Trellia and Trellia zoomed off, appearing and disappearing all over Arter and throughout space. Shenol lost track of her after a moment, took a breath, and reappeared in the Bahnder Tree. Shortly after Rax reappeared, then Noselar.

"You're doing great. Save the Swarm. You know what to do, Next Reader."

He bobbed his head excitedly. "I found hundreds of *attaten*. Someone was saving them!"

"Great! I'll see you inside," she said.

He beamed with pride and closed his eyes, entering the wake-dream.

"I can't do this," Noselar said. "I live a simple life, not the life of a hero. Can you do whatever you're going to do to me first?"

"Yes," Shenol said. She turned to the sumatta and said, "Ready?"

It sang a high note and curled its tentacles into a circle with a line through it. The Reader smiled. It said yes.

She stepped back, let the sumatta into the Bahnder Tree, watched it transform, then entered the wake-dream. It was time to save the world.

The wake-dream world was growing closer and closer to the real world. Even Shenol's dreams now were of the real world. She hoped that one day she'd be able to have wild dreams again. Today, though, she stepped into the almost-real wake-dream, then walked up to physical Noselar.

How do I bring them here? she thought.

"What appears is real," the sumatta replied. "Pure Energy is the force of Existence."

Shenol understood. She pulled the *draumr* from her forehead and envisioned pulling a clone of it in the dream. A replica appeared in her hand. She put hers back on her head, then reached out and held the replica out to Noselar.

"Take this and put it on like before. Zoom out until you cannot see yourself. Stay there and I will come."

Noselar reached out tentatively and took the replica from the ghost-like apparition that was Shenol's presence in the waking world. She put it on, and it worked.

Shenol had created something from nothing. Well, from Pure Energy, but it was... She had to stop marveling. She needed lots of *draumrs* and fast.

She took her *draumr* off and set it to floating in front of her. She envisioned it cloning, then of cloning the two, then of cloning the four, growing more and more, cloning all those from before it until she had hundreds of millions of them.

"Find anyone without a *draumr*," she commanded her *draumrs* as if they were minions. They all obeyed, flying off in every direction except down.

In the wake-dream, she didn't tire or run out of breath. That was good since hours turned to weeks turned to months as she went one by one, getting everyone to wear the *draumr* that had found them.

Some she couldn't save. Bodies littered Arter. No town, small or large, was spared, and no town didn't have some survivors. Most had almost two in three saved.

"We are done," the sumatta finally said.

"I'm surprised you could keep the field up that long," she said.

"I had Pure Energy. I could last as long as the energy."

It made sense. She went to materialize, but the sumatta interrupted.

"You cannot. See me now," it commanded.

Shenol zoomed in on the Bahnderia. The building was buried under rubble and soil. Only the sumatta and the Bahnder Tree, melded together inside the protective shield were untouched.

"When I release, it collapses," it said.

"Can you survive that?"

"Yes, and so can the Bahnder Tree. You cannot. You must stay ascended. You and the boy."

And there it was. Mountains had split the continent, the aurora was polluted with dust and toxic gas, cities torn to rubble, and every Arterian either dead, in a cocoon, or ascended.

Green cocoons were scattered all over the land. When they would open, she didn't know, but it was a striking contrast. Amongst all the death and destruction, life was spread like seeds ready to grow.

And there was chatter. Chatter all through space. The ascended were marveling, both in awe at their fate and their new powers.

Through her children—both those of Arter and those of her —Sumatta had kept its word. It had given its life to save Arter.

"How long do we stay like this?"
"I don't know," it said, then released the shield as it burst up and out of the Bahnder Tree into a Swarm.

The Igri

Unel watched as Noal and Strypan rotated into their full all-dimensional forms. The rotation was more of a rotation of their consciousness from being confined within their Arterian bodies to acknowledging their entire existence.

Noal took a moment adjusting, but Strypan had clearly done this more often or more recently. They appeared to talk to themselves, but Unel could not sense the speech or thoughts. They were communicating directly, without sound to carry the speech to others.

Strypan directed his attention toward Unel and communicated through a thought channel which encompassed all three of them.

"Igri Tufuer Unel," he said. "This is Noal, the Igri, the oldest. He has honored me by watching the coming of an age in my creation and joining in my symphony. He will teach you the ways of the igri tufuer."

Strypan's entire existence changed across all dimensions as if he were lessening himself and pulling back, making way for Noal. He was giving deference to Noal in every dimension.

Unel turned his attention to his son. "Igri, you honor me," he thought-said. He was still adjusting to how to communicate. Except for the brief moment with Strypan when he had greeted him, he'd not met any of the other igri tufuer.

"I have done nothing to earn your honor. I was simply born of your bonded."

"You came as a blessing to my house. That was an honor, Igri."

"You can call me Noal," Noal said. "And not Igri Noal, just Noal. I don't need a title."

Unel was in the presence of the oldest, the one Strypan had

been honored by. He must know so many things. Unel had tried to see, but he was too new at this. He had learned that everything left a trail through Existence, expressing itself in different dimensions. They were like shadows of every action left behind. Some were easy to read; some left trails in dimensions he did not understand well enough. He'd learned in his brief time as an igri tufuer to read some of the more subtle ones, but many still evaded him. Now was his chance to discover the whole truth.

"I cannot see Sumatta's trail far enough to see its history. What was it?"

Noal sent an emotion of denial, then teaching, and a summons.

Unel picked up on the summons and followed, turning his massive all-dimensional existence to another region of what he now knew was the Universum, the space between universes. There he could see the light trail from a universe which had once existed. He picked up on Sumatta's trail. He studied it for a while, but could not fully follow the trail.

Noal directed his existence to point to an unclear area. "Clarity comes from view. Change your view. You no longer see from one part of your existence," he counseled.

It was true. Unel could pick any part of his existence and see from there. He followed Noal's guidance toward another part of his existence and looked from there. The trail was clear, easy to read. He looked into the shadows of the once universe and saw Sumatta's trail clearly.

Sumatta had conspired against its own kind with the promise of godlike power. It had caused its universe to collapse in order to catch... whose trail was that? There were a number of trails leading out of the universe, but one amongst them was the focus. It was targeting Noal.

"They tried to kill you?"

Noal guided Unel back to another part of space. Arter's universe. There was a being that had been an old man. He had tried to kill Strypan during the Cycle of Ages. He had just tried to kill Noal and Strypan before they had ascended. He had an existence which was bigger than an Arterian. It was not as big as Strypan's or Noal's or Unel's, but it was very large. The creature would be able to move outside of his Arterian body as well. His trail went back through space as well, but got smaller. Unel couldn't follow it completely.

"An igri tufuer?" Unel asked.

"Torhe. They want our power, but our power cannot be given. Not until you. There has been no way to give another being the power to be one of us until you achieved it accidentally." Noal directed Unel towards a small part of space.

Unel had already seen this part. It was when everything had come together to push him into this state. It was a state of existence further than ascension, it was more like an actualization—he wasn't still his three-dimensional self, he was his all-dimensional self and fully self-aware.

"Will you let them have what they want?"

Noal signaled opposition. "Some symphonies should be silenced. They would destroy the Universum."

Strypan added his view, respectful in his dissension with Noal. "Everything can change. Why do we ask questions we know the answer to? Maybe the Torhe will change, maybe not. We will stop them where they do not and help them when they change. We hope for an answer better than expected."

Unel looked back, still curious about Sumatta. He saw the trail between universes, old and faded. He saw Strypan administer the oath of life to it. Sumatta was to protect life with its own life, give life with Strypan's power, and not kill. It was a punishment. A balance he'd sought through the Universum, the killer of all life becoming the protector of all life.

He missed Trellia. He'd looked at her trail so often. Having Col's baby to give Unel a child had been her guilt, but he was more upset that she had given up her life to search for him. He wanted her to go on and live. He had not figured out how to turn his consciousness back into his Arterian form; he had no way of communicating with her.

"Can I go back?"

"Yes. But you'll always return here."

"I see your trails. My trail will be the same, won't it? I will outlive her."

Noal conveyed an emotion through the channel, an emotion of sad acknowledgment.

"She must go on. I cannot go back. It will hurt her more. I cannot hurt her. What's next?" Unel said.

"I will help her," Noal promised. He signaled for Unel to follow him to everything. No, to everyone.

There were more igri tufuer? He was an igri tufuer, next oldest. Did that mean one day he would become Igri, oldest. Did old mean old? Was he an all-powerful being, capable of creating life?

"Am I a god?" Unel asked.

"We're all gods to something. Be the kind of god you hope you have," Noal replied, then signaled more firmly for Unel to follow.

Epilogue

Trellia spent countless lifetimes searching. Watching and searching. She watched as the momentum of the crashing mountains and the lava at Arter's core set the continents drifting, separating them by oceans and ripping glaciers apart. She looked on as continents collided with each other, forcing the land up into the sky and creating great natural mountains joining them until from space they looked like a wound healing. She saw the sky filled with smoke, dust, and debris warm Arter, melting the glaciers and raising the oceans turning some continents into islands. She watched in awe as the sky caught fire, burning through the aurora like a highly combustible fuel, its hues caught in a fiery orange.

And then she saw the turmoil begin to settle. The fire sky poofed out and the rains began, flooding Arter with a purity born from devastation itself. Glaciers reformed hiding parts of continents, rivers cut a home for themselves in the lands connecting fresh and saltwater together. Grasses and forests were rebuilt and the land was made anew.

Through it all, civilization was buried and hidden, covered in soil or ocean and wiped from memory. All of civilization except for the billions of cocoons and the spatiatta tending them. Arter became habitable again as if Arterians had never set foot on Arter, as if Sumatta had never brought life. Arter was no longer a barren planet inhabited by life, but a planet of life.

Watching over the transformation were the eight sumatta who found their places in new mountains and from there led the spatiatta as they curated the land and tended the cocoons.

Nowhere in all of that transformation or in the space of the Arterian galaxy did Unel, Noal, or Strypan ever show up.

Wherever they had gone, they had gone to a point beyond where Trellia could reach.

The cocoons started to hatch. The ascended Arterians saw the hatching and descended, taking on physical bodies again. Trellia joined them. Perhaps she would find her loved ones in those who came back.

The inhabitants of the cocoons had changed. They developed a green tint to their skin and seemed to have a na'aten link to the planet, making them stronger. They called themselves the New Race. Those who descended were the same as when they'd ascended, except for the couple thousand years they hadn't been grounded. They had trouble adjusting. The quibbling started.

Arterians of both races separated, claiming certain continents as their own and began fighting over them.

Nowhere amongst all of them did she find Unel, Noal, or Strypan. She had discovered Col and pulled him out of his coma from within a cocoon just a few years after the ascension. But the other three evaded her.

She built a house with Col and together they worked on projects to one day let them find Unel, Noal, and Strypan. She loved Col. He was Unel's best friend. He had helped her have a baby for his best friend. They worked well together.

She leaned back against their house and sighed. "Why can't I just have an answer? Am I that bad of a person?" she said to the nothingness.

"We're all good and bad, Trelly," Noal said as he approached the house. He was older, but not by the thousands of years she had spent ascended. He had grown into a strong adult Arterian, somewhere in his thirties. He still had white hair and gray eyes and a smile he must have stolen from Unel.

"Noal! Where have you been?" She got up and ran to him, throwing her arms out as she grabbed him and started hugging him, squeezing him as tight as she could. "I've looked everywhere."

He hugged her back with parental affection. "I know you have. You can't look where you can't see. I've been in the Universum," he said.

"What is that?" she asked, stepping back from him. He had been hiding in the Universum? Where was that university? She'd never heard of it before. Why hadn't she sensed them. "And where is Unel? Strypan?"

"It is the space between universes. Arterians can't go there." He chuckled as if at an inside joke. "Usually. Unel and Strypan are there. No, I cannot bring them to you. I came to bring you closure."

"Why? Why, if they won't? Why you? Why not Unel?"

"Existence is like a symphony. I like to see myself as a conductor. I guide the musicians into making a better harmony. A little push, nudge, or change and everyone does what they're supposed to to make things work better together. Sometimes that means making some play the rougher segments, others the nicer segments. In the end, it's like making a symphony with Existence."

"I don't get it." Was that some kind of Strypanesque answer to her question?

"Instead of letting you suffer and come to your own conclusion to move on, I came here to offer you absolution. Look at your life, birth parent. You gave your womb for your bonded. You gave your invention to save Arterians. You gave yourself to save your loved ones. You have found a way of making yourself pay a price to play the entire time. It was your role, but the music has changed now. Now that we've gone through the trough, it's time to seek a height. Thank you. Thank you for giving me birth. Thank you for saving your fellow Arterians. Thank you for never giving up. You are good, but you've done the bad thing of torturing yourself. We can't come back again, but you are loved, you are appreciated. It is time to move forward with life."

Move forward? That was why there would be no Unel. But

why not Strypan? He was older. It didn't matter now. He was telling her it was over. He was talking about himself like he was the conductor, like he had somehow been put in charge.

"I'll never see him again? Strypan? You?"

Noal kept a tenderness in his look as he nodded. She would never see those she loved the most again. That wasn't enough. He couldn't just send a one-way message.

"Tell them I miss them."

"They hear you."

They can hear me? she thought. *All this time he could hear me screaming for him and... it must have been torture to not be able to do anything about it.*

She turned her head up, arms spread out wide to the sky and screamed. "I miss you! I love you!"

Noal smiled.

Time to move on. How? All Col and.... That's what it was. He was giving her to Col. Did he know? He must. Noal would have told him. She closed her eyes and cried softly. Her bonded loved her so much that he would give her up to his best friend rather than see her spend her life chasing him anymore than she had.

Trellia sighed, licked her dry lips and swallowed to clear her scratchy throat. There was one more message she could deliver. Something Noal hadn't understood. She could be a birth parent again, but this was her last chance to be Noal's birth parent.

"Noal, I have a bit of advice for you. Remember that a conductor is not a painter."

Looking thoughtful with his hands behind his back, Noal gave her a considering bow. As he looked at her, still thoughtful, his body seemed to bend light like a prism and fold into it, then he vanished.

ATEN

Aten /AH-ten/

A spherical object created by Sumatta from a naturally-occurring substance which contains pure energy. Each aten harnesses one of strong, weak, and electromagnetic forces and works with specific elements of nature. There are 7 types of aten.

Attaten /uh-TAW-ten/

A type of aten. Eggs created by spatiatta. Pearlescent and solid. Extremely rare and contain small amounts of Pure Energy. Consumption of the pure energy by females results in fertility if the woman has entered or past the age of maturity. The further along, the more fertile the woman will get. Usage in devices binds to the force of life.

Ca'aten /CAH-ah-ten/

A type of aten. Appears in various tar pits throughout Arter. They come to the surface as hard brown spore spheres. Dangerous. Interaction with them by any living matter results in rapid decay via subatomic decay (the weak force). Usage in devices binds to the soil/land.

Hydaten /HIGH-dah-ten/

A type of aten. Dense gel spheres that come in green, blue, and yellow. Found in pools inside of cenotes. Contain an electric charge. Usage in devices binds to water.

Na'aten /NAH-ah-ten/

A type of aten. Brown bulbs found floating on the ocean. When dried, they will flake off and provide a good source of sodium. Bound to the strong nuclear force. Usages in devices binds to saltwater bodies.

Oxaten /ox-UH-ten/

A type of aten. Translucent bubbles with a thick skin that fall from the sky like rain. They contain an electric charge. Usage in devices binds to air.

Phoaten /FO-ah-ten/

A type of aten. Purple colored and teardrop shaped with electromagnetic energy swirling inside them. Produced by the Living Rainbow. Usage in devices binds to light.

Siaten /SIGH-ah-ten/

A type of aten. Fragile orange and red glass bubbles floating on the lake at the foot of Mount Sumat. Breaks down atoms in a small range around it. Usage in devices binds to glass and sight.

Alia /all-ee-UH/
Genderless Reader
Birth Parent
The parent who gives birth to a child.
Col /Coal/
Friend of Unel and Trellia.
Dise /DIE-ss/
Secretary of Education under Governor Muaske.
Gemtra /GEM-truh/
Psychedelic tea loving birth parent to Trellia.
Governor Muaske
Governor of Attadore, active proponent of Sumatta, chief
rival to Spratee
Governor of Attadore
Governor of the capital city-state. De facto president of
Arter.
Igri /EE-gree/
Translates from an unknown language to "oldest". Title
granted to the oldest living being in Existence. Always the
same species.
Igri Tufuer /EE-gree Too-foo-er/
Translates from an unknown language to "next oldest".
Title granted to all those of the same species as the Igri.
Next Reader
Title of the next in line to become Reader.
Noal /Nohl/
Son of Trellia on Arter. Adopted by Spratee and Noselar.
Rax /RAX/
The Next Reader at the coming of the Last Age.
Reader
The voice of Sumatta charged with reading Sumatta's
speech and interpreting it to the population. Resides at the
Bahnderia.

Shenol /SHE-noll/
   The Reader at the coming of the Last Age.
Spatiatta /SPAH-tee-ah-tah/
   Creations of Sumatta which look like Sumatta but are the size of a typical Arterian. Hive mind creatures which treat Sumatta as the hive queen.
Spratee /Sprah-TEE/
   Governor of Attadore and adoptive parent of Noal.
Strypan /STRY-pan/
   Parent of Unel.
Sumatta /SU-mah-tah/
   Non-native being that brings life to Arter through its foothold. Hive queen of the spatiatta.
Swarm
   The collection of spatiatta which serve Sumatta.
Tanseor /Tan-SEE-or/
   Covert military agent. Has traveled off world.
Torhe /tor-HE/
   Those seeking to become igri tufuer.
Trellia /TRELL-yah/
   Unel's bonded. Co-creator of the draumr. Birth parent to Noal.
Unel /EW-nell/
   Trellia's bonded. Inventor of the draumr.
Xarat /ZUH-rat/
   Gemtra's bonded. Trellia's parent.

PLACES

Arter /ARE-ter/

A planet in the Arterian solar system. It has one sun, one moon, and a single continent named after the planet. Inhabitants are called Arterians. Arter is divided into 18 city-states.

Attadore /AT-tuh-dore/

A city-state located on the eastern shore of the Sea of Lights. It is west of Sumna. The Falls of Attadore form its western border against the Sea of Lights.

Attatar /AH-tuh-tar/

Capital city-state of Arter. Also the easternmost city-state and second largest in population. Key attractions: Bahnderia, 2nd Dreamoria. Home of Trellia and Gemtra.

Bahnderia /bahn-duh-REE-uh/

Sumatta's home among Arterians. Houses the Bahnder Tree. Home to the Reader and Next Reader.

Caleston /cal-ES-ton/

City-state of Arter. Closest to Mount Sumat.

Hydrona /HI-drone-uh/

Western city-state. Vacation home of Spratee and Noselar.

Isle of Lights

Arter's only island city-state. The Living Rainbow arches in the sky above the island. Source of avak.

Living Rainbow

A dense section of the Arter aurora which forms a rainbow shape over the Isle of Lights and produces phoaten.

Mount Sumat

Home of Sumatta prior to the turning of ages. Housed the Cycle of Ages.

Oxyahyd /Ox-EE-uh-hide/

Western city-state. Brief war with Attatar.

Photania /FO-tan-yuh/

Westernmost city-state.

Si'inth /SIE-in-th/
Southern city-state. Location of Tanseor's hideout.
Sumna /SOO-m-nuh/
Largest city-state. Metropolis. Location of first Dreamoria.
Universum /YOU-nih-vurs-um/
The space between universes where pure energy can be found and where the igri tufuer and Igri reside.

THINGS

Avak /ah-vawk/

A bitter tea made from the roots of a plant found only in the Isle of Lights. Relaxes the muscles of the body and induces epic-length dreams.

Atenase /ah-ten-ACE/

A disk-shaped weapon which harnesses the fundamental forces of aten. Illegal in every city-state.

Bahnder Tree /BAH-n-der tr-EE/

A tree of an unknown metal made of the same metal comprising the footholds. The tree is located at the center of the Bahnderia. Forms a protective armor around Sumatta when it is in the Bahnderia.

Cycle of Ages

A formation in Mount Sumat which interpreted solar signals into a message in the Sumattan language. Destroyed during the attack on Sumatta during the message for the Last Age.

Draumr /DRAW-mer/

A device linking two Arterians together via their dreams. Creators: Unel, Trellia.

Existence

The collection of all things which exist in all universes.

Foothold

A solid metal plate in each mountain's main cavern made of an unknown metal. Draws Pure Energy from the Universum by way of electromagnetic gravitic force. Bound to the force of gravity.

Pure Energy

Energy in its non-matter form. Present in large quantities in the Universum.

Wake-Dream

The state between being asleep and awake; halfway between the real world and the dream world.

Thank You

Thank you for reading Arter, the first book in the Pure Impurity series. I hope you enjoyed it! The next book in the series is Ertra. You can get it by visiting my website:

https://sylas.art

Please take a moment and review your read on Amazon or GoodReads—your reviews are an enormous help to indie authors like me.

amazon.com/gp/product/B0B5QNB8SN

goodreads.com/book/show/61414705-arter

Newsletter

To get a copy of The Trasilian War for free and to stay abreast of all my latest works, signup for my newsletter:

https://sylas.art/signup

The Trasilian War Excerpt

Without hesitating, Fiador sang the tone to start.

Mettledore put all its force into its tentacles, leaning forward to reduce air friction and aimed for the first Ertain. The Ertain saw Mettledore coming and ran the other way. Mettledore sliced halfway through the rope and pursued the runner. The Ertain screamed as the rope lost tension and Mettledore swung its other wing at the Ertain's neck. The Ertain ducked at just the wrong moment and Mettledore's blade sheered right through the Ertain's face.

It didn't matter. That was five points—two for a headshot, three for a death.

Mettledore didn't waste time looking where Lownkey was. It spun around and zigged across the field at a slight angle. The next Ertain was short and huddled near the pole, squatting down. Mettledore trounced the Ertain, slicing straight through the pole and across the short Ertain's body. The Ertain flipped backward, sprawling out on the ground, and lay heaving. It hadn't died. Only one point for a torso shot. That was a potential four points lost.

The next Ertain was strong, stocky, and tall. It faced Mettledore down. This one must have been in the military. It waited in a fighting stance as Mettledore approached. Mettledore didn't hesitate. It just barreled through the Ertain, knocking him to the side. Mettledore spun around just as the Ertain was getting back to his feet and swept its blade around, a clean swipe at the neck. The Ertain's head flipped backwards, somersaulting through the air then landing with a thud. Mettledore noted the five more points, but kept on, not waiting for the head to come to a rest.

The last Ertain in its way was a tenacious-looking female. She stood demurely but held herself like a fighter. She was probably part of the military too. Mettledore couldn't afford another loss in points or time. It darted up to the Ertain and instead of going for her head, Mettledore slapped her in the back with the side of its wing. She started to duck, but abruptly threw her head up at the slap to the back. Mettledore swung its other wing around and took her head off. It went flying, and Mettledore only looked that way long enough to see that it was about a second ahead of Lownkey. Another five points made how many? It was only one kill down. It had to make the finish.

Mettledore bolted forward, pouring every ounce of energy it had into its tentacles, leaving a dust trail streaming behind it. The Ertain on the sticks were all ducking or proudly holding their heads up—they weren't consistent. With just two seconds before reaching, Mettledore did something it hadn't done before. Mettledore jetted into the air and flipped over. Its helmet fell off mid-air, exposing its head and giving it full sight of the playing field. It could see each of the Ertain and the head in the middle. Spinning as it flew upside down, Mettledore swung a wing around, stroking it up and down as it spun through the Ertains' necks and heads. It swung its body around as its wing completed its circle and brought its other wing straight down into the head in the middle.

It was a clean sweep.

Mettledore landed on the ground, its gills breathing frantically, its tentacles stinging hotly, and looked up at the playing field. Trasilians were rushing forward.

"That was great!"

"To create life, we must work with Pure Energy and Impurity, energy with mass. Life is what we call Pure Impurity. In the hand of an Artisan, life itself is created. When life ends, its mass is left in the three-dimensional plane and its Pure Energy returns to the Universum to be used again." - Noal, Terra

In the Curious Creators Epoch, the Igri Tufuer under the guidance of the Igri itself began creating life throughout the universe. The Igri Tufuer are beings so large that their existence spans billions of universes and they are able to see the path in time we leave behind. They began by creating more Igri Tufuers, but their curiosity got the better of them and they started making smaller beings than themselves.

The smaller beings came to be known as the Torhe, children of the Igri Tufuer. They spanned anywhere from a couple to a few dozen universes. They were large beings by any comparison, but they were nowhere near the size of their creators. They also could not create life itself.

The Torhe saw the great power of the Igri Tufuer and demanded to be given the power of life, but the Igri Tufuer through their best—the Artisans of Creation—explained that it is a skill which cannot be given or taught, but is native to the being itself.

The Torhe rose up to fight what they called a lie and were imprisoned indefinitely inside of a universe they could not escape. Yet given enough time, the Torhe showed just how much power they could wield and how artfully they could wield it, discovering a way out of the black hole of a prison in which they had been thrown.

Free from the confines of prison, the Torhe set out to force the hand of the Igri Tufuer, but they had learned far more than simply how to escape from prison. They had developed their own war games strategy. The best among them is a Torhe called Tanseor.

In the Pure Impurity series, we explore the life created by the Igri Tufuer and the Artisans of Creation and the conflict which arises from being a god who cannot—or will not—share all its power with others. From the first escape and attack on Terra, to the overt and destructive attack on Ertra, to the subtle attempts on Arter, Tanseor has engineered ever more sly ways of taking on his opponents and developed some deadly weapons along the way while his opponents shy awy more and more from a direct conflict.

One thing is certain: Tanseor will not stop. He will force the Igri's hand. When he does, how the Igri responds will set the fate of Existence on a final course forward.

I hope you enjoy the Pure Impurity Series and that it stimulates you to want to be the best you you can be.

Sylas

Ertra
Book 2

Released January 2023

Faster than light travel comes on the heels of the Trasilian desire to forage for a new home in space. Amrasia is selected to shepherd in this new era for the Trasilian, but so much rests on a rocky peace.

Go back in time to Sumatta's beginning and find the answers you've been looking for. First, you'll have to answer just how high can the cost of peace be.

https://sylas.art/books/ertra

Terra
Book 3

Released March 2023

Thousands of years before the Trasilian war, in a nearby universe, Terra waged a battle with the Torhe that almost tore the planet apart. Discovering universes beyond our own brings with it dangers far greater than knowledge; it brings the danger of the Torhe and with it, a new challenge for the Igri.

Return to the beginning and explore the fight between the Igri and the Torhe like never before.

https://sylas.art/books/terra

Released June 2023

The power to create life itself *can* be given. The proof is in Unel himself. The Torhe are aware of it, and the Igri still withholds this power. War is inevitable, but on a scale of universes, who can possibly win this game?

A fateful parley holds all the secrets that will bring the Pure Impurity series—and, perhaps, pure impurity itself—to an end. Can Noal rise to the challenge or will Tanseor finally make his move?

https://sylas.art/books/the-universum